SON OF THE MAYA

John McKoy

2nd Edition

Copyright © 2017 by John McKoy.

All rights reserved. No part of this publication may be reproduced, distributed, or transmitted in any form or by any means, including photocopying, recording, or other electronic or mechanical methods, without the prior written permission of the publisher, except in the case of brief quotations embodied in critical reviews and certain other noncommercial uses permitted by copyright law. For permission requests, write to the publisher, addressed "Attention: Permissions Coordinator," at the address below.

BookVenture Publishing LLC
1000 Country Lane Ste 300
Ishpeming MI 49849
www.bookventure.com
Hotline: 1(877) 276-9751
Fax: 1(877) 864-1686

Ordering Information:
Quantity sales. Special discounts are available on quantity purchases by corporations, associations, and others. For details, contact the publisher at the address above.

Printed in the United States of America.

Library of Congress Control Number		2017964147
ISBN-13:	Softcover	978-1-64166-315-1
	Pdf	978-1-64166-316-8
	ePub	978-1-64166-317-5
	Kindle	978-1-64166-318-2

Rev. date: 12/21/2017

Praise for <u>Son of the Maya</u>

"<u>Son of the Maya</u> is a fascinating tale of identity, migration, taking sides and striving to understand the full picture. Mr. McKoy brings his personal experience living in Guatemala and working with minority youth in Washington, DC…I greatly enjoyed this book," Jane Rubin-Kurtzman, Sociologist and Latin Americanist.

"The Spanish wasn't critical to understanding the action… I didn't want to put it down," Peter D. Livingston, Global Credit Union Expert.

"<u>Son of the Maya</u> is a fascinating read. Set partly in Washington, DC and partly in Guatemala, it is both a gripping adventure story and a profound inquiry into the best means to achieve social justice in both the US and in Latin America," Louisa Newlin, English Teacher and Education Consultant.

"John McKoy knows intimately the territories he writes about and the characters who inhabit them. In <u>Son of the Maya</u>, he brings life vividly to them both," John R. Nolon, Professor of Law and International Environmental Consultant.

"Very exciting. I can't wait to see your interview on the TODAY Show," Betsy Reveal, Financial and Management Consultant.

Dedication

This book is dedicated to Helen, John and Paul McKoy, whose memory brings me sustained comfort and joy. It is also dedicated to my wife, Andrea Gay for being a wonderful partner on every leg of this journey.

I'd like to acknowledge Jane and Cal Kurtzman for their detailed critical feedback; and Janet Goldstein for her invaluable publication advice. Finally, I wish to thank several other friends for reviewing early drafts of this work: Todd Kummer, Peter Livingston, Bill and Louisa Newlin, John Nolon and Betsy Reveal.

Chapter 1

(Roberto)

"Is this Mr. Prettyman?"

"Yes, it is."

"Mr. Bob Prettyman?"

"Yes. Who is this, please?"

"My name is Sergeant Murphy, Metropolitan Police Second District. There's been an incident involving Raúl Gonzales. He's in GW Hospital and says you're his closest relative."

"I'll be right over," I said.

"I'll wait for you here, sir. Room 5010," said the officer.

That phone call would not only change my nephew's life in ways we could never have predicted, but it would also accelerate a major life change for me. I'll never forget the year 2005. Most Americans remember it as a time of turmoil: the horror of Katrina, the deadly escalations in Iraq, and the killings in Darfur or Chechnya. They might recall the passing of civil rights icon Rosa Parks, presidential peace candidate Eugene McCarthy, or *Tonight Show* legend Johnny Carson. For me, it was a time of immense internal dissatisfaction, debate, and indecision. It was the year I turned fifty-two. It was also the year in which I had been recently divorced, had drifted away from my daughter, and was struggling to identify a professional direction that could reenergize my life. In short, I was experiencing an intense midlife crisis not unlike that endured by many "successful" Americans.

The emotional jolt of receiving the officer's frightening call and Raúl's subsequent close call with death helped me decide which way to go.

I threw on some sweats, grabbed my wallet and keys, and took the elevator down to the condo garage. It took only about twenty minutes to drive from Chevy Chase, Maryland, down Wisconsin Avenue to the West End neighborhood in the District. Sergeant Murphy was talking to the attending nurse on the fifth floor when I arrived at my nephew's room. He extended a calloused dark-brown-skinned hand and firmly shook mine. Not too much desk work for this hardened police veteran.

"Thank you for coming so quickly, Mr. Prettyman. Let me explain the situation. Please—sit here a minute before you go in."

My heart beat so hard against my chest that I thought the nurse would insist on admitting me too. I willed an exterior calm and sat facing the officer.

"There was some gang activity up on Adams Mill Road earlier tonight; your nephew was shot near his spine. He'll live, but doctors aren't sure whether he'll regain use of his legs. They'll operate tomorrow, after he's stabilized. The medical staff can fill you in. Unfortunately, I need to check some things with you before the medical proceedings get rolling, if you don't mind answering a couple of questions."

"I'd like to see Raúl, but sure. What can I help you with?"

"He's sedated now. I'll only take a minute. I realize what an imposition it is."

"Thank you. Okay."

"The incident was called in by neighbors, but by the time our people arrived, there were just two bodies and your injured nephew. We have identified the other two as illegals from rival gangs but have little else to go on. Do you know where your nephew was living?"

My mind didn't work. I was stuck on the image of Raúl, my cousin's boy, lying paralyzed and alone in a pool of blood on some District street while I slept in my sky-view, secure condo. Raúl had only stayed with me for a year while he finished his senior year at American University in DC. He'd then gotten a clerk job at an association on M Street downtown and rented an apartment on the fringe of Mt. Pleasant, a funky transition neighborhood. That had been two years, one promotion, and several girlfriends ago.

I had never actually met any of his friends. Raúl had been to my condo a couple of times, but normally when we met, it was at one or another restaurant in Adams-Morgan. We talked about his mother back in Guatemala, discrimination against Latinos in the region, local politics, and his desire to go to graduate school. I never paid enough attention to fully understand the crowd with whom he spent his time.

"He lives at 1745 Hobart Street and works at the Association of Home Builders in the administrative department. The rest of the family, other than me, is in Guatemala, but Raúl has a valid green card. As far as I know, he lives alone in a basement apartment."

"Great. Do you happen to know any of his friends?"

"Unfortunately, Sergeant, I don't. I now wish I did, but no, I really don't."

"Well, that's enough for now, sir. Where can we reach you during the day?"

"I have a real estate company in downtown DC. Here's my card."

John McKoy

"Thank you, Mr. Prettyman. Sorry to have to bother you, and sorry for your trouble. I hope the boy recovers. I'll be in touch after his medical procedures. Nurse Marcos will need to get insurance information."

I barely heard the final words, because I was inside Raúl's room, staring at his prone, tube-filled body. I pulled up a chair and placed my right hand on Raúl's arm.

"I'm here, Raúl. I'm here," I whispered.

I don't know how much time lapsed while I sat by his bed, praying that he would recover.

"Mr. Prettyman, my name is Dr. Ronald Jones, and I'll be operating on Raúl in the next day or so. If you don't mind, I'd like to explain the procedure to you. Maybe we could sit outside while Nurse Marcos changes your nephew's fluids." I must have nodded and mumbled assent, because I only snapped out of my trance outside the room as the doctor began to explain.

"In many ways, Raúl is fortunate. The bullet entered his side and managed not to sever any organs before it lodged against his spine. So if we can remove to bullet without affecting the critical nerves in his back, he should recover fully. I say *if* because there are risks, but if we leave the bullet in, there's a risk that he will never walk again."

"Well, Doctor, do I have time to get a second opinion? No offense, but I have no way of knowing how good your diagnosis is or your track record as a surgeon. I owe him that much—"

"No need to explain, Mr. Prettyman. You should absolutely check, but we can't wait longer than a day. I would appreciate it if you give me a call by tomorrow night, because we don't want to keep him sedated longer than necessary."

"I will try."

"Thank you. Here is my card. I know this is happening extremely fast, but I'm sure you can understand that to keep the chances for a successful operation high, we have to keep Raúl from moving about too much. On the other hand, we can't keep him sedated too long."

I stayed with Raúl for about an hour, watching him breathe peacefully. I studied his face more intently than I ever had when he first arrived in the United States. He had very straight, jet-black hair and prominent Mayan cheekbones, his mother's light-brown skin, and his father's hazel eyes, but he was taller and more muscular than either of them. While at his side, I decided not to tell his mother until after the operation. I hoped to save María Elena from worrying about any more serious a situation than necessary. Luckily, we'd arranged for me to have Power of Attorney when Raul first arrived from Guatemala.

I drove back, stopped the car, and parked on one of the numerical streets just off M Street in Georgetown. I walked down to the river, past the closed shops and restaurants. Occasionally, some chef's tangy tomato sauce pulled my head in the direction of a late-night café, or some loud, young suburban kids drew my attention as they struggled onto the sidewalk from their expensive watering hole. It was mostly dark and quiet, with a faint smell of honeysuckle under the Whitehurst Freeway along the Potomac River.

Back up near the car, I wondered when Georgetown had changed. The architecture was the same Federalist-period two- and three-story buildings, but the occupants had changed. Now they were Middle Eastern or Asian, as well as white American. All very young, young like Raúl.

I felt *old*.

On the drive back through Georgetown and Chevy Chase, I made mental notes of the doctors with whom I could check that were likely to have GW Hospital privileges. I thought of nursing services to call for Raúl's care after dismissal, in case he needed the most intensive care. I also made plans to have my COO, Marshall Robinson, run my business for the near term. I decided that regardless of the outcome of Raúl's operation, I would take responsibility for his care. I fought back the guilt attempting to overwhelm me, and I resolved to get his life back on track while he was on my watch.

It only took a few calls to check out Dr. Jones, and he proved to have a stellar reputation. Getting a second opinion was taking more time than Raúl had. After asking a medical colleague from the chamber of commerce to handle that research, I had to grit my teeth and wait as long as I could. The wait almost drove me back to the Catholic Church in search of relief. The next night, I called Dr. Jones and authorized Raúl's surgery. Each night after work, I drove by the hospital and then home to a glass of scotch. I cut out any unnecessary nighttime business meetings.

After my divorce a couple of years back, I moved into a spacious three-bedroom penthouse condo off of Wisconsin Avenue in Chevy Chase, Maryland, just across the DC border. It provided a breathtaking view of forest-like vegetation, with an occasional rooftop and a scattering of glass and steel office towers thrown in. It was close to a subway station, shopping, and restaurants. I was getting used to leaving the car in the garage and building much of my nonwork life around the neighborhood.

The second bedroom gave me a study, and the third was for guests. It was mostly used by our twenty-two-year-old daughter on her brief and increasingly more infrequent visits during her senior year at Berkeley. Scrapbooks and photo albums of my early childhood in Guatemala City lay about the condo. Relatives had really filled in much of what I remembered from those days since we immigrated to the United States when I was five. The loneliness, the awful, helpless churning in my stomach that I felt as I paced about the condo or stared out of the living room window approximated what I had experienced when my wife, Mónica, moved out. Only this time, I felt more responsible and more guilty.

Five days after the shooting, my secretary buzzed to tell me that Dr. Jones was on the line. My hand did not move quickly to the receiver, but it eventually got the instrument to my ear.

I'm sure that I only whispered, "Hello," in a very sheepish voice.

"Raúl will walk," were the only words I really heard on the other end of the line.

Chapter 2

Five years ago, Raúl Gonzales was pegged as a typical well-off, upper-crust teen preparing for post-high school education at some elite US college or university. He was not super smart, but bright enough and academically accomplished enough, and from a "good enough" family to be accepted in any number of schools used to full-paying Latin scions. If tradition and projections held, Raúl would learn the foundations of a profession; return home to study law, medicine, or finance in a Guatemalan graduate program; marry an attractive, college-educated, upper-class socialite; and live a life of privilege forever after.

He was permitted to be rambunctious or mischievous but was not to go too far off script for the rewards of class to be thrown his way. He could come in contact with, but not be affected by, youngsters from less privileged backgrounds. But Raúl never stuck to his lines. He was at the top of his grade academically and hung with the rich crowd of boys, yet he also starred in soccer and was known for the egalitarian way he treated all boys on the pitch, whether they were rich or poor, Indian, mixed-blood (Ladino), or pure Hispanic. This unusual sense of justice clearly came from his mother and often made his school colleagues scratch their heads about his behavior.

In one non-school league game, played in a rich neighborhood, Raúl's teammates thought it would be appropriate to rough up the star of the opposing "working class" team. When referees weren't looking, they tripped and shoved the youngster from all angles until he'd retaliate and invariably get penalized by the refs. Late in the game, one of Raúl's mates shoved the opposing player so hard and so obviously that the refs called him for a flagrant foul. The other player shoved back and a fight almost broke out, and Raúl stepped in, pushing his own mates away.

"That's enough. You've been trying to get them to fight all game. Let's just play," he said.

All players, on both sides, were stunned.

"Whose side are you on, Gonzales? You soft on this gutter trash?" The instigating—and muscular—teammate stepped into Raúl's face.

Not backing off, Raúl calmly said, "I hope you know what's right on the field, Marco."

As a circle formed, Marco, emboldened by an audience, took a swing at Raúl. A mistake.

Raúl easily ducked the swing and caught the bully in his belly with a right jab and in the jaw with a left hook. Marco's knees buckled, and he went down like a large elk whose legs had been shot from underneath it. The refs broke up any further scuffle and, after several minutes, allowed play to continue without incident.

Marco left the field before his teammates, and though they rarely spoke to each other, he never bothered Raúl again.

Back at school the next week, Raúl was approached after a history class by the other top male senior student, Oscar del Gato. Much more studious and less athletic in appearance and inability than Raúl, del Gato generally kept to himself around school.

"I heard about the soccer fracas. Unusual for someone from here to stand up for an ordinary Ladino. That took guts you don't expect," he said.

"You might not expect it, but my mother would. And, she's the boss in our house." Raúl smiled.

"I don't know if you're interested, but I'm involved in a study group on modern politics. You might enjoy sitting in sometime."

Raúl knew that Oscar had the reputation as a grind and a leftist sympathizer—not someone with whom his social set normally partied. In fact, he'd never seen Oscar at a party. He was intrigued, however.

"Thank you, Oscar. I'd like to sit in. Let me know when the next meeting is."

"Will do, Raúl. Will do." They shook hands and walked off.

Several weeks later, Oscar invited Raúl to a meeting held in a little-used neighborhood recreation center in a poor section of Zone 5. On the agenda was a debate on appropriate and effective revolutionary tactics with a student from Guatemala's Landivar University espousing gradual, but pervasive community-building and social change among the poor and a dynamic "participant" from Nicaragua championing radical violent action similar to Castro's Cuba triumph or the "Sandinistas" in Nicaragua. The audience was older than high school age, and many seemed to be university students. Some, however, appeared to be working professionals, because of their more formal, buttoned-down dress.

Raúl found the debate and ensuing discussion stimulating, but he was uncomfortable with how real and intense the discussion was. Judging by the questions, proclamations, and enthusiasm of their engagement, Raúl gauged that most of the fifty or so young men and five women in the hall were more committed to the radical approach than that of "social change." While everyone was friendly to him afterward, he realized that the mission of the most dedicated was to displace his social class.

"Well, what did you think?" asked Oscar as they walked the dark, crumbling streets back to the patch of dirt where he had parked his car.

Raúl was tense, walked with uncharacteristic caution, and didn't answer until they were driving back down toward his neighborhood.

"Fascinating. But, to be honest, it's the first time I've begun to realize that the change in wealth and power distribution that I believe is necessary would mean a radical change in the way you and I and our classmates live our lives. I have never really processed those possibilities. It's all been distant, intellectual, unrelated to my daily life. I suppose I need time to absorb and analyze the ideas and my reaction."

"Fair enough," said Oscar.

"I'm glad you invited me, Oscar. Thank you," said Raúl as he stepped from Oscar's car in front of his house.

The debate experience was sobering, but by no means did it immediately alter Raúl's life. He soon forgot the meeting, was conveniently otherwise occupied when Oscar advised him of future meetings, and had very few sidebar political discussions with Oscar during the remaining months of school. Late in the spring, prior to graduation, Raúl and some of his adventurous schoolmates, fellow soccer players, found themselves in a rundown part of Zone 5 to score marijuana. This sort of interaction with lower-class Ladinos, this "business transaction," felt natural to the preppy group and generated no apparent resentment from the sellers. After paying the agreed-upon price to the two sellers, Raúl and his six classmates walked nonchalantly toward Chico Bravo's, the group's vocal leader's, van. Before Chico could open the driver's door, they were surrounded by a rough-looking group of about fifteen youths.

"You guys are in the wrong part of town, no?" asserted the tallest of the bunch.

"Just passing through, slumming," returned the brash Bravo.

"Really? Well, see, that's funny, because this is home to us. This 'slum' is our home. We're forced to live here, so we claim it—and everything that's in it," the agitated spokesman said, steeping into Chico Bravo's chest. "And, since you are in our slum, we'd like back some property you took."

"Now, wait a minute; we didn't take anything. We made a purchase," said Chico, a few drops of perspiration rolling down his cheeks.

"I see, amigo. Well, if that's the case, just show us the receipt, and you'll be on your way," said the spokesman, grinning.

Chico turned to his buddies, now encircled by the group of neighborhood youth. All were paralyzed with fear, save for Raúl, who nodded with an expression of surrender on his countenance. Chico reached in his jacket and handed the other leader the bag of grass. The preppies turned to enter the van, when each was grabbed by at least two of the toughs. The spokesperson punched Chico twice in the stomach and once in his ear.

"Next time, you wait for an invitation before you come up here, understand?" the leader said as he started to walk away. Chico looked up and saw his buddies grabbing their midsections, gasping for air. Anger rose in his torso like a cresting wave, and he charged the spokesperson, punching him in the back. His adversary wheeled around and drew a six-inch knife from his jeans. Chico staggered a step back toward the van, his anger now overwhelmed by fear. He knew even an apology on bended knee would not stop the crew in front of them now.

The neighborhood toughs approached, all with some club or knife in hand. The preppies screamed that Chico hadn't meant to retaliate, that he was not thinking. The others still closed in. As they reached the point of engagement, of striking, a well-built, brown-skinned youth sprung from the middle of the tough's pack between the adversaries.

"Hold up. This is stupid. They got the message. We don't need more problems with the cops because of some sissy-assed preppies," he said to his crew.

There was an hour's worth of tension compressed into about thirty seconds. Then the interloper turned to the preppy group, pointed to Raúl, and said, "You did us a good deed once. We're even, now."

"Okay, Angel. You're right. Let's go," said the leader. "You're lucky you got that dude with you tonight," he said to Chico, pointing to Raúl.

Angel? Raúl tried to place the name with the face as they headed back to friendly territory. Then he recalled. The star soccer player that Marco had picked on weeks back.

When he got accepted to American University in Washington, Raúl hoped to use his first couple of years to sort out his own values. His mother hoped that living near her brother, Bob, would offer an opportunity for the development of a closer relationship, from which Raúl might gain maturing counsel. He graduated high school without firming up his views on social class, on social change, on the type of people he wanted to befriend, on the type of profession his wanted to pursue, or even on where he would settle. Events during his senior year, however, did prime Raúl for an explosive exploratory and potentially positive growth period. His scary encounter with Angel Chiapas and his crew in Zone 5 did not, however, suffocate Raúl's taste for recreational drugs.

Chapter 3

(Roberto)

"Raúl, I apologize for not being more deeply involved in your life, but—"

"Tío Bob, I'm a grown man. You don't have to babysit me. That's one thing I like about living up here. Thank you for convincing mi mama that it was okay for her to go back to Guatemala. I don't know if I could have taken another week of mothering."

We were sitting in my living room five weeks after his operation. The nurse had just left for the day, and I had come home early, as I had since turned much of the responsibility of running Mega Builders over to Marshall. María Elena had stayed for a month, caring for her son. She had, indeed, gotten on his nerves, but she and I had a wonderful time catching up with each other. Raúl, however, had been fairly closed-mouthed about any personal subjects while his mother was around.

"You know, I don't really know much about your life up here. Your friends, your hobbies, and so forth. I'm clueless."

"What do you want to know, Tío?"

"Like, where do you hang out after work? What do you and your buddies do on weekends?"

"Michael, Guillermo, and I do a lot together. Mostly clubs on U Street, Eighteenth Street, or out in Falls Church."

"Michael's the black guy, and Guillermo's from Salvador? Your college friend?"

"They're both college buddies. And, no, none of us are in gangs. Like I said, I happened to be at the wrong place that night—and without my boys."

"The police have arrested three or four boys from two rival gangs, but they don't have the shooter identified yet. They're pretty sure they have everybody."

"That's good, but I've let it go. I got to move on with life."

"Okay, let's not talk about it right now." Raúl hadn't fully regained his strength, and I could see that he was becoming a bit agitated. Changing the topic, I asked, "Let me ask you an unrelated question, though. Do you feel you've been getting opportunities like everyone else at work?"

"Tío, what is this? I'm treated fine at the firm."

I sat and looked at his expression. It was controlled and devoid of any perceptible emotion. He was neither interested in what I asked nor particularly upset that I was probing.

"You used to complain about the treatment you got at college, or about retailers following you in stores, or unnecessary police attention."

"Yeah, but you get used to it. And, that's generally in the 'hood."

"You mean like Columbia Heights?"

"Right. Okay, so, the stuff still exists, but you do get used to it. Tío. What are you driving at?"

"I don't know, but you read so much about kids without hope. Youngsters who feel the deck is totally stacked against them. That's why the gangs are growing. At least, the psychologists and sociologists say that."

"There's not a lot of optimism on the street. That's for sure. Some of it's straightforward. There's not a lot of support for kids just up from Centro—you know, Guatemala, Salvador, Nicaragua. Families are splintered, or working 24/7, or overwhelmed by the United States. The brothers turn to each other and gangs for support. Simple! Really!"

Raúl rolled his wheelchair into his room, and I sat by the living room window, gazing out at the night. Thoughts funneled into my head like black ink filling up a bottle, blocking out every ray of bright light. With every thought, my emotions absorbed another drop of depression. My treasured life partner, my former best friend, was gone; my daughter had distanced herself, and I didn't know if I could ever resuscitate that relationship; the fun of building "statement" office buildings or mixed-use complexes had drained from my system; and now my nephew, having barely escaped paralysis, maintained a protective firewall around his true self.

I couldn't lift my chin off of my chest for half an hour.

I finally looked out at the moonlit horizon, but its beauty had little effect on my mood. My housekeeper had left a salad and casserole in the refrigerator for our dinner. Once I had it laid out on the table, I called to Raúl, and we sat facing one another.

"Is it education, Raúl? Is that the key?"

"The key to what, Tío?"

"The key to staying out of trouble. The key for Latino youth to make it up here?"

"Tío, I don't know. You are the one that made it. You tell me."

"I'm a different generation. Things were different for me, and my parents were around for me. Well, my mom certainly was. And, they had some financial resources. I'm curious about your generation, your buddies."

We finished the meal and the evening without further discussion about any subject even remotely close to the fate of Latino youth in Washington. The next morning, as I was driving Raúl to his physical therapy session at George Washington University Hospital, he resumed it.

"It's work and self-respect. It's the dignity you get from knowing you can get it done just like the gringos. Education helps, maybe; but that's not it. It's work and the respect you get from being self-sufficient."

"Makes sense."

"How does that help anything?"

"Well, I don't know yet. I'll let you know when it clicks." I looked over at Raúl as I parked at the hospital's general admission door. "Here we are. Good luck in there today."

"Yeah. This is the day I trade the chair in for crutches."

As Raúl wheeled himself up the hospital ramp, I uttered to no one in particular, "I might do some trading in today, myself."

Since the age of five, when my American father and Guatemalan mother moved us to Washington, DC, I have learned to excel at most activities I tried. You might say I was a model Horatío Alger "Latino," even before the term became acceptable for Hispanic immigrants here. I was fortunate enough to amass tremendous wealth during my thirty years as a real estate developer, so from the outside, I was the portrait of middle-aged success. Inside, however, I was struggling to find deeper rewards in my life. I was not just searching for the next trail to take, but also how to appreciate the scenery and absorb the full experience of the next journey. I had been surrounded by beauty but had forgotten how to appreciate it.

In 2005, I felt too young to retire, too addicted to highly visible, complex challenges to teach, and too disconnected from the immigrant community in DC to know how to be useful. As in my business practice, I had begun calculating the pluses and minuses of my career options. I reviewed choices as I would have analyzed a challenging real estate investment opportunity to develop an "upscale" project in a dicey neighborhood. That process was deliberate and familiar, but inconclusive. But, by day's end, I had set in motion the steps leading to the sale of my company.

Months later, I was one of the wealthiest men in the region. I no longer needed a job, but my life's work had only begun.

Chapter 4

(Roberto)

"Just because I don't jump up and down and shout about injustice like some Boston Brahmin liberal or California crusader doesn't mean I'm not passionately committed to full enfranchisement for Latinos. That's pure bullshit, and you know it, Bob."

Max Ramirez was literally in my face, and every crease in his skin was stretched in anger. That was the moment I decided to invite him to join me in starting the foundation.

"Lighten up, Max. I have an idea you might find interesting," I said.

"You can't just change the subject. Chinga. After getting me riled up—"

"Max. Momento, calmate. Just listen for a few minutes."

"Jesús—"

"I want to start a foundation that helps Central American immigrant kids with job training and placement, primarily here in the Washington area. What do you think?" I took a sip of my merlot and looked out of the restaurant's open bay at the traffic on Eighteenth Street in Adams-Morgan.

After a few furrowed-brow moments, Max said, "There must be a dozen organizations doing that sort of training, and every foundation in town giving them money."

"Actually, no one is providing sufficient dollars to make a difference, and you know most of the training is worthless."

"So, why are you telling me?"

"I suspect you're not satisfied playing labor economist at Columbia, and I think you would make a hell of a good foundation president."

My old colleague laughed a deep, thunderous rumble and for the first time in ten minutes took a swig of his Tecate, licked the salt from the can's rim, and widened his coffee-colored eyes.

"Bob, you're the one during Latino Scholarship Fund board meetings who loves to tell me how I'm an academic who's never run shit."

"So, wouldn't you like a chance to change that?"

"You can't be serious. I have a career—"

"Max, I'm dead serious. I need a partner in this, and I want this project to have major impact."

"Bob, you're independently wealthy now. And, no disrespect, but you have only yourself to worry about. I have to support a family."

"I'm not asking you to risk anything financially. Tell you what. I'll increase whatever you're making by 50 percent and give you a four-year contract, so that if we go bust, you're still covered for four years."

"Well, I can't answer now. Tell me more about the idea."

"Not much more to tell. As you said, I've got extra bucks. I want it to do something that benefits Latinos in a sustainable way. I'm too young to not place my drive and passion into something I care about. I admit that I don't know anything about running a foundation, but neither did Jim Rouse, or Bill Gates, or even Edsel Ford when they started. And look at the impact they had."

"You are rich, mi amigo. They were, and are, wealthy beyond imagination." He laughed again. "Never mind. Okay, Bob. I gotta run, 'mano, but I'll think about it."

I watched Max stroll away toward his car with that brisk, focused New York walk, not sure if he'd ever call me about the offer.

The hip afternoon clients of El Rincon began to arrive a little before three. Corn and tomato-based aromas wafted through the restaurant as cooks prepared for the dinner crowd. Elevated speakers softly emitted guitar chords and the sweet voice of a DC-area singer, Eva Cassidy, and I sipped and pondered. A new waitress asked if I needed anything else as she looked down at the scribbling on my legal pad.

"I'm fine, thank you," I responded.

I tried to organize the categories of "to do's" on my pad:

Board

Legal

Fund management

Space

Under each category, I quickly wrote out tasks.

"A laptop would make that go faster."

I looked up at the hazel eyes and coffee complexion of Alice Brown, an aggressive young woman I knew from the chamber of commerce.

"Alice. What are you doing here in the middle of the afternoon?"

"I might ask the same of you, Mr. Prettyman."

"Bob, please. Here, pull up a seat," I said, pulling out the chair vacated by Max.

"Thank you, but I'm meeting a friend on chamber business." She smiled and flowed over to a window table. I wanted to stare at the firm movement of her buttock, but I thought better of it and went back to my pad. Ideas stopped coming, so I put down the pen and looked back out at the street. A few more business-casual men paraded by, and BMWs pulled into parking spaces that were earlier occupied by Toyotas and Accords. Within the half hour, I paid my bill, nodded to Alice, and left.

Out on the pavement, the languages were still a mélange-Amharic, Spanish, French, Arabic, and English. It was twilight, so I couldn't clearly make out the figures leaning on my beat-up Porsche Cayenne, but the three men appeared to be arguing. As I got closer, I could see that two blonde adolescents had a brown-skinned Latino pinned against the car parked next to mine.

"Give it up, Chico. You speak English, don't you, Jose?" one said.

"Don't act dumb, Jose; give up your cash, money. Give it to me before I shoot you with the gun I've got here," said the other blond, nodding at the object in his pant pocket.

Even though they were facing my direction, neither of the two crooks saw me as I approached. When I arrived at the parking space, fear, courage, and outrage melded into one unfamiliar, but powerful emotion.

"You boys better move on while you have a chance," I said in a voice a notch louder than my normally loud speaking voice.

"Who the fuck are you, old man?"

"I'm somebody that's giving you ten seconds to get out of here before I mess you up and then call the cops or an ambulance." All three turned to stare. The Latino registered confusion. One of the thugs glared in anger, and the other seemed disbelieving.

Although I'm fifty-five, I'm still a fairly strong man, six foot three, 210 pounds, and with long arms. I was considerably bigger than either of the youths standing not five feet from me. We faced each other for half a minute, and then the youth without the gun-like object cocked his arm to take a swing at me. I guess my briefcase must have caught him in the nose before he could complete his swing. He dropped to the pavement, bleeding and holding his face. I didn't have to say or do anything else. The braggart who had posed as a gunman pulled his open hand from his pocket and helped his friend to his feet, and they both took off running down the street.

"Esta bien, compadre?"

"You espeek Espanish?" said the shocked remaining youth.

"Si. Soy Guatemalteco."

"Yo tambien."

My voice was calm and had returned to normal volume, but I unlocked my hands from the handle of my briefcase and held it behind my back until they stopped shaking. Leaning against the other car, the young Latino told me his name was Manuel, not Jose or Chico as his attackers had surmised. He hadn't been in DC for more than a month and was staying with his brother while he looked for a job. He was a country boy from the hills around Chichicastenango, near Lake Atitlan. None of the skills he'd acquired in rural Guatemala were likely to promote his job search, but I didn't dissuade his youthful ambition. I cautioned the newcomer to be more careful when approaching strange men. We shook hands, and I got into my car.

John McKoy

Driving back to the condo, I smiled about how my life was constantly changing. Raúl, a few nonprofit boards, golf, and my prospective foundation filled my life, now that Mega Builders was sold. In a way, my life had become simpler. I didn't know it then, but my life would soon become more complex than it had ever been while I was in business. And my mother's birthplace, Guatemala City, would prove more significant and more dangerous to me than my adopted home, Washington, DC. But I'm getting ahead of my story.

Chapter 5

(Roberto)

"Hey, Tío. I left some Chinese takeout in the fridge with a couple of beers. I'm beat. Turning in early."

"Well, how did it go? I see you're hobbling on crutches."

"Fine. Actually, it's great to be at least partially upright again. But, man, it's tiring. I had to try to do some things, but getting the takeout was all I was up to. It will be a challenge back at work next week."

Just before closing his bedroom door, Raúl leaned on his left crutch, looked over his shoulder, and said, "By the way, Lisa left a message for you."

"Lisa, Lisa who?"

"Lisa, your daughter, the West Coast stranger. You know, Tío, her Spanish is pretty good. I didn't recognize her."

"Well, how long's it been since you saw each other?'

"I couldn't have been more than ten."

"Ok, thanks. Good night, Raúl."

While I ate some Sichuan noodles and swilled a cold Corona, I filled in a couple of more items on the to-do list. For about an hour and a half, I cleaned up bills and played with investments. When I couldn't handle the anxiety any longer, I dialed Lisa's number. It was 11:45 in DC, but I was wide awake.

"Hello, Dad." Caller identification technology that enabled parties to tell who was calling without so much as a peep from the caller's end always stunned me for a second.

"I was surprised, to say the least, to get your message. How are you?"

Even in the period directly after the divorce, the most estranged and strained period, Lisa and I had been able to have a civil sentence or two. She fully sided with her mother, however.

"A lot of changes there, huh? Raúl getting hurt and moving in, you retiring … what else is going on?"

"That's about it. How about out there?" I wasn't giving up anything until I knew her mission and whether it involved some reconnaissance for Mónica, as well. I was still smarting from the times I had shared information in confidence with Lisa, only to have it come back to harm me emotionally or financially during Mónica's divorce proceedings. Information was just hard to give up.

"Dad, I have to be in DC for interviews in a month, and I wondered if we might have dinner."

"Of course, Lisa." I started to ask her to stay with us but held back. We set the details and chatted impersonally for a couple of minutes about politics and her graduate thesis, "Income Effect of NAFTA on Mexican Urban Workers."

"Dad, I look forward to seeing you."

It wasn't "I love you," but it was something.

"Both your cousin and I look forward to it."

As a joint economics/anthropology degree candidate, I knew Lisa would be intellectually interested in and probably have constructive thoughts about the foundation. I wasn't up to sharing over the phone.

Over the next few weeks, I read as much as I could about the mechanics of operating a foundation and paid visits to some of the area's key foundation executives. My years of board activity and financial contributions enabled broad access to a network of officials in the local foundation community.

The details of day-to-day activity were beginning to push out any time for reflection or strategy. I had to find a way to get better organized and to manage my time. I knew whom I needed to get involved. Two days later, I sat down in the Madison Hotel's tony restaurant for breakfast with Alice Brown.

"I must admit that I was totally surprised to get a call from you, Mr. Prettyman. How can I help you?"

"First, by calling me Bob. Then, by passing the sweetener."

"I'm sorry. I guess I can be too focused sometimes."

"Nothing wrong with focus." For a few minutes, we sipped coffee, placed orders, and got comfortable in our chairs. I waited to see how she would deal with silence and ambiguity. She didn't keep me waiting.

"So, now that you've sold the company, what are your plans, Bob?"

"That's partly what I want to talk to you about, Alice. But first, tell me where you see yourself in the next few years; whether or not you stay at the chamber."

"Well, as you know, I've recently been made head of business services. So, I want to build up the suite of things we offer members to be better than any of the competition. That will take some time. I'm happy doing what I do."

"Where do you want to go? What sort of contribution do you want to make in this community? You strike me as someone who wants to do more than 'a job.'"

"Wow. I … this is not one's normal breakfast meeting conversation."

"No. It's not." I focused every ounce of my attention on the pretty young executive facing me.

"Okay. Well, sure, I'd like to make an impact. But first, I believe I have a lot to learn about managing, leading—"

"Why? I hear you're quite a take-charge person."

"Thank you. I guess."

"Yeah, it's a compliment. The chamber budget is what? Two million?"

"Actually, this year, we're about 2.5."

"And you manage what? Five hundred thousand dollars?"

"Yes. How'd you know?

"Not important. How would like to influence more than ten million a year and have it mostly go to underserved youth?"

"Wow. I'd want to know details, but that sounds great."

"But, suppose it was a small operation and your bread-and-butter responsibility was to build and run a top-notch office? And your main portfolio was managing me?"

Son of the Maya

Alice dribbled a bit of egg yolk down her chin before she regained her professional composure.

"Alice, how's your Spanish?"

"Well, I had two years in college, so I understand a bit, but I'm not fluent."

"Well, you asked me what I am going to do. I'll tell you." I ate a few bites of English muffin. Over my coffee cup rim, my eyes remained fixed on her curious young face. She was no longer put off and nervous. Just curious.

"I want to address the problem of Latino youth facing dead-end futures in this town. I want to find ways to build their skills, their confidence, and their earning power. I want to produce a tsunami-like change in the life outcomes for Latinos in the District. I'm going to do it through a foundation called the Quetzal Fund. And I want you to be my executive assistant. To start, I'll pay you 25 percent over whatever you make now." I pulled out a couple of tens, placed them on the table, and stood up.

"Why don't you think about it for a few days and call me on Friday."

Alice sat in her chair, folding her napkin and looking wide-eyed, but serious. She said something like "Thank you," and "I'll be glad to," but I was halfway out of the dining area by the time she finished her sentence.

That evening, I decided to test out my theory of change, my thoughts about how to radically improve life outcomes for Latino youth, with my nephew.

"Raúl, you know how I've been asking you a lot about your life here? How I've been sort of prying?"

"Really, Uncle Bob? I'd been too busy recuperating to notice."

"Funny! Well, it's not just idle chatter. I've pretty much decided to start a foundation that will invest in quality workforce training and placement for Latino youth in the area. Without the tools to compete in this economy, these kids are accused, tried, and sentenced to failure before they get started. Gangs, crime, and poverty will spread, and the eventual backlash will be comprehensive, severe, and unjust. I can see it so clearly. Do you disagree?"

"You've hit one of the problems, Tío."

"What am I missing?"

"Well, there's the quagmire of issues around legal status. How long kids can stay, under what conditions, with what authorization, related to the location and status of parents, what constitutes proof of a life-threatening situation in their home country," Raúl said.

"Those are valid issues, but I'm in no way qualified or prepared to deal with immigration law. There are others, like MALDF, that raise funds and staff legal action in that area," I responded.

"Yes, but that legal quagmire adds to the psychological state, the anxiety of kids and parents, and can affect every aspect of ability to adjust and integrate," Raúl persisted.

"I see that, but I'm a business guy, Raúl. I need to go after something more tangible."

We looked at each other for several minutes.

"What else am I missing?" I asked.

"There's good old white bigotry, for one. Do you think that even if the Latino brothers are well-trained, there's a tolerance for many of us in the marketplace?" Raúl's complexion reddened. "Either the buttoned-down white guys snub us downtown or the skinheads mess with us out in the counties. And there's no love lost between us and the blacks. Of course, the Asians I saw at A.U. seemed to be the kids of engineers, scientists, and financial immigrants. If the academic landscape were totally open, the whites would be screaming for affirmative action for themselves. That's tangible, as you well know, Tío."

"It's tangible, no question. But I don't know how to attack it head on, outside of the courts. I keep coming back to employment. It may seem like there are abundant bright, well-placed graduates flooding the market, but I really think there's more demand. There are jobs going begging. There are CEOs dreaming up all sorts of programs to import 'employable' immigrants, because they feel they can't find job-ready people in this region."

"Tío, I appreciate all you're doing for me, believe me. And I know you've been very successful, by any standards. But I don't think you understand the depth of the psychological barriers most young Latinos, particularly immigrants without papers, confront."

"So, I hear you saying that I haven't figured out the details of how to support young Latinos as they enter the world of work, trained or not."

"Si, pero hay mas, Tío. How do you deal with the institutional racism that beats kids down, that tells them that they are nothing at every turn, or that tries to brainwash them into believing that they are 'the exception' if they do demonstrate talent? When was the last time you saw an articulate Latino on the news, or a 'soap' that showed a normal, middle-class Latino family?"

"Well, last time in LA—"

"Yeah, but LA has a big middle-class Mexican and Chicano population. Companies have to market to them. We're practically ignored here."

"I don't think it's ever been easy for immigrant groups. But kids can't just throw up their hands. Tough love, Raúl. Tough love."

"Good luck." Raúl limped to the picture window facing out over a canopy of green blanketing Bethesda.

"Uncle Bob, I'm not saying don't try. I'm just skeptical right now. No question that we need more skills, but that alone won't get it. You may just hasten the frustration that leads to desperate violence in kids. But, in truth, I don't have the answer."

"Well, fair enough. I'm just toying with ideas so far. I appreciate your thinking about it."

"No problem. I'm heading in. Full day at work tomorrow."

I tossed and turned a bit that night. I knew that Raúl was partially correct, but I felt strongly that the way to beat the skeptics and the racists was to get prepared, to be able to outperform the expectations. Was I so different from this generation of Latinos? Surely, the barriers of bigotry had been tougher thirty years ago than they are for these kids.

"Hey, Mr. P. Retirement agrees with you. Looking sharp. You got a bunch of calls. The only one I recognize is from Max Ramirez," said Tonia Gutierrez, my former secretary.

"Tonyita, you're a dream, as always. Thanks."

Tonya had stayed on to work for Marshal Robinson after I sold Mega Builders. I had gladly accepted his offer to keep office space there until my new venture was off the ground. Before I returned Max's call, I placed one to the number left by Alice Brown.

"Hello," she whispered into her cell phone.

"This is Bob Prettyman returning—"

"Bob, let me call you in half an hour. Okay?"

"Fine."

I wanted to know her response before launching into a heavy conversation with Max, so I fiddled around with other calls, mail, and minor checklist items until Alice called about an hour later.

"Sorry, but that was an important meeting."

"Understood. So, what's your decision?"

"This is probably crazy, but I can join Quetzal Fund in about a month."

"Great. I can certainly hold on 'til then. Let me send you a bunch of things to start your casual reading."

"This is probably the riskiest thing I've done in my career—"

"I'm sure you can guess my view about risk and reward. I'll do my best to make sure you don't regret it."

"I shouldn't have said that. I'm actually very excited, and thank you."

With one piece in place, I now felt more comfortable returning Max's call.

"Did I get you at a bad time, Max?"

"No, this is in-between. It's perfect. Now, are you really going through with this foundation idea?"

"Papers have been filed, I just hired an executive assistant, and I'll start looking for office space soon."

"Well, I'm flattered that you asked me. And, it has some appeal, but I need to know a lot more."

I smiled to myself. "You want me to come up there, or—"

"I'll be in DC in a couple of days. How about lunch Wednesday?"

John McKoy

"Good by me. What about Olives off K Street?"

"See you there at 12:30?"

"Great."

When we met, Max had a lot of questions that I had never thought about concerning investment criteria, oversight policy, and investment partnering. I felt even more confident that he was the right person to run the foundation. He didn't agree to come on board, but he suggested we visit a couple of well-known Latino youth training projects in the Bronx and Harlem. I agreed to go up to New York in a couple of weeks, after he'd had time to set up the visits.

A few days later, Raúl, who by this time had moved back to his apartment, left a message asking if I could meet him at 8:00 p.m. at El Tamarindo on U Street. "El Tam" had become a nighttime hangout for many Latino men in Adams-Morgan. I had no idea what he wanted to discuss, but I left word at his office that I'd be there. As I reflected on the fully recuperated, vital young man who had spent so much time at my condo without revealing much of his inner workings, my thoughts drifted back to my own early Guatemala experiences.

Chapter 6

(Roberto)

My mother and father met at some US embassy function in Guatemala City in 1952, and apparently it was love at first sight. Mom was a young embassy secretary from a middle-class family. She had had two years of Catholic college education and was the smartest kid in a family of six. The fact that my very conservative grandfather had allowed her two years of college was extraordinary, but he was a history professor at Landivar University. Grandma wanted my mother to get more education, but Grandfather felt that young women needed only to prepare to be wives and thought that two years was much more than adequate. Somewhere back on her side of the family tree were some Caribbean people from Belize, because Mom had gorgeous, dark complexion. Dark enough to draw stares of admiration, but not so dark as to elicit the upper-class bigotry against "Morenos."

Phillip Prettyman was a six-foot-three brunette marine from Washington, DC, who'd recently graduated from the US Naval Academy. His first post had been aboard a cruiser based in Guantanamo Bay, Cuba. The Guatemalan embassy was to be an in-between assignment until he received his next military posting. He had Caucasian features, and he stood out at the cocktail party as tall, dark, and handsome. Dad had a marvelous facility for romance languages and had the sort of permanent tan that allowed him to "pass" for Latin, Southern European, or even Eurasian.

When Papi and Mom were first introduced, the attraction was apparently instantaneous. They dated for several months and got married late in 1952. During those early days, Papi told me later, they socialized with an interesting mix of local and international businessmen, foreign service families, and university-based intellectual elites. They were exposed to all positions on the political spectrum and soon decided to publicly remain politically neutral. I suspect they were slightly left wing, given family dinner table conversations.

I was born in 1953, the same year as my cousin, María Elena Gonzalez. Many of my early days were spent playing with Mom's large extended family. I didn't have relatives on the Prettyman side, since Papi had been an only child whose foreign service parents had died in a car accident while he was still at the naval academy. Even after Dad was assigned to the Pentagon and we moved to Alexandria, Virginia, I spent summers with my grandparents and cousins in Guatemala City, my uncle's cottage on Lake Atitlan, or Granddad's second home in Antigua. I saw poverty among the Ladino kids in the city and the "indigena" kids in the countryside, but no big deal was made of it. To me, they were kids who simply lived differently. We weren't really wealthy, but I had a joyful and privileged childhood.

Papi stayed at a desk job during the Kennedy administration but left for Vietnam in 1963, when I was almost ten. Mom and I moved into Washington, on Connecticut Avenue, and that's where I grew into young adulthood. My North American friends, my political beliefs, and my professional aspirations were formed during those years. My father was killed in Vietnam in 1968, as I entered high school. At first, I was overwhelmed with grief, then anger at our government. I knew that my parents didn't think America should have been there in the first place, but Papi was patriotic, and they both had hoped the war would end soon after he shipped out. I dedicated my years at Wilson High to Papi and what I thought he would want. I played team sports and held the star positions in baseball and football, I learned the saxophone, and I studied history.

In college, at Georgetown, I broadened my exploration of international affairs and expanded my language portfolio by taking French, Portuguese, and even Chinese. For the first two years, I imagined myself a foreign service officer or delegate to the United Nations. By junior year, however, I became as skeptical about diplomacy and politics as I had become about the military. I lost the optimism and idealism of my classmates, but I never became as cynical as my Guatemalan cousins. I decided to just focus on making a living and submerged myself in business courses. My grades were good, so I had plenty of options with banks and consulting and accounting firms when I graduated.

The building industry fascinated me, because it offered complex problems with verifiable results. Projects either made money in the marketplace or they didn't. There was no gray area about economic success. You had to build attractive, customer-pleasing structures, price them right, develop the right market appeal in your sales, and build your financial relationships with lenders and investors. It seemed to offer lots of challenge and big rewards. And from the distance of real estate classrooms, there didn't appear to be prejudice against tan-skinned Latinos. So, I first joined a real estate brokerage and then a commercial developer.

I totally immersed myself in work and the social scene surrounding it. I only went to plays or concerts if I thought some industry networking would result. My sports outlets became morning runs and occasional evening gym workouts or weekend basketball games with real estate colleagues. Visits to Guatemala became less frequent, and the Latino part of my identity disappeared.

After learning the real estate development business, I took out a loan, bought a strip of commercial land in Montgomery County outside of DC, and began developing mixed-use projects. I worked hard and constantly. Luckily, I quickly grasped the knack for assessing good sites and had an innate talent for finding and hiring young and eager skilled financial, construction management, and marketing people.

I soon became a rich man, emotionally impoverished at his core. I played around and dated lots of Anglo women, a few Latinas, and some African-Americans. I enjoyed moving in and out of various social sets, going to cultural, entertainment, and sporting events that I could never have afforded as a kid. I was never bored, but my life, my passion, was my work and building the company. I was, however, emotionally impoverished until I struck it rich and met a young first-generation immigrant female med student from Miami. Mónica Sanchez was the only child of a Cuban businessman and his socialite wife, to whom I was introduced by a friend who taught at Georgetown University Hospital. We had many late-night conversations about Latin American politics, a subject she knew far better than I. While her parents were conservative Cubans, consumed with a dislike for Castro and what he did to their generation, Mónica focused more on the plight of Cuban-Americans in Florida. She was passionate and had none of the prejudices of her parents, but was definitely driven to be a financially successful doctor. We dated and got married, and she eventually began her practice in the Washington area in 1980. For twenty mostly wonderful years, my life was enriched beyond my dreams. But, more on Mónica later.

In 1977, shortly after I graduated from Georgetown, my mom moved back to Guatemala. "You're now equipped to live your own life and to contribute as God sees fit, mi hijo. I'm always a phone call away, but I want to go back home," she told me.

Mom was an anomaly on the Guatemalan social scene. Although without a college degree, from middle-class (as opposed to wealthy) parents and of mixed ethnic heritage, she commanded attention and demanded respect. She was still a relatively young widow, elegant and beautiful in appearance, delightfully articulate in English and Spanish, and fiercely intelligent. María Elena's mother hooked Mom up with Guillermo Schaefer, then a young start-up businessman, who had been a friend of both María Elena and mine. Mom became his right-hand everything: bookkeeper, editor, and secretary/assistant. The Schaeffers were part of an influential immigrant German community that had come to Guatemala originally to work in the coffee industry. Guillermo had been set up in business by his wealthy father, so he had the ability to pay my mother well. He was also an enlightened boss, in that he encouraged Mom to become active outside of work, particularly with the Maryknoll community—a group of missionaries from a progressive branch of the US Catholic Church.

For her fundraising and social advocacy on behalf of a socially conscious diocese, she needed little encouragement. It was through this vehicle that Mom was able to funnel assistance to her beloved Belize, the poor stepchild Caribbean nation that borders Guatemala's eastern perimeter. Although we stayed in close telephonic touch, Mom was so busy with both Guillermo and the church that I rarely got to see her for any extended period when I visited Guatemala. She never married again but seemed fulfilled and happy.

"Berto, your father and I had a special, wonderful relationship. I loved him more than I can ever imagine loving anyone else. And you were a joy to raise. Now that you are a successful person, I really can't ask the Lord for more. My work is challenging, it stretches me intellectually, I feel useful in the community, and I'm able to promote values so important to the development of our Guatemala. Values held dear by both your father and me. I live among true family and friends. No, Berto, don't worry about your mother. The Lord has been very good to me," she once said to me.

I'm not sure how she fit it in, but after coming to Miami for Mónica and my wedding and after coming up to DC for a few weeks after Lisa's birth, Mom was always available for visits. She loved her daughter-in-law, even though she and Mónica, being of similar constitutions, were cautious around each other. She adored her grand-daughter. When Lisa was with us on summer Guatemala trips, Mom always either spent time with her or had a list of fascinating and fun things for her to do. And if

Mónica and I needed time to ourselves, Mom made sure that a loving, trusted relative or friend was available to watch over Lisa.

While she was the clear backbone to Guillermo's business, it was her volunteer work for the church that gave Mom the most pleasure and for which she became known. In fact, María Elena feels that Mom's organizing, advocacy, and fundraising for the Maryknolls enabled them to be effective advocates for the poor and provided support for a progressive Catholic bishop. His success was so impactful that he was assassinated in the late eighties, a decade before the assassination of Bishop Gerardi. I think mourning his death exacerbated Mom's breast cancer, and she died in 1989.

Chapter 7

(Roberto)

As I look back on that July evening a couple of years ago when I went to meet Raúl at El Gato Negro, I think I was trying to find more than a connection to my past and my roots, a connection to my other self; the self nurtured by my mother but partially buried by material success. The jukebox was playing one of those typical Mexican "aye aye aye aye" rounds, but the Spanish bouncing off the glasses on Formica tables was from Guatemala, Nicaragua, and Salvador. The green and brown colors of the Mayan village motif wallpaper had long ago faded from years of cigarette smoke.

"So, now you have a little feel for where I hang, Tío," Raúl greeted me as I approached his corner table.

"We're only missing a Texas mariachi band to complete the cultural mix."

"Not bad. I'll mention it to the owners. Please, sit. Like a Tecate?"

"Thanks."

"Salt and lime on the rim?"

I nodded approval.

He waited for my beer to arrive and the waitress to depart before speaking again.

"Tío, I think your Quetzal Fund is a good idea. But, I am not sure if you're doing this to help the young *compadres* or to help with your loneliness. Maybe assuage some guilt, too."

I sipped and stared. Raúl's expression reflected nothing more than the question his words had asked.

"I'm not sure. Probably there's some of each motive involved. Actually, does it matter, as long as I'm genuine about it?"

"No, except that the motive may influence how long you'll stick with it when the bumps and bruises come." The young man, recently recovered from a near-death encounter, seemed wiser than his twenty-something years entitled him to be.

The music, chatter, clinking of glasses, and scuffling of feet across a gritty floor were just loud enough to seal the two of us in a cocoon of our own private conversation.

"If he comes by tonight, there's a friend of mine I'd like you to meet, Tío. Hector is not on the college tract, but he can tell you a lot about the guys you think you want to help."

"Raúl, one thing doesn't add up to me."

"Just one?" My nephew gurgled down half his bottle of beer and smiled broadly. This was his environment.

"Why do kids keep coming? Why send for family and partners if things are so rough? I mean—"

"Tío, that's easy. You don't need a survey or a study for that one. It's simple. Tough as it may be here, there's still much more opportunity than in congested barrios or agricultural wastelands back home. Then, there's the violence and drugs that are everywhere. The gangs have enormous reach, and they grease palms and line pockets in very corner of power, regardless of social class. And the life here is intoxicating, even as the promise of riches proves to be empty."

"I just think—"

"Hold up. Hector. *Aqui, hombre.*"

A short, well-built, clean-shaven, brown-skinned, *mestizo* youth approached the table.

"Javier Hector Romano, *te quiero presentar a mi tío,* Roberto Prettyman."

"*Tan formal. Mucho gusto,* Hector." I shook the youth's small but hard calloused hand.

"*El placer es el mio,* Senor Prettyman."

"*Me llamo* Bob."

"Okay, Bob."

We broke into English when Hector's Budweiser was brought to the table. Not wanting to insult Hector, I made no assumptions about where he worked (if, indeed, he did).

"So, are you at the National Association of Home Builders with Raúl?"

The two boys looked at each other and smiled.

"Bob, when I got here from Salvador, I had ten dollars, a high school degree from a barrio school in San Salvador, and five cents' worth of English."

"How long ago was that, Hector?" I interrupted.

"About ten years ago. And, I've not had a Hora—what do you say the guy's name?"

"Horatio Alger," Raúl finished his friend's thought.

"Yeah. No rags to riches here."

"But, your English is very good now," I broke in.

"Thank you. I have had a chance to work on in it through plays at Gala Theater. Do you know it?"

"Yes, I used to go quite often. So you're an actor, Hector?"

"Only small parts. No, I make my rent money in the produce section of the Safeway on Columbia Road. I've been able to work my way all the way up to manager of the section."

"So, that sounds pretty good for only ten years in the country."

"Bob, it's not bad if one sets one's goals very low. And that's a big problem with most of the *muchachos* who come up. I have a revolving set of roommates and guys in the apartment, 'cause no one can get steady employment. Even for guys from urban backgrounds, it's tough to get work that pays well, much less offers a career path. Even those who do well, are smart at carpentry or building or calculation, they don't find gringos who expect them to be promotion material."

"Sounds like a little prejudice and some inadequate training."

"Can't argue that the guys from Centro are behind in training, but it's a class thing. Gringos decide if you are a laborer, and that's all the chances you ever get. You don't get trained for jobs that white guys with the same education get."

"Now, that doesn't surprise me," I said.

"The other problem is that guys buy into the future that gringos paint for them. So even real smart guys set their sights low. What's the point of trying hard, you know? So, after awhile, a guy may work hard at some dead-end bullshit, but he's so happy when the weekend comes that he drinks, parties, and plays away whatever he made."

Raúl broke in. "Unless he's got a savvy lady who manages his cash."

"Yeah, right." Hector laughed.

"So, what do you think can be done, Hector?"

The young boy's brown irises, which had been surrounded by perfect circles of alabaster white, seemed to grow out to the perimeter of his black eyelashes. His body tensed for an instant, and then he stood and said, "I'll have to owe you for the Bud," and sprinted to the kitchen behind the bar. Ten seconds after he disappeared, two large DC policemen entered the front door. One Caucasian and one African-American officer surveyed the tables from just inside the door. Glasses seemed suspended and conversation dropped several decibels as the African-American walked over to talk to the bartender. He brushed the table next to ours, and his holster passed within two inches of my nose. The guy might have played tackle for the Redskins. He was tall, wide, and solid. His partner stood menacingly by the door. After a brief chat that only those closest to the bar could hear, the black officer turned and walked to the door, and both officers left. Looking out the window onto Florida Avenue, across from a schoolyard, I could see that the police remained in their car for only a minute or so before they sped off up Eighteenth Street, into the heart of Adams-Morgan.

I had almost forgotten that Raúl was still at the table with me.

"What was that about?"

"I'm not sure, but Hector does hang with a politically active crowd that the District keeps tabs on for the feds, I suppose. It's too bad he had to leave, because he could shed light on the numerous scenarios that lead to street shootings. It's not all gang turf or drug related. The feds and cops pull some crazy shit sometimes."

I realized that I was holding the tabletop tightly enough to separate the Formica from its wood base.

"That's interesting. But at least they don't think you're a 'person of interest,' as they say."

"Tío, I'm not really into that sort of politics." After a few more sips, he said, "Well, I got to get going, Tío."

"Can I give you a lift?"

"No, I'm just a few blocks away. Take care."

"Thanks for the introduction. Let's talk more later."

I watched Raúl walk off and head up Eighteenth Street, paid the bill and walked to my car.

Chapter 8

(Roberto)

Alice Brown's first assignment upon joining the fledgling Quetzal Fund was to research all of the youth job training programs in the area. Two days after she had gotten the assignment, my executive assistant gave me a detailed description of dozens of programs she had found on the Internet. When the information was available, she had identified those that targeted Latino teens and specified the source and amount of their grant funding. She had categorized everything from the District's federal job corp. program to the new Latin American Youth Center's Ben & Jerry ice cream franchise entrepreneurial project. Alice lined up a few weeks' worth of site visits using her chamber contacts, a list of well-known foundation and nonprofit program experts, and a few references I provided. Max Ramirez and foundation colleagues in DC had advised that I carefully investigate current job training programs to see if there was an existing model that simply needed an infusion of capital to scale up and make the impact needed in the Latino community.

"Welcome, Mr. Prettyman and Ms. Brown." Marta Hernandez, CEO of La Puerta Abierta, extended a friendly hand as we entered her vestibule of a converted warehouse just off Mt. Pleasant Street in the Columbia Heights section of Washington.

"Thank you for seeing us, Ms. Hernandez. We've heard such wonderful things about your results with young people." We all went through the obligatory courtesies, and then Marta Hernandez took us through her well-funded after-school music, art, dance, and exercise facility.

"The green border along the top of this corridor leads to the dance studio, while the red leads to the music practice rooms, yellow leads to the gym, and so on."

"There's so much I'm curious about, Ms. Hernandez," I said.

"Marta, please."

"Okay. Marta. How do you measure the impact you're able to make? And why start with teenagers? Aren't the difficult behavior patterns set by that age?"

"Afternoon, Ms. Hernandez." A rough-looking black youth with a pronounced Spanish accent politely addressed the center's director as we passed a row of hall lockers near the gym. The director warmly addressed the youth and then turned to us.

"Let's go to the administrative offices, where we can talk more openly."

Several Latino and African-American boys gave both Marta and Alice a quick head-to-toe inspection as we passed through the multicolored halls. As we approached the floor-to-ceiling glassed-in administrative offices, a group of vocal boys and girls reduced their chatter only a couple of decibels as we cut through them. While in the middle of a crowd of a couple of dozen kids, Marta assertively called out.

"Manuel and Aisha, can you come to the office a moment?"

The whole crowd stared at the director as if she had just given them some terrible news.

"Now, Ms. Hernandez?" they said in chorus.

"If you have the time. Yes, right now, please."

We sat on thick cushions covered with rainbow-striped Mayan seat covers inside the sparse, but tastefully appointed conference room. Each wall was a different bright color, buttressed by sturdy hand-carved Mexican chairs and end tables. The twenty-four-seat capacity wrought iron and glass table sat under soft recessed ceiling lighting in the middle of the room. We were each brought a tall glass of ice water. I wondered for a moment who financed the decorations of this famous nonprofit youth center.

As she settled into the seat at the head of the table, I realized for the first time that Marta Hernandez was a very attractive woman. Her old-fashioned horn-rimmed glasses and hair pulled back in a "schoolmarm" bun gave her a severe look. When she finally smiled, however, her light-hazel eyes, pinkish mouth, and caramel complexion projected classical Latin beauty. Her smile was so wide and warm that the teens lost their tension and talked freely.

They talked about how their test scores in school had shot up, how they loved coming to the center, and how they were glad to be someplace where it was ok to excel at something. We asked them a few softball questions, which they hammered with the finesse of experienced interview subjects.

After the kids left, Alice asked the logical follow-up.

"So, what would allow you to take this to scale?"

"If you mean, would more resources permit us to reach a lot more kids? Perhaps. But, to be honest with you, I am not convinced that we can find or handle more kids without getting them ostracized by their peers. I just think we've hit a saturation point and that there is a strong culture of mediocrity, backed by a sub-current of youth violence, that would keep our numbers where they are. None of these kids, for example, talked about the boys who leave the program each year because they have been beaten up."

John McKoy

"But if you got to more kids, couldn't you tip the predominant culture to one of achievement, of that old-fashioned American dream?"

"I'm afraid, Mr. Prettyman, that that's what it is for most of these kids. Old-fashioned."

"You don't sound too hopeful."

"For the majority of the kids in this building, yes, I am. It's that they are such a small minority in the community."

"Well, we appreciate your honesty." I couldn't think of what else to say.

"This is, nonetheless, a fabulous program. And your results are quite impressive." Alice was able to be more gracious.

"Please, come by anytime," said Marta, extending her hand.

As we got into my car, I glanced over to my young assistant.

"She's going to be our first grant. What do you think?"

"She sure deserves it. But I guess we have a great deal to learn, if we're to make a real impact on youth employment. And she's pretty convinced that there's a real saturation point, beyond which you won't find any willing kids," said Alice.

"That's what's going to make this fun."

Chapter 9

Weeks passed, and Raúl's diligent rehab exercising paid off. One had to know he'd been injured to notice any difference in his stride, strength, or stamina. And even then, his recovery was 99 percent, so he was soon back into the swing of his old life.

"That's crazy, *mano*. Nobody's goin' to think there's any political significance to it. They'll think it's crazy Latino hoods."

"You sound like your uncle, man. The only way to get some real change is to threaten, to cause revolution. We'll all be dead by the time the evolution works." Javier Hector Romano was forcefully pushing his point to Raúl Gonzalez at one of their favorite watering holes, El Rincon on Columbia Road.

"Look, Raúl, no one gets hurt, but it sends a message. And in case they're too dense, we e-mail the TV stations about the need for better schools and jobs up here," Hector persisted.

"Tío Bob may be stuck in the past in many ways, but I think his approach can work."

"No doubt. But for how many dudes, and how long can it take for one organization? We need to push the government, man."

Raúl thought about his friend's plan for a few minutes. He sucked on the lime from his can of Tecate.

"It would get the mule's attention," he finally conceded.

"Look, all you have to do is send the e-mail blast."

"I guess; I can do that from an Internet café up at Eighteenth Street. Nobody would notice."

"Yeah. Man, it's not like we're into this suicide stuff. Me and the boys want to live to enjoy the revolution. Can't be as sure as the Muslims are of what's on the other side of death." Both young men laughed and chugged their beers.

Two days later, at 6:35 p.m., Mayor Anthony Williams' two-car motorcade turned left off of Sixteenth Street, slowed down and moved carefully up Mount Pleasant Street toward a meeting at Bancroft Elementary School. As the lead car drew within fifty yards of the intersection of Park Road, an old red Toyota Corolla parked near the corner exploded and burst into flames. Plate glass from four or five stores next to the corner filled the air and a couple of other parked cars were torched, but the boom, the dust, and the trash blown into the air gave the impression of a larger blast than had actually occurred. Two teenage boys were cut on the arms, but other would-be pedestrians had been diverted from the area by some temporary barrier cones mysteriously placed on the sidewalk fifteen minutes before the mayor had turned onto the strip. No one in the mayor's two vehicles was injured, and his chauffer quickly executed a U-turn and sped back down Mount Pleasant, away from the scene. Police who had been stationed along the route near the intersection could find few witnesses and no real suspects. Their lab later determined that a very small incendiary bomb had been ignited by a radio remote device.

As the mayor's car raced back toward city hall, his aide for Latino affairs flipped on the radio to an all-news station.

"Minutes ago, a car bomb exploded in front of Mayor Williams's limo as he was approaching a meeting on youth employment at the Bancroft Elementary School in Mount Pleasant. No one appears to have been seriously hurt, but the intersection of Mount Pleasant and Park Road is now blocked off by police."

"Well, WTOP sure gets tips fast." The mayor was finally breathing normally. "You know, we weren't actually that close, and I'm not sure that was a lot of explosive, but it got my attention," he said with his wry sense of humor.

"This just in." The radio cut them off. "A blast e-mail we've received takes credit for the blast and demands that the city provide real jobs for Latino youth. It further claims that nothing planned so far approaches the level of training and job placement needed to really help. And who's the claimant? *La Gente.* The People," said the announcer.

Early the next morning, the mayor placed a call to an old colleague, the CEO of Mega Builders. He had moved on to a pile of papers stacked for signature on the large oak table in the middle of his main office. Soft Oscar Peterson piano notes floated about the spring air, sweetened by wisteria cut from his wife's garden.

"He's no longer at the company, but he has set up a foundation. Something like '*El Pretzel.*' Do you want me to try to reach him there, Mayor?" his assistant asked.

"Fine. Yeah, please find him."

Two minutes later, the mayor was connected.

"Bob? How are you? It must be two or three years."

"It's been awhile, Mayor. Are you okay after that explosion yesterday?" I inquired.

"Yes, yes; I'm fine. But that's what I'm calling about, in a way. Whatever happened to that idea you used to talk about of starting some job training thing for Latino kids?"

"Well, Mayor—"

"For Christ's sake, call me Tony. This isn't a public meeting."

"Okay, well, El Quetzal is a foundation set up to fund youth training and job development efforts in DC."

"So, you're funding someone else to do it?"

"That's the idea, but we haven't made any grants yet. It's so ironic. You're the first mayor in a while with a specific agenda to help Latino kids, and look at the reward."

"Well, that whole business yesterday is clearly a direct result of our lack of attention in that area. This whole business about tightening immigration laws is crazy. These kids need education and jobs. I'm willing to put money into it, if you just show the way. I'd love it if you'd get back to me as soon as you have something that can make a big impact quickly."

"Mayor … Tony, I might just have something soon."

"Good. Get back to me. Make it me personally, not any of my departments or staff. Thanks. Bye."

Prettyman let the quiet of the early morning in Columbia Heights settle over him for several minutes. The folder on his desk next to the phone was labeled "Potential Grantees," and its top document was a detailed twenty-page brief on La Puerta Abierta. Alice Brown had developed an excellent analysis of its current operations and capacity, as well as an estimate of the resources it would take to increase its service level to amounts that might make substantial impact on the unemployed male

Latino population in Mount Pleasant and Adams-Morgan. She had also completed more background information on Marta Hernandez.

Marta was thirty-three and had grown up in a Mexican-American Los Angeles neighborhood, attended UCLA, majored in sociology, and graduated Phi Beta Kappa. She started doing nonprofit work at Centro Nia (a Columbia Heights program for young children and mothers primarily from Central American immigrant families) while in graduate school at Catholic University in DC. She later got into youth employment work through a job with the Boys and Girls Club, where she was rapidly promoted into management. Her reputation was that of an innovative, fair, and very tough leader. Marta had said that she didn't want major expansion, but she recognized that the environment was getting out of hand.

Prettyman needed a vehicle, and he could wait for the programmatic details to be filled in later.

"Alice, do you have Marta Hernandez's cell number?" Without waiting for an answer, he barked an instruction. "See if you can get her for lunch or early afternoon today."

"Today?" she asked, to be sure of the urgency.

"Absolutely. These kids won't wait," insisted Prettyman.

Chapter 10

(Roberto)

Cosi is a franchised coffeehouse and sandwich shop made popular in the District in the early 2000s. The new affluence that moved into Columbia Heights Metro Rail station condos provided market for a comfortable shop on Fourteenth Street. From a table looking out onto the busy noontime street scene, I watched Marta Hernandez cross the main drag and approach my spot. I gave her a perfunctory buss on the cheek and helped her into a chair.

"Thanks for seeing me on such short notice. I think, however, things are heating up and bode ill for the summer jobs season."

"Well, I was a bit surprised to get Ms. Brown's call. Clearly, I'm happy to talk. I don't see how I can impact the current tension, however," she replied.

"Do you think a million dollars over two years could impact?"

For the first time since I'd met and observed her lovely face, Marta Hernandez registered wide-eyed shock.

"Oh, Bob, thank you for your confidence and for your flattering view of La Puerta Abierta, but we can't absorb $500,000 more per year. We don't have staff trained—"

"Will the facilities accommodate a hundred-plus more kids per day? I figure you now spend no more than five thousand per kid per year for your most expensive programs."

"That sounds high. But, okay, let's say a hundred to 150 more children. Space is not the most pressing issue. It's staff. It's taken us years to build this core. Then there's the time needed to build the interaction with the kids that permits real youth development. Then there's staff team spirit." Marta was clutching for reasons not to take a million bucks.

"So, you can't help? Even if we throw in top-notch management help?"

Marta Hernández looked away at the clouds floating by a blue background behind new sandstone-colored, five- to seven-story commercial structures. Then she turned back to me. I couldn't tell what was happening behind her hazel eyes, but there were neurons firing rapidly, for sure.

"Let me talk this over with my staff. I mean, I know the need is out there, and I do think we can help certain children, but without careful screening, we could get an impossible group and do more damage than good. And more success could easily breed resentment and negative reaction from some quarters in the neighborhood."

Marta fidgeted with her napkin, looked off toward the street, tightened her lips, and then turned back to me.

"I am not ungrateful, but this would be a big jump. Let me get back to you," she finally said.

"No problem, Marta. You should be sure and committed to the increase in service. Take your time." I tried to be reassuring. "Shall we order?" I was used to doing core business quickly and then building the relationship with business associates. Marta was too absorbed with her work to be able to enjoy a "social" lunch.

"I think I'm going to take a rain check. You've given me quite a bit to think through. I appreciate the offer, but there's a lot to figure out."

"You promise that I get a rain check?"

Again, that glorious smile. "Absolutely."

I stayed and ordered half a ham sandwich and a cup of corn soup. I moved to a corner booth, pulled out my grants folder, and sipped on a Coke. I'm not sure how long it took for me to get the sandwich, but within minutes, my mind jumped from other prospective grantees to Marta, from Marta to Mónica. Their smiles were eerily similar, I thought. Their business constitutions, however, were radically different. Mónica made lightning-quick business or investment decisions, because she usually anticipated options and developed contingencies far in advance of face-to-face meetings. Probably not a fair comparison, because Marta didn't know ahead of time the real purpose of the lunch. And Marta's social justice IQ far exceeded Mónica's. I still mulled over the comparison. Then I found myself focused solely on my ex-wife.

"Berto, it's beautiful. I don't believe I've seen foothills this lush in my life." Mónica smiled and planted a kiss on my cheek as I steered the compact car around yet another mountain curve near Quetzaltenango in central Guatemala.

"*Papi,* can you take these curves more slowly?" fourteen-year-old Lisa pleaded from the backseat.

"Okay, *preciosa*. We'll be at the lake soon. Then you can rest, walk, and swim for several days," I said, slowing down slightly.

"Watch out, Berto. There's a jeep blocking the road around the next bend," said Mónica, and the cheer drained from her face.

By the time I braked and stopped in front of the empty jeep, I knew we would be trapped by guerrillas. The second jeep pulled up behind us and three camouflaged rebels leapt from the vehicle, rifles drawn.

"Stay calm," I said to Mónica and Lisa seconds before the leader ordered us from the car.

"*Como puedo ayudarle?*" I quietly asked the leader as I opened the door.

A five-foot-six, dark-brown-skinned Ladino youth of twenty-five or so motioned me to the front of the car, turned me around to face the hood, patted me down, and commanded me to wait. He instructed his partners to get Mónica and Lisa from the car.

My daughter seemed defiant in a silent way, but Mónica began orally protesting as she got out.

The calm commander lost his cool and yelled for her to shut up. I tried to signal for her to be quiet, but Mónica got more agitated and began to struggle.

To draw attention my way, I said, "*Ellas no tienen dinero.*"

"What makes you think we're after money?" The leader did focus on me. After a few exchanges, he told us to stand by the side of the road. Mónica's gorgeous violet eyes and sparkling Pepsodent smile tightened to slits of intense anger. Her expression was etched in my memory, and I felt her belligerent reaction rapidly increasing the danger to us all.

I wrapped my arms around Mónica and Lisa while the guerillas rifled through our clothes and papers. Even though I tried to calm them, I could feel Lisa relax slightly and my wife grow progressively more tense. When a couple of teenage guerillas not much more than Lisa's age discovered a felt bag with Mónica's earrings and necklaces, she screamed at them and tried to break my embrace. Only when the two youngsters pointed bayonets at Mónica did she freeze and quiet herself.

John McKoy

To this day, I'm not sure how we escaped losing only jewelry and a few dollars from my wallet. Not more than fifteen minutes after we were stopped, we were waved on and hurriedly made our way to our pension at Lake Atitlan.

"Why didn't you try to do something?" Mónica's anger rekindled itself as I drove.

"*Mi vida*, we're all safe. What would you have me do? Take on three armed guerillas and get us all killed?"

"I felt so helpless, as if I was the only one fighting them," she said, near to tears.

"I don't see how we could have had a better result, once they had us boxed in. Please, Mónica. Let it go."

"Papi, Mommy. Please, don't fight. Those men were scary enough," Lisa pleaded from the backseat.

When we finally reached the hills above Lake Atitlan and descended into the village of Panajachel through roadside groves of trees smelling of orange blossom and eucalyptus, the family was more relaxed. When we waded into the azure-blue, chilly water for the first time, we were holding hands. And by dinner out on the patio overlooking a pink and purple sunset, our collective capability to compartmentalize had chalked the afternoon's adventure up to "life in a developing country" and filed it away for future reference and stories.

I suppose I had hoped that that trip would show my Cuban wife and American daughter the beautiful, culturally diverse and rich part of the countryside that I had so often associated with my homeland. Mónica knew about the legacy of cruel dictatorships, the oppression of indigenous people by the mixed-blood Ladinos, the almost endemic corruption, and the growing violent drug trade. That history is not the whole of Guatemala, and I had hoped to provide other more joyful and romantic images to provide contrast and reveal the complexity of modern-day Mayan country. Luckily, our family had several other trips that provided a diversity of memorable and enjoyable experiences.

The waiter's subtle coughing brought me back to the present, and I left a tip, stood, and walked back to the Metro station to catch a train to my office.

"Lunch go well?" Alice Brown's quick glance was genuinely inquiring, even though her fingers never missed a key on her desktop keyboard.

"Pretty well. Marta Hernandez is going to think about it," I responded as I headed into my small corner office.

"Oh, Max Ramirez called with some dates. I booked you on a Friday a.m. train to New York for your visit," she said.

Chapter 11

(Roberto)

I hadn't heard back from Marta by Friday morning when I boarded the Amtrak Metroliner at Union Station for New York. Those couple of days had given me an opportunity to think about the previous week's chain of events. The brief restaurant meeting with Raúl's friend Hector, which was aborted by a police search; the bombing of a car in front of the mayor's motorcade; Marta's hesitance to take a grant to expand La Puerta Abierta; and the pending visit from Lisa all seemed important. I couldn't begin, however, to make sense of or draw conclusive meaning from the events. The three-plus hour trip up to New York provided no answers.

I took the Broadway Number 1 train up to Columbia University, spent an hour browsing in the university bookstore, and then met Max at a faculty lounge for lunch.

"You're looking chipper, amigo," said Max, greeting me with a big hug.

"Well, that ride is so relaxing, and with no business deals to contemplate, it is sort of refreshing. I must admit, however, that I'm glad to see you and will be interested in the projects, because we're not having an easy time finding our first investment."

"I also hear there's a bit of Central American action bubbling up in DC."

Son of the Maya

"Oh, what have you heard?"

"Just that some of the Salvadoran and Guatemalan radicals are organizing the young unemployed to develop foot soldiers for the hills in Guatemala. You know it's been rather calm in your homeland for almost seven years. The violent cycle is due to return soon. That is, if the last fifty years is any indication of the future."

"Well, that would explain one part of the curious environment right now. I don't think anything in real estate was as tough to navigate as simply trying to help kids in the District."

"We'll take my car. I think you'll see quite a few changes since you were last in Harlem."

Riding east along 125th Street was enlightening. New office buildings with chic upscale shops set the streetscape, while trendy-looking yuppies in beat-up-looking jeans and tattered sneaks that cost hundreds of dollars walked tiny, defenseless dogs among the hang-out brothers and strolling *senoras* attentive to baby-carriage-hugging young kids. It wasn't the rich East Side, or the well-off Upper West Side, or the rundown Harlem of old. This marginally gentrified Harlem was something new, something blended. We drove past a complex devoted to a charter school and family support programs called "Harlem Children's Zone" and a spiffed-up public elementary school playground.

I felt like the real estate and the minds of children were getting equal attention and perhaps redefining community identity in this new Harlem. As we moved deeper into East Harlem, it was clear that the commercial renewal extended only so far. Storefronts with loosely attached signs, rusted window bars, and crowded merchandise displays still dominated some blocks. Max told me that while crime statistics were down, elementary school test scores were stabilizing and beginning to rise; however, the full impact of Harlem's latest renaissance was still inconclusive.

We parked near a mid-block brownstone townhouse on a quiet side street and climbed the steps to what appeared to be a well-kept residential four-story unit.

"*Buenas tardes,* Senor Ramirez. *Adelante,*" was the greeting of a jeans-clad young woman at the door. No holes or patches, just pressed denim blue jeans.

"*Quiero presentarle a mi amigo,* Roberto Prettyman," Max introduced me.

Alma Santiago took us on a tour of La Cultura's program performance spaces, reading nooks, computer labs, video theater, ceramics studio, and lounge areas. Only a few kids were in each space because it was only 2:30 p.m., an hour or so before kids began to arrive from school. The young staff members I saw preparing for their next activities or talking with the few kids present seemed caring and sharp. Those with whom Max or I spoke all seemed to possess intensity below the surface of their conviviality.

"Every time I visit, it seems like you've found some new way to engage and inspire young teens' social and emotional development," Max said to Alma.

"I'm very impressed by the variety of activities. I'm curious. Do you have any way of measuring the impact you're having, Alma?" I asked.

"Good. Looking for the numbers. Let's go to your office, and Alma, maybe you can pull up the last grant reports," Max suggested.

Typical of many great program administrators, Alma had spent little money on her cramped office, compared to the investment evidenced in the student areas. We crowded around her laptop and reviewed school performance, absentee, and arrest data Alma kept on her young people. All of the indicators were heading in the right direction.

"I would caution you, however, Mr. Roberto, not to expect to see rapid improvement for at least two years. We have changed the culture for our youngsters, and we've built their capability to withstand the pull of the strong negative environment in their schools and on the streets. They all have to find ways that work for them to pretend, to ignore, or to avoid the approaches of bullies and the like. I am very proud of our children."

"With these results, you should be. Very impressive," I said. "So, what do you think makes your program special? How are you able to succeed so well in getting kids into good high schools?"

"I don't know, because many of the programs we have, you'll find elsewhere in the community. I suppose I spend a great deal of time recruiting the right staff. And in a big place like New York, you can find smart, dedicated people who don't need large salaries to work."

"Alma is modest," added Max. "She spends lots of effort finding, building, mentoring, and maintaining staff. Sometimes, we on the board think she searches for as many ways to reward the staff as she does the kids. But it works."

We thanked our host and left her to attend to La Cultura's late-afternoon agenda, now in full swing.

Max suggested we drive back to a little café near Columbia for a drink and reflection. On the way, we stopped by another after-school program devoted to reading and sports for older Latino boys. As we traversed Harlem and then the Upper West Side, the sounds of young people laughing and bantering, the beat and rhythm of club "musack" and apartment phonos, or the dribbling of playground basketball and thumping of steel drums and the smells from sidewalk vendors and restaurant kitchen doors enveloped me.

As I sat at a sidewalk café, Frank Sinatra on the speakers, students debating at one table, professors pontificating at another, government officials agonizing at another, I waited for Max to return from placing the bar order. I smiled, closed my eyes, and inhaled New York. The bright neon colors of Forty-Second Street, the classical elegance of Lincoln Center, the "time is money" focus etched in the brows of executives on "the Street," the European style strutting along Madison Avenue, the brash and boisterous fans filing into Yankee Stadium, and the collage of tongues bouncing off the buildings along Broadway all rushed by on an imaginary screen as I daydreamed.

"Jack Daniels on the rocks." Max brought me back to the present.

"Cheers, my friend. Thank you for an interesting afternoon."

"My pleasure. So, did you conclude that staff talent is the key?"

"Max, before I go there, I've been reflecting on how New York is so different from much of the country. Certainly different from my little capital city. I mean the scale alone. Your mix of glamour and blatant materialism, the bigger-than-life display of culture—music, theater, movies, dance—are all over the top. It goes on and on. So many lifestyles and lives co-existing, yet not *really* mingling. The twenty-four-hour city with beauty in unsuspected places: small galleries and big museums; opulent, brilliantly lit interiors inside deteriorating classical structures. The unmanageable city with problems of impossible scale, with decades of historic social programs and heralded mayors. The dying, yet indestructible city. NYC, the Big Apple. Why would I try to find answers for our little Latino population in this world-size metropolis?"

"Wow. Take a sip of your Jack. You need to slow down the current in that stream of consciousness." Max smiled and raised his mojito in a toast.

"The size of the neighborhoods and the dollars required to fix our ills may be larger. The keys to success, however, are more than likely the same. And you'd be surprised at the mingling that does go on, particularly with the younger sets." Max stopped and waited for my response.

"Well, a couple of hours of touring projects don't even touch the surface, but you're right. If I had to pick the main ingredient, it would be talent.

Probably like my old business, talent alone isn't sufficient, but you can't create a winner without it."

"My friend, as much as program components can and should make a difference, starting out, I'd find your most talented youth program leader and surround him with support, resources, and more talent."

"Her."

"I'm sorry?" he asked.

"*Her.* I think it's surround *her* in this case."

"*Perfecto. Lo que sea.* Surround her."

"Cheers, my friend. And thanks for an insightful day."

Chapter 12

(Roberto)

The message from Marta on the office voice mail simply asked me to call, so I called her cell phone Saturday morning. She answered, and I apologized for disturbing her weekend.

"No problem. I was just getting ready to run by the office for the morning. But I want to take you up on your offer. That is, if I can grow the center at a pace I feel comfortable with."

"I think that's a very reasonable condition. I'll get a grant letter out to you early in the week."

"Thank you for trusting in us. We all think it's a great opportunity. It took some thinking through, because we've seen success kill lots of good projects. After your offer, I walked around some of the Columbia Heights side streets and ran into so many teens. They aren't benefiting from the new coffee shops, or the Harris Teeters, or the upscale menu/downscale décor fun places in the neighborhood. They're hanging out, waiting to find trouble or to have trouble find them. The Latin American Youth Center helps lots of young kids, but there are still so many, more hardcore youth that need to be reached. We have no option but to try."

"Well, I'm delighted. I am confident you can have impact well beyond what you probably believe, but one step at a time. My job now is to get you the resources and step out of the way."

"We can use all the advice you can offer. Talk to you next week. And, thank you again."

I asked Alice Brown to draft the letter according to the outlines from the grant makers' regional association. She also set about establishing accounting and grant deliverables folders so we could track performance. The initial grant amount was ready with the stroke of a pen, so I began thinking about how and where to attract other funds to ensure that Marta's payments could flow unimpeded for a couple of years. The mayor's offer would help but certainly not be sufficient. So I had made several lists of different categories of potential contributors the old way, on a legal pad, and had just taken the lists to Alice for her to add the phone numbers when my line rang.

"Hello, Papi. Do you have time for dinner tonight?"

"Well, how are you, Lisa?"

"I'm fine, had a good flight in from the coast, and I would really like to see you."

"Nice to hear your voice. Of course we can have dinner. I know you don't want anything too fancy. How about Cubanos in Silver Spring?"

"Oh, I remember that. Perfect. See you at about 7:30?"

"See you there, Lisa."

Why is it so awkward when we first meet or talk? We're not really estranged. Then again, we're not close, either, and I feel like we should be. Then again, I wasn't ever really close to my father. For the moment, I had to put my relationship with Lisa in its mental cubicle and move on.

The fundraising calls went well. That is to say, people were cordial and expressed interest in my ideas, but were curious as to why I didn't simply run projects myself. They'd say something like, "With your private-sector experience, why not design and run your own project?"

Other philanthropists often remarked, "You've got more money to put into your initial projects than I give away in five years. I have plenty of grantees I can send your way."

The discovery that the foundation community perceived The Quetzal Fund as already well endowed, not as a facilitator to whom they would contribute, forced me to reconsider my investment strategy. I began investigating partnerships with foundations and others in a way that I hadn't considered months before. I realized that I hadn't developed a realistic strategy yet, to leverage my money. While the calls were initially frustrating, the problem they crystallized provided the sort of business challenge I enjoyed solving. The hours flew by in thought. Seven p.m. arrived quickly. I left the office and drove up Georgia Avenue to the Maryland suburb where I was to meet Lisa.

I got to the restaurant first, ordered a drink, and settled into my chair to review the past few days' events. I didn't know how long I'd been engrossed in the past before Lisa was taking a seat across from me.

"Hello, Papi," she said while reaching across the table to touch my hand.

I got up, took a step, and gave her a peck on the cheek. "You grow more beautiful every time I see you, *mi hija. Como estas*, Lisa?"

"I'm good, Papi. What about you?"

"Great, but what would you like to drink?"

"You know; I haven't had sangria in a long time."

After I ordered her drink, I rested my gaze on her light-green eyes.

"Where do we start?" I asked.

"Tell me about this project. Raúl said that you have started a foundation or something."

Her hair had grown and accepted reddish highlights into the deep-brunette base. Her figure was still trim but more curved than I recalled. She was a beautiful young woman.

"All right, but then I want to hear all about school and your life out there."

I gave her a twenty-minute capsule of starting the foundation, finding Marta's organization, and my trip to New York. I didn't tie in any of my Raúl or Hector Romano encounters.

"That's certainly more interesting than commercial real estate buildings." Lisa looked away. "I'm sorry, Papi. I'm very happy that you're trying to make this work. And, as hard as it is for me to admit, I'm proud of what you're doing."

After that icebreaker, we were able to have a fascinating, even instructive discussion about the diagnosis of urban juvenile issues and theories of change.

"Papi, it's strange, because with my double major, I can appreciate what I think are the macroeconomic forces that bring a lot of these kids to Washington, while I also see the cultural collisions their migration brings about, on the ground. The dynamics of big-time agricultural add a different dimension in California, but the tensions are similar."

"You've also got a bigger, more established Chicano community in the mix, and the Hispanic community has been there long enough to build a middle class and political power. We don't have that here. And a small foundation has so little influence that you're forced to think small, at least in the beginning. First, you have to figure out solutions, and then you have to find leadership to carry them out; finally, you get to worry about going to scale."

"Papi, you don't have to do the second step."

"What do you mean?"

"I mean, *you* may be the leadership. You yourself."

"I don't have the energy, at this point, to devote my whole being to this fight."

"Maybe. But if it's about leadership in the end, then it may be up to you, Papi." Lisa took a bite of the plump chicken enchilada covering her plate. "You didn't build Mega Builders into a success by turning it over to Mr. Robinson or anyone else before you had gotten it to where it is today, I'll bet. You had to implement your own vision."

"Listen to you and all of this business psychology." I stopped to eat my chicken in onions and to absorb what my twenty-four-year-old daughter was suggesting.

"That's funny that you still roll your food in tortillas." Lisa pointed a fork at my chicken-and-onion tortilla wrap as I washed down the first bites with a couple of gulps of a cold Tecate.

"I suppose some habits endure. Okay, mi hija, tell me about you."

"Well, Papi, there's not much to tell. I go to class, research in the library, take care of my apartment, and see a few friends. I might go for a hike or a swim here and there, and occasionally eat out. Nothing exciting."

"How do you like Berkeley? Do you ever go into San Francisco?"

"You know that I love the Bay Area. If you and Mama weren't out East, I probably wouldn't even think about moving back. I am interviewing for jobs on both coasts later this year. And, no, there's no guy in my life."

"I didn't ask a thing about men," I protested.

"No, but you were thinking about it."

"Well, it is, you must admit, a reasonable thing to ponder."

"You know whose life I am worried about is Raúl's. I saw him yesterday, and although he's got a lot of activity in his life, Raúl seemed lost to me."

"Lost?"

"Yes. He wasn't really into his association career. And I don't think he's clear about his current activity and which friends are into lefty political action versus who's just part of some drug ring."

"I'm obviously concerned too, but tell me more."

"Well, I've learned a great deal about various West Coast connections to Central American politics, not just what's happening in Mexico. Raúl never probed me, but he seemed jazzed about the impact of some explosions that shook up your mayor's schedule one day and made national news."

"So, you think he's a bit immature in his understanding of revolutionary politics?" I asked.

"This is only based on one short visit. Maybe *unsophisticated* is more descriptive than *immature*. He seems to overlook the complexities involved in social change, and I don't think I'd be comfortable with his grasp of 'tactics' for even any protest in which I might be involved. I have to admit that I fully understand the dilemma of being rich enough to benefit from access to a prestigious US education, yet recoiling at the apparent axis of indifference (those in power) that condemns Latino youth, both here and in Guatemala, to underclass status."

"I see," I said and tried to convince her that I also understood, given my path to success. Lisa insisted that my situation, my era, was different. I let it go.

"I took a taxi. Could you give me a ride to the Metro, Papi?"

I looked up from the table and around the sparsely populated restaurant.

"Boy, I didn't realize it was so late. So, what are you doing after your conference?"

"I'm flying to Miami to spend a couple of days with Mama."

"Well, I'm delighted that I got some time to see you, Lisa."

"Me too, Papi."

We chatted more about her outdoor hiking and water sport activities as I drove my daughter to the Washington Hilton.

Later in the week, I thought I'd get Raúl's reaction to the Puerta Abierta project by having him meet me there after work. He agreed, so I asked Marta to arrange a little tour.

Chapter 13

(Roberto)

My conversation with Lisa, a few more chats with Raúl, interviews with new colleagues who had been involved with Latino, particularly Central American, youth brought me to the conclusion that I needed more information on the situation that was driving the current migration north. Was it gangs, police violence, unemployment, inflated stories from migrants already in DC, or some combination of the above? I also felt I needed to better understand the viewpoint of my cohorts who had chosen to stay and seemed to live comfortably in my hometown of Guatemala City. During a phone conversation with my cousin, María Elena Gonzales, she asked if I ever thought about my mother during these spring days, which represented the anniversary of her passing.

"I have to admit, María, that I think about her so often that no, I don't have any particular focus on the anniversary of her death."

After I hung up, however, I thought that an obvious way to gain some clarity on the Quetzal mission would be to visit Guatemala, to get reconnected, so to speak. My old pal and Mom's former employer, Guillermo Schaefer, and María Elena were logical touch points. So I had Alice book the flight.

The red, green, and white spring planting around the airport looked and smelled the same as always—capturing and magnifying the sun's rays brilliantly and smelling like freshly cut lilacs. The low-scale suburbs surrounding the highway into the center of town offered no hint that Guatemala City was any different than half a dozen other Central American metropolises. Single-family homes hid behind six-foot trellised walls topped with broken glass, hiding lush gardens, tiled patios, and stucco facades. The first in-town boulevard cafes displayed young professionals in white seersucker suits munching nuts and sipping rum or an occasional coffee. The life one saw from the taxi window was manicured, lush, ample, and *tranquillo*. Even the youngest tourist, however, would notice the police and soldiers scattered about the city and wonder, *Why the heavy armed presence?* But I allowed myself to inhale the beauty, to admire the trees and flowers and the comfort of a smooth ride back home.

Guillermo Schaefer's office was in a seven-story steel-and-glass bank building in the heart of Guatemala City. The feel was urban, but not as crowded as Mexico City, not as sparse as Tegucigalpa, nor as low-scale as San Jose, yet had all the charm of twentieth century Caracas. On Guillermo's little section of *Avenida Reforma*, I saw the passing of the ethnic mix which kept the country bubbling beneath the service: native *Indígenas*, pure white Europeans, and mixed Ladinos. The door to Guillermo's outer office was sturdy and plain. It only said "Señor Schaefer." He could be a dentist, accountant, or lawyer by the outside appearance. Inside, his receptionist, administrative assistant, and walking Rolodex, Olivia de Marcos, gave me a warm welcome, as if I were a returning veteran. She took my bag and then walked me past the other employee's, Daniel Valenzuela's, office on our way to the large memento and book-laden inner sanctum of Guillermo Schaefer.

"*Cuanto tiempo, amigo*! God, it's great to see you, Roberto." We embraced.

"Gil, everything looks so green, full of life and promise. Even the soldiers look relatively calm. It must be a good period in the capital."

"For now, you're right. But, as you know all too well, that can change in a second. Berto, give me one second; I have to check one thing with Olivia, and then maybe we get an early dinner, eh?"

I swiveled the deep leather chair toward the floor-length picture window, which overlooked a picturesque boulevard leading toward a dominant gothic cathedral, farther toward the center of town. Turning away toward the opposite wall, I saw, at each end of his leather couch, two circular walnut tables that held speckled *Oaxaca* figures, South African dolls, and replica Xian soldiers. The shelves behind the couch reflected his eclectic English and Spanish reading tastes. *Understanding International Conflicts* by Joseph Nye; *Negotiating Globally* by Jeanne Brett; *Diplomacy* by Henry Kissinger; *El Presidente* by Guatemalan legend Miguel Ángel Asturias; *I, Rigoberta Menchu* and *The Hydra Head* by Carlos Fuentes; *The Feast of the Goat* by Mario Vargas Llosa; *Long Walk to Freedom* by Nelson Mandela; *The Kite Runner* by Khaled Hosseini; and *Globalization and its Discontents* by Joseph E. Stiglitz were a few that caught my eye as I scanned.

Behind his desk, next to a small photo collection of four scenes showing beach, jungle, mountain, and cornfields, Guillermo had framed a large collage of typical Guatemalan woven textiles. The juxtaposition served as a subtle reminder of the brilliant and delicate mix of cultures, societies, and landscapes that make up this Ohio-sized country.

"Okay, it's all set. We'll register you at the hotel and can eat dinner right next door at a bistro that I don't think you know yet. I'll have Olivia pick you up in the morning and take you out to María Elena's for breakfast. She's dying to see you. Then you can still get a mid-morning start on whatever you've got planned."

"Well, Gil, you should be in the tourist business. Not only are you keeping up on the literature and politics around the world, but you also know how to organize private trips."

"At your service, amigo. However, as you can imagine, I'm nowhere near as well organized or as informed as when your dear mother helped me get started."

We both laughed raucously.

After a quick stroll to the little restaurant next door, we ate, drank, and talked of the complexities of Latin American trade, swirling politics, and shifting alliances. As we approached ten o'clock and the end of a wonderful visit, I asked Guillermo about the political situation in Guatemala.

"From the little you told me on the phone, I gather that you are concerned about Raúl's dealings. Well, the hills near Escuintla are the only active training grounds for revolutionaries that I know of now. Their focus, however, isn't the U.S.; it's Nicaragua and Mexico."

"Interesting. Why there?"

"Nicaragua is always in play. At least, it has been during most of our lifetime. And Mexico still offers slim promise of providing housing and jobs for its rural masses. The idea is to keep pressure on the government from the left and hope that the United States continues to ask more of the Mexican domestic economy to decrease the States' immigration problem. However, I think sophisticated guerillas understand that the attraction for the poor to endure the many risks of migrating north is likely to be reduced only by a combination of factors: improved Mexican economy, waning of US low-skilled opportunities, perpetual violence along Mexican border states, tightening United States border enforcement, and the continued perilous nature of the trek north. Given those dynamics, the theory goes, perpetual pressure from our lower classes will force change."

"That still seems like a long shot to me," I said.

"In the short run, you're right. But should migration through Mexico continue to be a high-risk proposition, the demand for and the willingness to die for change could increase here, Berto."

"Wow, the stuff has really gotten complicated, hasn't it? So, you think Raúl's involved in this in some way?"

"Without much more information, it's hard to tell. But I doubt it. He is not employed in an American company where he'd have access to useful information. If he were in some government office or international bank or working as an international trader, he might be useful. But from what you say his level is in his company, it's highly unlikely. Now, he might *think* that he's involved. My guess is that he's either knowingly or hopefully unknowingly involved with some cartel or gang. They're sophisticated enough to cloak their brutal dealings in political intrigue, while they're really carrying out some low-level criminal agenda. That's my guess."

"Thanks, Gil. I really appreciate your guidance."

"Needless to say, you have to be careful in polling around. On my cocktail napkin, I've written the names of some useful contacts for your stay. Pick it up as we leave the table."

"Maybe we can have lunch with Berta before I go. I'd love to see her."

"We'll try and make it happen. She's visiting her mother in Miami but should be back at the end of the week."

We rose and embraced. I walked a couple of blocks to my hotel.

The next morning, Olivia was waiting at the front door at eight in her Corolla and drove me the twenty-minute ride to my cousin's house. Out of habit from years of visiting Central America, I regularly checked the rearview mirror.

"Have you noticed that navy-blue BMW that's been following us for ten minutes?" I asked Olivia.

"Yes. It's probably police, since you came out of the hotel with a suit on and are not immediately recognizable to them. Many visitors to Senor Schaefer are followed."

"Well, I don't want to cause my cousin any problems. Maybe I'll get off near the train station, lose them, and get a taxi."

"You don't have to bother, Señor Prettyman. I have lots of experience losing 'tails,' as you *norteamericanos* call them."

The next five minutes were harrowing, but Olivia did indeed lose the tail. We arrived unaccompanied at my cousin's with the back of my shirt fairly wet from anxious perspiration.

"Outstanding job. My compliments." I gave her a light hug before she drove off, leaving me at the gate of María Elena's modest, but walled front yard on the western outskirts of Guatemala City. A maid escorted me through the garden and onto a side patio where she had laid out bread, jam, sliced papaya, and strong coffee.

"La señora will be out in a moment, Sr. Prettyman."

"Thank you, Graciela. I'll be fine here."

I sat inhaling the honeysuckle and listening to mourning doves coo as they went about their early chores. The rich voice of Spanish crooner Raphael drifted out from the little stereo María Elena had inside the living room, directly inside the double glass doors behind the porch lounge.

"My cousin. So sorry for keeping you waiting, Roberto."

We embraced and I held her at arm's length to see how prominent the worry lines around her eyes were. She looked five years younger and infinitely more relaxed than when she'd left Washington almost eleven months back.

"The year back home seems to have been good to you, María; you are as lovely and youthful as ever."

"Roberto, you still have your touch; thank you." We sat. "I think I have made peace with the fact that Raúl's life is in Washington, and I can't worry him back to Guate."

"That's quite rational and brave of you, but I wouldn't be surprised to see Raúl move back in a few years. He's not really found himself there, although he's happy for the time being."

"And what about you, my cousin, any new women in your life?"

"Ah, María Elena, I'm an old man. Women aren't—"

"Save it, Berto. Women *are* whatever you were going to deny. It's not good for you to be alone. You're still a young man. Maybe I should throw a party for you while you're here. Introduce you to some lovely women who'd love to move to the States."

"It's not that there aren't women in Washington, María. I suppose I'm just not that interested yet. But, come. Tell me about you. Who's in your life?"

"Well, there is a new gentleman that I've been seeing. He's quite good company."

"Company. And is it serious?"

"Oh, you're so silly. Why do I need a serious relationship at my age?"

"María, you're younger than I am, and who said it had to be serious? What does he do?"

"He's a professor at the Catholic University, Landivar. If you stay long enough, we'll have dinner."

"I'd like that."

We nibbled, sipped, and enjoyed reconnecting. It seemed like she was a very different woman from the scared and devoted mother who had stayed with me only a year ago, when she nursed Raúl back to health. Only after a couple of hours' conversation did I bring up the issues of rebels and of drug gangs.

"María, I'm a bit worried about Raúl."

"You mean, because he's not moving up in that business, or because he doesn't seem to have a girlfriend, or because of his ideas about revolution?"

"Well, you certainly have been keeping tabs."

"Well, I am his mother. Yes, he has a bit of indecision going on right now. But I think he'll straighten out. After all, whatever he's into up in 'Los Estados' is more promising and safer than what he'd have to deal with here."

I was beginning to think that talking to María Elena was not going to be fruitful, and I certainly didn't want to plant worry where there currently was none.

"Is Guatemala so bad right now that Raúl couldn't get a job with some trading company, or maybe some new computer business?"

"Berto, the drug gangs have their tentacles into everything. You have to know who to pay off just to be able to go into business," she replied.

"But, at least the violent political killings and kidnappings have died way down." I was asking more than stating a fact.

"For the moment, but you know how we are. If they get the drug gangs under control, then some army guys will get upset, because their extra income is cut. They'll find some political reason to have a coup. It goes on and on."

"You, my cousin, seem to have made peace with the situation. Maybe Raúl could."

"He's twenty-three or twenty-four and got his whole life ahead, not like me. No, better he makes his way, like you did. Besides, with the growing Mexican population, maybe more Cubanos leaving Castro, Latinos will soon be the biggest minority up there. That will be good for us."

"So, are there any questionable *muchachos* that Raúl stays in touch with here?"

"Since the shooting and his recuperation, I know very little about his relations here. He's becoming like you used to be. No news, no way."

I couldn't see the point in pursuing the issue more.

"There's another issue we've never really talked about, but I don't know if it's too delicate." I waited for her signal to continue.

"*Dime*, Berto."

"Well, I don't remember anything about your husband, Raúl's father, Mauro."

"There's not much to remember. He was a kind and charming man, but rarely at home. He was a top executive with the Embarcadero Coffee Company. We had an active social life that put me in contact with all of the government and military, as well as business leaders. Although I wasn't as vocal as your mom, my politics were far too leftist for that crowd, so I stopped attending many of his events. You don't remember him, because he was always working when you came during the summer.

Anyway, as the company grew and as Mauro's role increased, he drank more and really neglected his health. He died young of a heart attack."

We took a stroll around the garden so that María Elena could show me the new flowering plants she'd put in since my last visit, as we waited for the taxi she had called.

"You know, I just remembered this very serious graduate student that Paul is always talking about. He's impressed with his knowledge of United States politics and his fascination with Cuba. Paul thinks he's involved somehow with the Central American leftist movements. But you should talk to him. The student's name is Oscar something."

"And Paul is your friend at <u>Landivar</u>?"

"Yes. I'll tell him to call you at the hotel."

The taxi arrived, and María Elena and I hugged good-bye. On the shorter, more direct trip back into town, I pulled Guillermo's crumpled napkin from my pocket. One of the names of the two recommendations he made was *Paulo Lancea, Landívar*. Now I was anxious to meet Elena's Paul and his student, Oscar. I had the driver drop me on the edge of La Limonada, the *favela*-like ravine of dense urban slums. He insisted on waiting until I came out, given the reputation for crime and violence this city-within-a-city had. I wandered down garbage-strewn dirt paths, past stick and corrugated tin-roofed shacks, chatting with young and old as they stopped to greet me. I was not in business clothes, but I was clearly more expensively dressed than the average resident.

The lush green islands separating traffic lanes on boulevards in other sections of town and the brilliant floral trees adorning the hotel areas were spectacularly absent. Dust was everywhere, and I forced myself to reject all thoughts of the pathogens I might be inhaling with each step. The physical deprivation was depressing, but I could detect nothing of the sloth or violence the newspapers would have assured would cross my path in my stroll. I stopped in a store, which appeared to be a community gathering place. Rather than complain about the gangs, men talked about the lack of education and job training as their biggest complaint. They saw La Limonada as the first step toward better opportunity, so few said they wanted to return to their home villages.

The taxi driver was visibly relieved to see me emerge from a path a few hundred feet from where I had entered the ravine. I had him drop me at a newsstand several blocks from the hotel so that I could stock up on a number of political journals and newspapers only available in Latin capitals. The walk down La Reforma to the hotel was pleasant, and I was happy not to detect any cars following me. In the hotel's interior patio, I had a chicken sandwich and cold bottle of my favorite apple drink, Manzanita, for lunch.

María Elena had worked quickly, for as I spread out the magazines on my bedside table, I noticed the message light blinking on the phone. There was a brief voice mail from Prof. Paulo Lancea, asking if I might join him for afternoon tea at about four p.m. He indicated that he would enjoy meeting me and might have a guest in his office. I couldn't reach him but left a message that I'd be delighted.

Lancea's office overlooked a green quadrangle on the university's main campus in the zona 16 on the northeastern edge of the city. It sat at the end of a long corridor of 1960s-looking oak doors with frosted windows. Paulo stood up from his desktop computer and gave me a warm two-handed shake. His complexion was that of a suntanned European, with sandy brown hair, light brown eyes, and slightly crooked, off-white teeth. His smile was friendly, yet his gaze was piercing and unwavering when he was listening to you.

"To say the least, I'm delighted to meet the famous cousin of my new dear friend, María Elena," he said, ushering me to a deep, well-worn tan leather armchair.

"The delight is fully mine. I'm so happy to meet the man who has brought back the joy into María's life."

"Would you like a beer?" Paulo offered.

John McKoy

"No, thank you. Water would be great, though."

From a cube-shaped refrigerator in the corner by his desk, Paulo retrieved a small bottle of mineral water. He settled in a chair similar to mine, placed forming a semi-circle.

"Well, I was able to reach Oscar del Gato, and he should be here in half an hour or so. That should give us time for me to brief you. María told me why you are interested in this star pupil."

"You must have an interesting class. Political Science in a traditionally Catholic university," I offered as a straightforward icebreaker.

"Really, Sr. Prettyman. We're a modern university. Landívar was founded in 1961, while you were still here."

"Actually, we had moved to the United States by then. But you've done some homework."

"Well, I am an academic."

"Fair enough."

"Anyway, we have a fairly rich offering of many of the public policy courses you'd find at a graduate school in the U.S." He paused to hand me a two hundred-page school catalog to flip through.

"Oscar's focus is Latin American History, Hemispheric Relations, and Modern Military History. The boy's a genius. The army has expressed interest in providing him a scholarship to study in the US, but no one is quite clear what his politics are. Oscar has been careful not to align himself with any particular faction publicly."

"So why do you think he would be helpful to me?"

"Oscar knows a great deal about current revolutionary activity in the region, and while he's not declared any ideological preferences, he's certainly not hostile to the left. His activities are loosely monitored by the state, but he confers as much with government-leaning students and intellectuals as he does the left. For that reason, I doubt that he's on the 'inside' with any camp. He's valued, however, by all sides. So, until he graduates and takes some sort of job, he'll probably be able to move fluidly about."

"I take it, Paulo, that you think he'll know something about María Elena's son Raúl and his pal Hector Romano in Washington?"

"That, I can't be sure of. He will likely know a bit about what's going on in Washington and who expects what from your capital."

"So why would he talk to me?"

"Good question. Oscar has a certain intellectual detachment about today's activities. He's a student, not a soldier. He's fascinated by the puzzles of international relations but has yet to experience loss or life-threatening challenges encountered because of his beliefs—whatever they might be. And I suspect that he's got a certain amount of arrogance and assumes he's too clever to be caught in anything really blatant."

"Since we have few minutes, would you tell me about your connection to Guillermo Schaefer?"

For an instant, the affable professor looked taken aback. He had not apparently registered that connection.

"Guillermo is a friend of yours, or a business colleague?"

"We've been friends for decades. In fact, he's the first one to suggest that I talk to you about the various Guatemalan activities in Washington."

The tension drained from Paulo's face.

"You gave me a brief start, because Guillermo is one of the best connected and most strategic businessmen. No matter who's in power,

Guillermo survives and is courted. Young Oscar might have found interesting notions on the web or had informative bull sessions with clever university thinkers, but Guillermo has dealt with the top powers in the world. He has extraordinary access."

"Well, he obviously thinks you do as well."

"I'm flattered, but in comparison … let's see, how to describe my relationship to Guillermo?" Paulo stood and walked around the back of his desk chair.

"When your friend gets involved in major trade deals, he not only thoroughly studies the economics, the markets, and so on; he also likes to know as much as he can about the politics. He wants to know who's in power, who's behind the scenes, who's in the wings. Guillermo never gets off a plane without a very detailed marketing plan and fallback options. He thinks like a combination of a general, a spy, and a TV interviewer. Quite extraordinary, actually. So, occasionally, he's visiting someplace about which I happen to have some useful information."

Just then, the phone rang, and Paulo returned to his desk.

"Thank you. Send him up please."

"Mr. del Gato?"

Paulo nodded and softly said, "You might elicit more by identifying yourself as a foundation executive and talk about your youth project."

As he stood in the doorway, everything about Oscar del Gato said "student." His frame was thin, his jet-black hair was unkempt, and his beard desperately needed a trim. The thin smile he offered when we shook hands quickly receded as we began to engage. I realized that Oscar had access to money, because even though the shoes whose soles he placed against the edge of Paulo's coffee table were worn and unpolished, they were expensive Mephisto brand boots. As my host had instructed, I introduced myself as the founder of the Quetzal Fund, but

I also offered that I had a nephew living in Washington. I thanked him for coming and asked him a bit about his background before delving into the areas of interest.

"I have basically been in Guatemala all of my life. My parents' families initially made money in coffee, but my father was a lawyer. They moved to Buenos Aires three years ago, so we don't see each other that often now. My little sister lives with them."

"So, what got you interested in international affairs? Professor Lancea says you have built an extensive body of information on current activities on the hemisphere?"

"Well, I'm not sure anymore where my interest in international stuff came from. The professor is too kind." He saw no need to offer anything of value yet.

"I'd be curious to know if you have looked at the student activity in the U.S."

"Only what is well-known, that pro-Mexican and pro-Nicaraguan activists are seeking resources and allies."

"Exactly, but no Guatemala-focused activity?"

"No, not on the political front."

"Is there some other front?"

"Well, of course, there is drug activity."

"Ah, of course. But that's not a student-run business, is it?"

"Hard to tell. But, pardon me, Sr. Prettyman. How does this affect your youth activities?"

Paulo, who had taken a seat behind his desk, fidgeted.

"Ah, forgive me. The kids I'm trying to help in the Latino barrios of Washington need job skills and an introduction to the culture of United States companies if they are to be successful. If their idle behavior is stoked by political or underground economic objectives that conflict with this simple objective, my job is a great deal more difficult," I explained.

"Interesting. Yes, I see that."

The brilliant young student could only confirm what I already knew, that both the political and drug markets were active. He did clarify, however, that the drug trade involved primarily teenage and young twenties-aged boys, whereas the political activity usually involved many older, a bit more sophisticated men and an occasional woman. Paulo let us talk without interruption until about six, when Oscar had to leave. I thanked him and wished him well.

"Paulo, I look forward to hearing more about your work," I said, extending a hand in thanks.

"That would be delightful, and I think María Elena is trying to arrange something."

"I'll look forward to it."

I strolled around the campus until I found the main gate and headed for the large avenue along which I was sure to catch a cab. I had been waiting for only a few minutes when someone in a twenty-year-old navy Fiat with tinted windows honked at me. The last thing I was about to do was approach some stranger in a mysterious car, so I continued to try to flag down cabs. Before I could get an empty taxi, the driver stood outside of the front door of his vehicle. It was Oscar del Gato. I cautiously approached the car.

"Senor Prettyman, let me give you a lift further in town. It might take quite awhile to get a taxi out here."

After I thanked him and settled into the passenger seat, Oscar carefully pulled away from the curb.

"I couldn't tell you in front of Professor Lancea. There are several lieutenants in the drug trade who stay on the fringes of the revolutionary activity. They tend to be better educated youth who understand more of the macro forces that drive our brothers to illicit activity. Most don't have any real power, but they attend meetings and participate in study groups here and there."

"Why are you telling me this? And why now?"

"Well, I sense you are sincere in wanting to help my generation. I also know and like Raúl Gonzales. No offense to you or his mother, but Raúl is not clear about what he wants to do. And one of his amigos, Hector Romano, is one of those fringe players I mentioned. Hector is ambitious, but I'm not clear that his motives are true to the progressive political movement in Central America. He likes power, and he loves the money his drug activity brings him."

"So, you think Raúl's in danger?"

"Probably not yet. He's not full-time in either politics or drugs like Hector. For now, I think he's not even a fringe player."

"So how do you know all of this?"

"I read a lot, am on the web frequently, and know lots of *muchachos*. That's about all I can tell you." He turned from the wheel and indicated that I could get a cab at the next corner.

As I bent forward and stepped out of the sedan, I asked one last question.

"Why couldn't you say these things in front of Paulo Lancea? He seems to admire and respect you greatly."

"And I admire the professor, but he is complicated and has … let's say he's got competing consultancies. Good Luck, Mr. Prettyman. Please, feel free to pass my best wishes on to Raúl."

I had so much new information to digest, hard facts and innuendo that I simply needed to sit in my hotel room with a scotch and a chicken sandwich and think. I found an ex-pat jazz station on the radio and settled into my lounge chair to take some notes on my laptop. I finished recording my conversations with Guillermo, Paulo, and Oscar and typed some initial thoughts about getting Raúl more involved in Quetzal Fund programming, and I began to think of places I'd like to visit over the rest of my week in Guatemala. It had been many years since I had visited the ancient capital, Antigua, or Lake Atitlan. My list was growing when a prompt reminded me that I hadn't checked my e-mail. The first message had been sent at noon from Alice Brown. The message was clear.

"Recommend you return in the morning on the 10 a.m. United flight. La Puerta damaged. Marta in trouble.

—Alice."

Chapter 14

(Roberto)

By the time I contacted Mary Elena and Guillermo to let them know that I had to rush back—for business—picked up a couple of gifts, got my ticket, and hustled through immigration at the airport, I looked somewhat disheveled and a bit distraught. I hadn't lived with that sort of stomach-knotting tension for a couple of years. Even the vigil over a recuperating Raúl hadn't tied up my nerves like this. The flight felt like it took three days.

Flying over the Gulf of Mexico, the Florida Panhandle, Georgia, up through the Carolinas, I had time to reflect on how little I knew about the complex world El Quetzal had stumbled into. Oscar del Gato, never having left old "Guate" and spending most of his time in classrooms, at the library, or in front of his PC, knew all about Raúl, Hector, and the world they inhabited in one small District neighborhood in DC, worlds removed from Guatemala. My retiring cousin just happened to be dating a university professor who not only knew the radical thinkers in Guatemala, but was well known to the pragmatic, successful, and thus politically connected establishment. The establishment always prevailed because of its ties to the military. Clearly, my old friend, Guillermo Schaefer, was at least knowledgeable about drug activity, campus politics, and whoever was critical to business, and thus had impunity before the military. Somehow, revenue from DC drug activity was at least one strand of string in this ball of twine. Could our funding the growth of Marta Hernandez's La Puerta Abierta have tightened somebody's jaw way down in Guatemala?

Alice had a car waiting for me when I landed late that afternoon at Dulles Airport. I reached her at the office on the way into town and she gave me a quick summary of the events at Marta's the day before. There had been a small explosion and fire. Marta Hernandez had suffered from smoke inhalation while scurrying about to ensure that all of the kids reached safety. She was resting comfortably at George Washington Hospital, so I had the driver drop me there directly.

"Oh, Mr. Prettyman, you shouldn't have come back. We have everything under control at the center," she said upon seeing me.

"That may be, but I'm most concerned about you. The center is bricks and mortar. How are you feeling?"

"I'm okay. Just a little tired. Luckily, no one was seriously hurt."

I sat and listened to Marta's version of the fire, her herding kids out and then collapsing from the smoke as she neared one of the exits. After the ten-minute tale, she closed her eyes and drifted off. I stayed around until a nurse came into the suite and then quietly left the hospital.

Back at my office, I asked Alice Brown to fill me in on what the police had told her so far. They heavily suspected arson and had already found a can of kerosene in the basement of a nearby apartment building. On an intuitive hunch, I called Raúl to see what he knew or could scare up in further detail. He said that word on the street was that the drug leaders were feeling a potential, if not an existing, threat from the expanded outreach of La Puerta and wanted to shut it down, without intending to harm Marta or any of her people. He promised to get back to me later.

"Alice, I'm going over to the center. Don't wait for me today."

"Do you think it's a good idea to go over there now? It's almost eight o'clock and will be dark before you get there," she cautioned.

"You think the streets open up and spew goblins after dusk?"

"It's not funny. This is serious stuff. These may be kids committing these crimes, but they can cause 'grown-up hurt.'"

"You're right. And, I don't mean to make light of it. I suppose I'm a bit tired from the trip."

"All the more reason to wait until morning before going over there."

"I appreciate your concern, Alice. But I'm only going for a minute and will be fine."

Manny Cortez, Marta's most senior youth-worker, met me at a slightly charred front door to the center.

"Not much to see, Mr. Prettyman. A couple of burned classrooms and a few smoke-darkened hallways." He spoke with a slight Spanish accent that wasn't Central American. I wondered for only a second where he was born.

"Thanks for seeing me, Manny. How long will you be closed?"

"Not at all, Mr. P. Well, the police have completed crime scene work, so we'll reopen for activities tomorrow."

"Don't you want to give it some time? After all, it's only been a couple of days," I suggested.

"Mr. P, the sooner we get back to the kids, the sooner the healing can start. That's how Ms. Hernandez and all of us feel," the young devotee said with the assurance of a family doctor.

I took a slow stroll around the facility and found that other than in a couple of rooms, there really was no major damage and that activity could, indeed, resume in most of the building during renovation. The area used to train carpentry, electrical, and plumbing caught my eye, because that had been one of the suites requiring the most capital investment.

"Manny? When I did my initial research, most job trainers said that the District of Columbia has been spectacularly unsuccessful in training and placing young blacks and Latinos in the building trades. Tell me, honestly: Do we have a shot at success?"

"Absolutely, Mr. Prettyman. Look, I'm not a craftsman. I'm a highly skilled soldier," said the mature young man. "After my early years on the Mexican Yucatan peninsula and then high school here in DC, I enlisted. I may be young, but I've spent much of my life learning and implementing the tools of war. Not bragging, but I was encouraged to join and then ended up a fairly well-decorated marine. I'm positive that the discipline, attention to detail, listening, and observation skills that saved my ass any number of times overseas are useful here. We have skilled craftsmen as trainers, thanks to a lot of the builders you put us in contact with. As good as they are, however, they won't be the key to success for these boys." Manny took a breath.

I sat on the edge of a desk and fixed my undivided attention on Manny.

"What we're teaching them and the confidence they're getting from La Puerta has more to do with life skill and job readiness attitudes. You'd be surprised ... well, maybe you wouldn't be, but most folks in the trades who have successful union careers would cringe at the lack of awareness these boys have about the world of work. We're giving them that exposure and building confidence. That, quite frankly, is why the druggies are trying to shut us down. Trust me; that's what this fire was about.

"Check it out. You don't see training programs in Southeast attacked, and the drug activity over there is scary compared to here. We're making headway, and the word is getting out that Ms. Hernandez and La Puerta is for real. So, we need to open up as soon as possible."

"I'm sorry about the fire, but I'm glad it got me over here. Thanks, Manny, for the tour and for the insight into how you all operate. I think we'll make arrangements to provide a little better security, just in case one marine isn't enough. You should also go get some sleep; looks like you've got a big job ahead," I said and grasped the young man's hand. His was a tenacious grip, one I'd remember.

"I will, Mr. P. We have a night watchman arriving in a few minutes, so I'll wait for him."

I had the driver drop me off in Chevy Chase, checked mail, and quickly fell asleep.

At the office the next morning, I had Alice see if she could line up Raúl for lunch, before I headed over to the hospital. I suspected that there had to be something drug-related in the whole affair. I also felt that the center of power concerned about La Puerta could well be in Guatemala, not Washington, DC The hospital visit ended up as solely a trip to the nursing station. Marta Hernández was too sleepy from her meds to carry on any conversation. So, after about an hour outside her room, I returned to the office.

"Any luck with Raúl?" I asked Alice.

"He can meet you at the Zebra Room on Wisconsin at about one o'clock, Bob."

"Thank you," I said and closed my inner office door.

It occurred to me that this would be a perfect time to finally talk to Raúl's friend, Hector Romano. I e-mailed my nephew to see if he could bring Hector to join us.

I arrived a few minutes before Raúl and settled into a corner table looking out at the edge of the Cleveland Park section of Washington. I was surprised but happy to see both young men enter and approach me a few minutes after 1:15. After a few minutes of salutation and obligatory inquiries about health and family, I got to the point.

"I'm not looking for anyone to rat on his compadres, but we have an injured Latina sister in the hospital. Why? Because she is trying to give a few Latino youths a new chance at a mainstream life, a view that just might lead to permanent employment. Because she is trying to turn a culture of violence and failure into one of hope and success. Going after a woman was certainly not considered macho in my day."

"Mr. Prettyman," said Hector. "You are assuming that the villains are Latinos."

"Hector, I may be old enough to be your grandfather, and I may look slow and stupid, but give me some credit."

"Okay. I'm sorry."

"Tío, I really don't know who's involved," Raúl chimed in.

"Okay. Fine. Let me say this once. If I find out on my own who did this, and if I find out either of you knew, or even should have known, no rock in North or Central America will be big enough for you to hide under. Are we clear?"

Both young men looked at each other. Neither had seen my generally well-controlled temper before.

"All I've heard is rumor. But the rumor is tied to some very dangerous people," said Hector, averting his eyes to avoid my stare.

"Hector, I appreciate that. And I won't divulge where I got the information. Let me restate that I'm fed up with this self-destructive behavior and don't intend to have some half-assed drug lord 'wannabe' ruin the lives of hundreds of Latino youth, much less threaten that of someone who's trying to do a bit of good."

"Okay. It's rumored that the torching was ordered by Víctor Zam—"

"Zamora. *Víctor Zamora?*" I cut Hector off. "I don't believe Víctor's smart enough to tie his shoelaces without help. So there's got to be somebody else calling the shots."

Hector Romano just stared down at the vinyl tablecloth.

"Tío, all I've heard is that it's all got to do with Jaguar II, but I have no idea what that means," Raúl added meekly.

"Okay. Raúl, I need to talk to you at another time. I just got back from Guate, and your mother is concerned about you."

The waitress came over, and the others ordered burgers and Cokes. I had nothing.

"Look. I don't believe you guys are in any way connected to this incident, but let me warn you that I am pretty sure that what may appear political on the street today, may simply be illegal business for which someone may well pay with the rest of their life. There is traffic going on between here and Guatemala that is being monitored by the feds. It won't go on forever, and folks will get caught, tried, and convicted. Be careful."

I stood, dropped a twenty on the table for their lunches, and left.

Back at the office, I was only minimally concerned about Víctor Zamora, a local thug, who the police could pick up and keep in jail on any of a dozen charges. My real focus was on the "Jaguar II" label, code, or name that Raúl had mentioned. I knew enough Guatemalan history to know that the ferocious spotted cat, the jaguar, was a revered symbol of strength in ancient Mayan times. Its image appears on glyphs on many of the Mayan temples, walls, and pyramids that dot the jungles of Guatemala, Honduras, and Mexico. My head was swimming with all of the loose ends from apparent connections in Guatemala and DC How many kids could Marta possibly reach at this point who could affect the real drug profits? Not many, I reasoned. I needed to know more about Jaguar II, more about Mayan history. We may have had a less than warm-and-fuzzy relationship at the time, but I hoped that Lisa would want to help keep Raúl out of trouble. So I decided to share with her enough of my Guatemala City findings, the La Puerta fire, and her cousin's range of unseemly friendships to whet her appetite for helping. I sent her an e-mail asking for any research she could provide on Jaguar II.

Having no idea what Jaguar II meant in today's context, much less two thousand years ago, I felt I had to also use my re-established Guatemala City resources. Guillermo would be trustworthy and probably tell me what he knew, if he could. But, as I had discovered, his network was not as deep with the younger political crowd. I had only just met Oscar del Gato, so he had no reason to offer useful information. On the other hand, I didn't feel he would purposefully deceive me either. I fired off separate e-mails to them both.

Street activity outside The Quetzal Fund was buzzing in the late summer breezes, as tulip and poplar trees neatly planted in sidewalk tree boxes offered limited shade. Bicycling messengers and strolling business partners occupied more space than normal for 4:30 on a weekday afternoon. I walked a block and a half to my favorite Caribou Coffee Shop, bought an iced coffee, and grabbed an empty sidewalk table. Alice Brown joined me after a few minutes, and she updated me on the last couple of weeks of minor fund transactions. Alice was relaxed and confident that nothing she mentioned really required my attention. I listened to her intently, made a couple of suggestions on follow-up items, and then gave her a full briefing on Marta and La Puerta Abierta happenings.

"I don't want to keep all of this stuff in my head, because I think it's all going to get a lot more complicated before this is all over."

"How do you mean, 'it's all over?'" she asked as we walked back to the office.

"I wish I knew, but I'm positive there's some Guatemala connection to the arson. So, if you can just keep track of the other project ideas we're scouting out, I'm probably going to spend more time on this deal until Marta gets back on her feet."

When I looked at my inbox, my hunch about Oscar was rewarded. His e-mail was brief, but it was enough to suggest that my suspicions were properly directed.

"Be careful. Word is that the Jaguar Paw is a major rebel, with a very successful drug-financed operation up near the Petén. So far, he's beyond army or government reach."

I'd have to wait until I heard from Lisa on the origin of Jaguar Paw before investigating more, so I decided to put a little pressure on Mr. Zamora.

"Danny? Danny Joseph. *Aquí soy Roberto. Como andas?*" I had reached an old Panamanian buddy, who still worked for the DC Police Department.

"How about meeting me for a drink at about six at the Heights in Columbia Heights?"

"I might be a little late, but you're on," he said.

"Hey, you. Skinny kid. You look like you can play; I'll pick you. What's your name?"

"I'm Bob, and I'm not very good at soccer."

"Bob. Bob or Roberto? You have a little accent."

"Call me either," I said shyly.

"I'm Danny. Nice to meet you, Roberto."

The big, dark-skinned kid stuck out his muscular right hand, and we shook. He had a rag-tag group of black and brown kids, half of whom didn't speak English, on his side. They were usually smaller and older than the grinning hustler. The other pickup side was made up of mostly white Catholic kids from the prep school over on North Capitol Street. They didn't wear uniforms, but it was clear that they played together as a team, often.

"Roberto, let's kick some gringo ass," he whispered in Spanish so that only I could hear.

A pickup game of soccer on P Street Playground, not far from Columbia Heights, or three-on-three basketball on cement playgrounds all over northwest DC, really didn't matter. Danny Joseph played fiercely and usually won. He had only a slight accent, even though he had been raised in a military family in Panama, so most kids thought he was African American. Danny would play along, speaking English for most of a contest, and then when he was about to score the winning goal or basket, he'd break into his fluent Spanish, grinning all the while. I wasn't yet great at soccer, but I was a good athlete, so Danny and I played well together. We spent many an afternoon in our youth playing sports and joking around. After high school, Danny joined the army, and we lost touch until recently.

He looked a little heavier, a bit balder, but basically still the handsome six-foot, well-built stud of old. As he strode toward my corner table in street clothes, ladies' heads turned. We slung some friendly macho bull before I told him about my dream for helping Latino boys and the whole Marta Hernandez story.

"Yeah, I heard about the fire, but I didn't know of your backing for the project."

"Do you still keep tabs on *Victor Zamora?*" I asked.

"Pretty much. Why? Is he mixed up in this?"

"That's the word I get."

"Well, Roberto, if you give me something, we'll pick him up."

"No. He's too cocky. I want to scare him. Scare him enough so that he whines to his folks in Guatemala."

Danny smiled but said nothing.

We talked about changes that had come to DC since we both had become adults: the rebirth of the Fourteenth Street corridor from a riot-torn hooker hangout wasteland to an urban revival with a yuppie flavor; the start of a professional soccer league team; immigrant populating of Columbia Heights and Adams-Morgan; incipient signs of the redevelopment of the same area; the growth of Latino gangs; and the slow decline of Marion Barry-era politics. We talked, laughed, and drank for almost an hour.

"Good to see you, mi amigo," said Danny. "I'll see about our friend. You take care."

After we embraced, he was gone. I paid the bill, walked across the street to pick up some Salvadoran carry-out, retrieved my car, and headed home. The breeze across the front seat was crisp and cool, so the slight buzz I had from our drinks heightened my senses. I was alert to the cultural and class neighborhood changes as I drove from working-class African American townhomes, to low-income Latino apartments, by moderate-sized single-family three-story Caucasian-owned houses east of Rock Creek Park. The long wooded park from the National Mall up into Bethesda, Maryland still acted as a buffer between the ever-changing "ethnic scene" in northwest DC and the relatively stable middle and upper-class family white neighborhoods "west of the park." My neighborhood bordering Bethesda, Maryland did feel like another world from that in which I now spent most of my days.

The e-mail I found from Lisa pushed me deep into yet another world. She expressed serious concern that I might have involved her cousin, Raúl, in some dangerous activity for which he would be ill-prepared to deal. After a short lecture, however, she forwarded information about the Jaguar Paw that validated my trust in her research skills.

"The first Jaguar Paw was the fourteenth Mayan king of Tikal in the Petén jungle during the "Early Classical" period. Named Chak Tok Ich'aak, he ruled between 360 and 378 AD. His great contribution was to construct a temple/palace of such magnificence that it was never built over by succeeding kings. My guess, however, is that the reference is to Chak Tok Ich'aak II (Bahlum Paw Skull, sometimes called Jaguar Paw II), who ruled Tikal from 486-508 AD. This is part of the period in which Tikal was the dominant city in the entire Mayan kingdom—Mexico, Belize, Honduras, El Salvador, and Guatemala. Its architecture, pottery, trade, and military influenced the whole kingdom.

To give you some other historical perspective, this is the period when US textbooks would say the important events in the world included:

European Middle Ages

Britons fighting the Saxons

The Byzantine Empire was fighting Persia

It was 120 years before the Vikings invaded Ireland

125 years before Muhammad's vision, dictation of the Koran, and the subsequent spread of Islam

50 years before Buddhism was introduced into Japan

Only 30 years after Attila conquered Eastern Europe

So, conquest and violence were a part of daily life around the globe. People were not used to dominating with concepts and ideas alone. They used violence to push their particular concepts, philosophies, ideas, and beliefs. Has it always been thus—the Crusades, Colonization, Liberation, Jihad, etc.?

While not as central as to the Aztec culture, nor as an obvious tool of torture (as we would see it), sacrifice to the gods of captive neighbors' blood and organs was not uncommon during this period in the Kingdom of the Maya. Whatever his significance in the early sixth century, Jaguar Paw II was certainly but one of many influential kings during the over two thousand years of Mayan dominance in Central America.

Your whole country is, in some way, fully descendent from this rich Mayan heritage. If someone is trying to copy Jaguar Paw, his approach will depend on how much he knows and which part of history he chooses to emulate. Violence is more than likely a natural and very important tool he uses.

Papi, please be careful."

I sat back from my PC, peered out across the suburban tree tops and tried to find a meaningful context for this Mayan mystery. I had gotten what I believed I could from Oscar del Gato. Now it was time to ask Guillermo Schaefer what he could unearth about this latter-day Jaguar Paw II from the Petén. I fired off an e-mail and turned on the news to try to clear my head of gory Mayan sacrificial images.

Chapter 15

Later that night, back down in the Columbia Heights, Danny Joseph, operating on a tip from a youth informant, waited for Víctor Zamora outside a quiet bar on Fourteenth Street. At about eleven o'clock, Víctor emerged with his three-person entourage/bodyguards. Before he finished his fourth step toward the street, Danny confronted him.

"Where you headed, amigo?" Danny asked, blocking his path and towering over all four youth.

"Well, well. Officer Joseph. Isn't it past your bedtime?"

Víctor's crew laughed.

"It is, actually. Which is why this will be a short conversation."

"Well, how can I help you, officer?" responded a cocky Víctor.

Stepping to within an inch of the boy's face, the intimidating officer whispered, "We know you started the fire."

"What fire are you talkin'—"

"I didn't ask you to talk yet." Danny hissed in his face, grabbed his right bicep, and stared off the "bodyguards."

"Now, before I arrest you, you can do two things to help yourself. One now. The other in a week."

"I don't know what you're talking about." Victor strained to maintain a blank stare.

"Fine. If I leave here now, before daylight, your house will be raided, your sister will disappear, and your stash, your cash will be stolen and distributed to every black gang in the DC market. Oh yeah, and they'll all have your address as well." Danny gave him a "love tap" on the cheek and said, "Good night, Victor. Sleep tight."

Danny Joseph had walked only two steps toward his car when Victor called to him.

"Okay, okay. Let's talk."

"You sure now? 'Cause I'm tired and, as you said, I need to get to bed."

"Yeah. What do you need?"

Danny returned close enough so only Víctor could hear him.

"First, you deposit a million dollars in a rebuilding fund just set up for La Puerta by a week from today."

"Where am I supposed to get that sort of money?" Víctor seemed genuinely stressed.

"Now, you are a resourceful dude. That should be chump change for you. Second, I need the name of your Guatemala leader, right now."

"I don't know nothing about no Guatemala leader. You got the wrong dude."

Now Víctor's glare was one of fear, not arrogance or even hate. He was frightened, truly frightened.

John McKoy

Danny knew he had gained a solid upper hand but simply stared at the youngster.

Minutes crept by.

"All right, since you're such a nice, clean-cut kid. I'll give you until the same deadline as for the cash to give me a good name. After that, Victor all bets are off. Now, if I was a betting guy, insufficient cash to help the club or a wrong name and I'd say you need to make yourself scarce. Have a good one." This time, with a smile on his face, Danny reached his car, pulled away from the curb and left a visibly shaken Victor Zamora standing on the sidewalk mumbling to his posse.

Chapter 16

(Roberto)

I was still on my first cup of coffee at the office the next morning when I noticed a short e-mail from Guillermo.

"Call me."

I tapped out his cell number, in case he was not yet in his office. His phone rang five times before he answered.

"*Bueno.*"

"*Que tal, Guillermo? Como va la cosa ahí?*" I asked.

A few exchanges of chitchat took less than a minute, and then Guillermo lowered his voice to give me his information.

"I was sort of hoping that Felix Gigante's name would not come up in any DC connection. Roberto, this guy is a very dangerous, very bad apple. He calls himself the Jaguar Paw, because he's from Flores and his father worked in Tikal as a biologist/ gardener. I don't think there's much of a deep meaning behind the association, other than the original Paw having been a successful and domineering king, back when the Mayans were a significant power in the Americas."

"Why do you say he's a bad apple, Guillermo?"

"Oh, he fancies himself a great leader, but he's simply a vicious drug lord, best I can tell. He seems protected by the authorities and does enough in trade to pay off police, army, whomever. I can't find that he's ever been arrested. You can imagine that making any charges stick against him would be challenging. My contacts tell me that he's cunning, ruthless, and controls the drug trade for hundreds of miles around the Petén."

"But, outside of Flores, there aren't many people for him to control in the Petén, are there?" I asked.

"No. That's one of the reasons he's been so successful. He's not ventured into heavily populated urban areas to speak of, as far as I know. So, while he's dangerous, the authorities have much more disruptive drug-related gangs to worry about."

"Any way I can get a message to him that might get him to move his activity away from Washington?"

"None that I can think of, other than a gun to his temple, or perhaps some ice cubes on his cash flow. Neither of those two approaches would be pulled off easily, because I don't think our boy travels outside of his home region much."

I thanked Guillermo. By the time we hung up, I had pretty much concluded that I'd have to make another trip to Guatemala.

Alice Brown left me a note that Marta was going back to La Puerta on a shortened-day schedule starting that afternoon. Before I could leave the office, however, she buzzed my line to let me know that Max Ramírez was on the line, from New York.

"Berto, everything okay with you?" Max avoided any small talk.

"Sure. And, how are you, my friend?"

"I saw a piece on the news about the training project director returning to her program today. And it sounded like your key project."

"Well, the press got that part right. No, I'm fine, and it looks like Marta will be too. But I'll tell you. It never really occurred to me before just how much our own people, so to speak, want to keep us from progressing."

"You mean the almighty quick dollar gets some kids' attention more easily than reading, writing, and earning a proper living?"

"It's not just that, but you have the drug trade in Central America trying to pick off programs they think will horn in on their territory."

"But of course."

"Anyway, Max. Nice of you to call. Anything new happening up in the big city?"

"No. But, you be careful down there, my friend."

"Thanks for the call. I will."

After a few more desk chores, it was almost noon when I finally got in my car to drive over to La Puerta.

Chapter 17

A stocky five-foot-seven, brown-skinned man with Mayan cheeks, thick black hair, and brilliant amber eyes stepped from his tent beneath heavy palm tree cover at 6:30 in the morning. Red-and-green parrots and white-faced brown monkeys were already busy in high-altitude conversation. An aide brought the man a cup of steaming coffee and a plastic dish with a warmed-over corn tortilla.

"*Gracias*," said the man in a quiet tenor voice.

"*Mi Capitán*," responded his aide.

The jungle air was already humid and hot and buzzing with insects. The man seemed not to notice as he ascended a small dirt path to a hilltop. Perched above the nearby jungle, he could see for a mile in every direction. What he saw was green jungle cover, and he heard every manner of animal dawn-breaking sound common to this part of the Petén. He knew there were pigs, monkeys, ocelots, and, of course, jaguars hidden under the mist and the canopy of green. He breathed deeply so that his nostrils could inhale the sweet honeysuckle-like fragrance of his surroundings. The coffee provided another type of stimulus, awakening the man's tongue, throat, stomach, and mind. If one had to forgo the finer things of a twentieth-century life, why not do so in a gorgeous natural setting, with a band of committed colleagues, fighting for the freedom of one's homeland?

Why not, indeed? he thought. *My forefathers conquered their enemies in this territory. Surely, we are no less clever, no less strategic, and no less resourceful than they.* He smiled to himself.

Many of the *campesinos* and Ladinos from all over Guatemala who had joined him in his jungle camps, including those soldiers whom he had defeated in skirmishes and peasants to whom he donated food or clothing, built schools, and financed wells knew that he had been christened Felix Gigante de Santos. Everyone recognized his activity as that of the Jaguar Paw. Felix now assumed that the territory he now surveyed would always be his home, his office, and his neighborhood. His business planning was conducted in the burrows, caves, and hollows of this jungle. He would die among these banana trees, palms, and cassavas and be buried on some hill such as that from which he now scanned the Petén. Only victory over the culture of oppression, fear, and greed that had gripped Guatemala for centuries would allow him to live freely. He long ago stopped trying to handicap the likelihood of that victory coming during his lifetime.

Felix smiled more broadly as he reflected on his father.

Had the drunken soldiers left him alone, had not pestered him and driven the proud Petén biologist to react to their taunts, he might still be alive. Indeed, Felix would have finished law school and perhaps become an attorney in the capital. He might have emigrated and escaped the cycle of poverty, uncertainty, violence, and defeat in rural Guatemala. Instead, Felix cut back on his course work and became an adjunct lecturer on social movements at San Carlos University. After a little more than a year, he joined a revolutionary band, and plotted and executed his revenge on the four who had killed his father. In a moment of dramatic rage, he had drawn the shape of a powerful jaguar in the sand next to the bodies of his decapitated victims.

Over the next decade, the Jaguar Paw terrorized government officials and private landowners whom he viewed as part of a corrupt and insidious system that oppressed decent Indians and Ladinos in the northern reaches of the country. To those he helped, the Paw became a liberator or Latin Robin Hood; and to the "system," he was an irritant to be obliterated from the face of the planet. After years of failure to find, capture, and destroy Felix, the government adapted a policy of "live and let live." Bombing the jungle near the town of Flores was not seen as a politically practical option, but there seemed no other strategy that might finally rid the authorities of his raids, disruption to communications, or mastery of the drug trade that had provided extra income to local soldiers. So they decided not to continue to pour resources into his capture, so long as they felt his influence was limited to the north.

After four years in exile, the Jaguar had begun to run out of funds. The donations of supportive Guatemalan leftists were insufficient to finance his operations and provide resources to the poor. It didn't take much analysis for him to recognize that the Central American provision and transport of drugs to the United States was a lucrative trade devoid of ideology. As long as drugs were harvested, transported, and delivered, few in the chain cared about politics. The Jaguar cared little about the negative consequences, the havoc on poor communities that drugs created in the US He established a business that could finance the good he was doing in Guatemala.

To those in his camps and inner circle who questioned this strategy, the Paw argued that he was merely taking advantage of illegal commerce that would continue to go on with or without their involvement. Gigante understood that the geopolitics of the drug trade were much more complex than he let on around his jungle campfires, or with the various characters up and down the drug chain with whom he dealt. He may have been bothered by the collateral damage that ensued, because he used the drug trade as a means of financing a revolution to help people like those harmed by the cartels. He had, however, cultivated that ability to compartmentalize primary means and ends from secondary results. Thus, he was able to sleep soundly, without an annoying guilty conscience.

The Jaguar traveled to the capital, to other countries, and even to the US on occasion. These field trips were to evaluate his network from every financial and operational aspect of his "business." The indirect collateral damage caused by his operation would bother him, if he allowed himself to focus on it. He did not permit such a focus. Luckily for him, as in the days of the earlier Jaguars, Gigante's empire, though productive and impressive in its own realm, did not command center stage, even in the western hemisphere, let alone the globe. Thus, since the United States, Mexico, and Guatemala were willing to fight radical insurgencies with only modest budgets, the Jaguar was easily able to stay several moves ahead of his enemies.

The exacting planning and thoughtful attention to detail that marked the Jaguar's operational activities played no role in his personal career planning. What did the concept of retirement mean for a guerrilla? Where could he possibly live if peace and justice came to Guatemala? What would he do to earn a living? Useless questions, or at best relegated to another day.

As the Jaguar Paw returned to camp, Ángel Chiapas, an aide, approached him with disturbing news.

"*Mi jefe*. There's trouble in the Washington, DC operation," reported the aide.

Chapter 18

Víctor Zamora had indeed been shaken by the evening encounter with Danny Joseph, but at least he had a week to figure out what to do about his demands. Joseph was right in thinking that finding $1 million to compensate for the fire would not be difficult. Giving up the Jaguar, however, was a nonstarter. Víctor was concerned that the police already had so much information about his family and clearly had him under constant surveillance that they could close him down at any time. His operation must be low on their priority list, and they clearly only cared about him only to get to someone else. Really, they didn't care about him at all, so he and his family were totally expendable. They had the reach to take him out anytime they chose. But, if he served up the Jaguar, Joseph would either arrest Víctor or leave him to be dealt with by his own vicious boss. Víctor was confident that he was accurately assessing his situation, and he was not comforted.

Sitting in his car, speakers throbbing all around him, alcoholic buzz slowing his synapses, Víctor thought, *I screwed up, big time.*

A week ago, his plan to shut down the youth employment project that Marta Hernández ran had worked well, but he hadn't anticipated the woman getting injured in the fire. No matter how tough or ballsy a chick was, nobody liked you targeting women or children. It made you look weak. Anyway, at least the idea and the incident put a dent in the threat she posed. *Glad I didn't run that by the Jaguar,* he thought. Now would certainly not be the time to offer that information. The more Víctor could resolve the current situation without requesting Guatemalan assistance, the better.

Unaccustomed to having to construct contingencies, Víctor forced his brain to focus on several "what ifs." His gangster tactics had always worked for him in the past, but it was now clear that some, if not all, of his antics had been permitted and tolerated by the "authorities." He had fooled no one who mattered. He knew the Jaguar wanted the DC market, so there was no chance of giving it up or moving to some other territory. "Taking out" the black cop would be a death sentence to him and his family. No answer came to him.

Víctor turned down the salsa music a bit, took a drag from his cigarette, filled his cheeks with cold Corona, pushed back his seat, and stared out the driver's side window into the night. Young white and Latino couples returning from an evening of clubs and restaurants strolled by his unassuming vehicle on a very quiet Adams-Morgan night. Lights were extinguished in the front rooms of his apartment, but Víctor continued to ponder his situation. Then he sat up with a start and smiled at himself in his rearview mirror. He placed a call to a number in New York City and quickly borrowed a million dollars against future drug sales. Part of his problem solved, Víctor skipped up his building's front steps and let himself into his apartment.

Víctor didn't sleep well and was struggling to be of good humor with his eleven-year-old son, Rodolfo, at breakfast when he got lucky.

"Papi. It makes me mad that my gringa language teacher always confuses me with that idiot Marco Garcia. He doesn't look at all like me, and he never has the right answers."

"Mi hijo, lots of these gringos can't tell us apart. Don't let it bother you. Do your work."

After Rodolfo left for school, an idea hit Víctor.

"Stupid. 'They all look alike.' Of course. I'll feed these gringos a different name. No need to involve the Jaguar at all. They'll never trace him."

Víctor's plan might have worked and saved his operation, but he failed to check a few facts and neglected to look at enough "what ifs." When he delivered the money for La Puerta to the PO Box designated by Officer Joseph, Victor waited outside the post office until he saw Manny Cortez, Marta's top aide, enter and head for the correct box. Satisfied that his troubles were half over, Victor drove to a small Asian restaurant near the Gala Theater on Fourteenth Street to meet Danny Joseph.

Sitting across from the cop, Victor summoned his most concerned frown, looked around the room carefully, and then said, "The name you want is *El Rey*. He's in Oaxaca, Mexico."

Joseph looked at him in silence for a minute, sipped a Diet Coke, and asked, "What's his real name?"

"*No lo se*," Zamora honestly replied, since he didn't actually know.

"Bueno. We'll be talking."

Victor left the restaurant feeling ten years younger.

Ten minutes later, Danny Joseph left feeling a lot happier and more relaxed than he had felt in months. He had checked with an FBI colleague about *El Rey*, who indeed was a drug lord based in Oaxaca. His operation, however, spread no further east and north than Atlanta, although he had previously tried to enter the New York City market. And his colleagues were only Mexican; he never worked with Central Americans. Danny now enjoyed the notion of shutting down Mr. Zamora's operation—at least for a few months.

Several nights later, Felix Gigante climbed a makeshift ladder twenty feet above the jungle floor to his cassava tree "office." Most of his comrades had long ago gone to bed when he turned on his powerful laptop computer to check his mail. After scrolling through and deleting most messages, he noticed an entry from a former student friend, Oscar del Gato. Oscar seemed to be a perpetual student from a wealthy family, but he shared none of the right-wing politics of his parents. While the Jaguar knew that Oscar communicated with a wide variety of thinkers of varying philosophies, and while he knew that he couldn't be trusted as any sort of strategic partner, he comfortably exchanged ideas and collected information. He knew that Oscar sometimes felt the Jaguar was behaving more like a thug than a revolutionary. More than a few times, Oscar had reminded him that he had nowhere near the political, nor the military infrastructure that Castro did. A ridiculous comparison in the Jaguar's mind. Nonetheless, Oscar's recounting of Bob Prettyman's visit helped fill in the picture that Ángel Chiapas had begun painting several days earlier.

This Prettyman guy and the youth project he funded with Marta Hernández was serious, and they were not going to easily be dissuaded from trying to help Latino boys in that community. It seemed clear that any interference with his drug operation was incidental to Prettyman's goals, and that Victor Zamora's scare tactics had not deterred him in the least. For an instant, a very brief instant, the Jaguar acknowledged that the actions of the parties created an obvious irony, given the parallel common objectives. The revolutionary was obstructing progress of the capitalist's social justice initiative in order to promote the security of his insidious illicit drug trade.

The jungle outside his tree office was alive with peepers, owls, rodents, boars, and even jaguars in search of a meal. The noises were like background music or white noise to Felix. His keen senses enabled him to detect a sudden rustling near his tree. The noise was too light to be a man, but too noticeable to merely be an animal passing by. The Jaguar sat up erect in his chair. His ears, nose, even eyes were alert to the darkness outside and twenty feet below. The noise subsided, and Felix decided that some carnivore had met with hunting success, while another animal had met death. He smiled and thought about the similarity to his revolution. To survive, he had to occasionally kill. But the survival of his movement, of his mission, trumped any incidental collateral human damage along the path to a more equitable Guatemala. In some ways, the Jaguar viewed the survival of his movement as the jungle cat might see its requirements for survival.

When he returned to thoughts of Washington and his threatened operation, Jaguar Paw decided to escalate his offensive against any further opening of La Puerta. Raúl Gonzales, Prettyman's nephew, would have to be used. Before he shut down his computer, the Paw sent a cryptic e-mail to Hector Romano. Saving el pueblo of Guatemala would have to take precedence over any do-good efforts in far-off Washington, DC

Chapter 19

Hector Romano had known for months that more would be demanded of him than to merely cultivate smart, young disaffected Latinos and Latinas in DC neighborhoods. Even the occasional assistance to drug kingpin Víctor Zamora was an underutilization of his skills. He wasn't totally prepared, however, for the coded instruction he received from the Jaguar Paw. In essence, Hector was to kidnap his friend, Raúl Gonzales, and deliver him to a pre-established contact in DC.

Though committed to the Jaguar Paw's revolutionary cause, Hector had never had to harm anyone. He truly liked and admired Raúl, but his allegiance to the Paw was paramount.

Hector had grown up in Antigua, a colonial capital and popular tourist attraction that was perceived to be quieter and safer than Guatemala City. His father had been a professor of Latin American History and a sought-after lecturer throughout the Southern Hemisphere. So, Hector had traveled widely, read precociously, and thought extensively about political ideology as a young man. He had found an exhilarating lecturer and mentor in classes at San Carlos University in Guatemala City who breathed life into intellectual theories Hector had studied. So when that lecturer, Félix Gigante, took to the "hills," Romano was an easy recruit for his cause. He spent several months with the Jaguar in the Petén before Gigante decided that Hector's language and social skills could best serve him as "eyes and ears" in Washington, DC, locus of a profitable drug operation. Raúl Gonzales was one of many bright young Latinos that Hector met and researched before recognizing the potential value of a friendship with him. Once he had targeted Raúl as a valuable asset, Hector easily secured a spot in the Latino Internship Program at the Association of Home Builders.

Raúl was happy to get Hector's call, since they hadn't met for several weeks and he was anxious to catch up, now that La Puerta was back in operation. Marta Hernandez seemed more determined than ever to save the boys in the barrio from drugs, gangs, and failure. Since no one had gotten seriously hurt in the fire, Raúl still felt that, on balance, the Jaguar Paw's cause back home was more important than Marta's workforce development efforts. Naturally, he didn't view the two projects on an either/or basis.

"*Que tal, mano?*" Hector warmly greeted Raúl at a Mexican bar/restaurant in Wheaton, Maryland.

It was five in the afternoon, so they ordered chips and salsa to go with their Coronas. Legs straddling plastic-covered kitchen chairs, they sipped their cold brews and began to update one another on their activities. To stretch the conversation out, Hector offered a long monologue on the ills of DC government and its insincere attempt at improving relations with the Latino community. After forty minutes of inconsequential chitchat, Raúl had to go to the men's room to relieve himself. When he returned, new mugs of freshly poured beer were on the table. It took but three sips for Raúl to feel the drowsing effects of the spiked drink.

"Let me just put my head down a second," Raúl slurred to his friend.

In three more minutes, he was snoring.

Hector asked two apparent strangers at a nearby table to help him carry his friend outside for some fresh air.

Raúl was not even semiconscious again until thirty-six hours later when he was awakened by the blast of wind sweeping off the bouncing sea surrounding the freighter he was aboard. He didn't know it, but the ship was anchored in the port of New Orleans. He rolled over on his elbows, since his hands were bound in cords in front of his chest, and then rose from a forced crouching position in what seemed to be a locked storage room somewhere beneath the deck of a ship.

He quietly called out to Hector. Where was he? Why had he abandoned Raúl? Who, in fact, was Hector? Of course, no one answered his all but inaudible questions. Raúl was too scared to scream and too woozy to trust eating the tray of cold chicken and rice on a solitary table jammed between crates of merchandise. The only other occupants of his makeshift dorm were several small rats. They were small enough to be disinterested in Raúl, but he struggled mightily to not focus on their occasionally noisy presence.

After putting out to sea (actually, the Gulf of Mexico), the ship, by Raúl's estimate, took two days to reach its next port. Two men entered the room, placed a sack over Raúl's head, and marched him off the ship. He protested and asked where he was, insisting that they had made some mistake. But a hard punch to his ear quieted his attempts to communicate with his captors.

Raúl couldn't tell if it was day or night outside, but he did suspect that his next resting place was the back of a canvas-covered truck. He further guessed, due to the melodic lilt of their accent, that his handlers were Mexican. Calculating time at sea, harbor smells, and surrounding accents, he further calculated that the long truck ride originated in the port of Veracruz, México. It would be the most northwestern port on Mexico's gulf coast. Before he passed out again, Raúl called forth a virtual mapped image of Central America.

"Guatemala. They are taking me to Guatemala." Raúl then dozed off for countless hours.

When he next awoke, Raúl was sweating heavily, and his stomach ached from hunger. The breeze passing through the canvas roof merely moved the hot air around. It didn't cool. He didn't recognize either the smells or sounds accompanying the truck on its journey. Even when Raúl was growing up in Guatemala City, he rarely ventured out to the mountains or jungles of the dense interior. He knew very little about the inhabitants of those areas—wild animal or human. Sleeping off and on, Raúl totally lost track of time. He occasionally recalled the bar where he and Hector had been drinking.

Héctor's from Antigua. He knows this Jaguar personally. That's where they're taking me. But why was I kidnapped? Raúl was gaining confidence that he knew the right questions. As of yet, he had no answers. His trip on the ship felt as if it had taken place a year ago, when the truck finally came to a stop.

The Mexican voices spoke to him from the back of the truck, telling him to move to the rear and descend. He was disoriented and kept falling down when he tried to walk. His handlers lost patience, entered the truck, and dragged him roughly over the tailgate and let him fall to the dusty dirt road on which they were parked. No head cover or masks were needed, for the handlers knew they were never going to see Raúl again. As they untied his wrists, the ruffians instructed him to sit by the side of the road and wait. They then mounted the steps to the truck's cab and drove off, secure in the belief that Raúl would only wander in vain if he attempted to hide from the next pickup.

It was dusk, and Raúl began to appreciate and recognize some of the sounds. The vegetation bordering the road was dense palm tree and cassava jungle. Raúl heard at least ten types of bird calls, various frog croaks, large, winged insects, and numerous patterns of monkey chatter. In other circumstances, Raúl might have enjoyed the beauty of his surroundings. As light began to fade, however, he became more and more frightened. Had he not spied a green boa constrictor in a roadside tree, he would have climbed the low-hanging branches and sought a perch for the night.

Maybe I can find a cave or construct some sort of thatched banana leaf tent for the night. If I build a fire, then I can keep large creatures at bay, he thought.

Raúl gingerly stepped into the brush near the road and sent a family of guinea hens scurrying. He only managed to get ten feet into the jungle before he noticed that the sun was rapidly sinking in the sky. The jungle would soon be pitch black, and he had no real cover or protection.

Best return to the road, he decided.

Raúl found a tree stump by the road, sat down, and pulled his knees up under his chin. Although he could think of no reason why anyone would benefit from his being abandoned in some Central American jungle, he began to worry that he might never see another human being. Exhaustion magnified his fear, and it displaced his hunger. And then it began to rain. It was a fine, warm mist of a rain that made his smelly clothes stick firmly to his slumped body.

It might have been an hour, or maybe three, that passed when Raúl wakened and sat erect to the terrifying scream of some wild cat.

Jaguar, Raúl thought.

Off in the distance, he saw two yellow eyes slowly coming directly toward him. Raúl was too tired, stiff, and frightened to do anything but stare into the blazing eyes of the approaching cat. After several minutes, he couldn't withstand the tension. He stood and reached around for a stick that he might use as a weapon, but found none. He balled up his fists and let out his boldest bloodcurdling scream. The animal kept advancing. Raúl had convinced himself that his only hope was to charge the cat, yelling at the top of his lungs. He braced himself for the charge. Then he realized that the cat was not purring or growling, but humming and grinding, like a motor. Savior, captor, or unconcerned passerby? It didn't matter. Raúl was thankful for the vehicle's arrival.

A jeep-like vehicle rolled to a stop in front of Raúl. Two hooded men armed with AK-47 machine guns again bound his hands, covered his head with a sack, and roughly pushed him into the vehicle. For another two hours, the vehicle seemed to climb through the jungle without regard for road, stream bed, or uncut rocky terrain. Thankfully, Raúl had no food in his stomach, for he would have thrown up several times before they came to a final stop. He was then forced to walk another hour and a half deeper into the jungle beyond the end of the vehicle's termination point. Whether this was because the terrain was impassable or because his captors wanted to torment him further was unclear. But after stumbling through thick underbrush and climbing several slippery inclines in suffocating heat, Raúl collapsed and lost consciousness when they finally stopped.

When he next awoke, Raúl's hands were untied, and the hood had been removed. He sat up on a cot and tried to take in his surroundings. Sounds, humidity, and odor told him that he was in a tent somewhere in a rainforest campsite. Although his legs were wobbly, he was able to stand. But before he could reach the flap in the tent, it was thrown back to admit a medium-height, handsome, bearded man of about forty years old.

"Welcome to our home, Señor Gonzales."

"And who might you be?"

"Oh. Come now, *compañero*. Surely there are not many men who could have you abducted from Washington and safely delivered to the jungles of Petén."

"The Jaguar Paw!"

"Pleased to meet you."

"But why me? Why all the way to Guatemala?"

"Get some rest, and enjoy some of our forest cooking. Build up some strength, and then we can talk. You have had a long journey, Señor Gonzales. You will be able to freely move about the settlement, but I caution you against trying to negotiate the jungle on your own. Even though you are a city boy, you know enough about the Petén, I am sure, to know how dangerous it is. Until later, then."

And then the Paw abruptly left.

A very short, dark-brown-skinned Indian woman wearing a colorful red, green, and yellow woven top whose pattern Raúl didn't recognize brought him rice, beans, and a mysterious spicy meat stew. After he wolfed down the meal, Raúl pushed back the tent flap and stood beneath a palm and banana tree canopy in what seemed to be a clearing in a dense emerald jungle. Men and a few women were busily attending to physical tasks—hauling water, chopping wood, smoking meat, and repairing thatched roofs atop bark-and-leaf huts.

As he strolled about the camp, people politely acknowledged his presence but never engaged him in conversation. Surprisingly, Raúl saw few automatic weapons. Inhabitants interacted as if they were all members of a big family. He counted about seventy-five people in an hour walk about the grounds. Upon his return to the tent, Raúl noticed that his rice bowl had been removed and replaced with a banana leaf topped with fresh coconut, pineapple, and guava. He chewed on a chunk of coconut, lay back in the cot, and passed out.

Chapter 20

(Roberto)

The phone rang early that Tuesday morning, and I knew it was Danny Joseph halfway through his first sentence.

"The chump is now cheese, and he's fermenting in jail," said the policeman.

"Clever, my friend, but what in the world are you talking about?" I asked.

"When I heard about the kidnapping, I went on instinct, strapped on my pistol, called two uniformed officers, and told them to meet me at Víctor Zamora's house at 4:30 yesterday afternoon, when his kids would be returning from school. During the early afternoon, my plain-clothes unit and I rounded up about a dozen of Zamora's key goons that we have been monitoring. We got everyone without fanfare and before they could tip off Victor.

"You should have seen his face when the blue-and-white cars surrounded him as he sauntered up his steps for dinner. His whole family and assorted neighbors got to see him handcuffed and carted off to jail. The boy has some *cojones* because he managed to yell at us, for the benefit of the street audience, 'You can't haul me off. I got rights.' I loved it, since I politely told him in Spanish to call the DC police, if he had something to say. By 6:45 last night, the Jaguar Paw's DC operation was out of business. Unless I'm sorely mistaken, old Victor will be out of commission for quite awhile."

"You know, you have a mean streak in you," I chided him.

"Only with respect to criminals, my friend."

I had made my normal list that Monday morning, but the purpose of the calls on the list was anything but normal. I was making dozens of calls to contacts in the State Department, the Guatemalan Embassy, and colleagues in Guatemala City. Three days after Raúl's disappearance, I had a very good notion of where he was and why he was there. Long before any ransom note, it was clear to me that the "Paw" had tired of the inconvenient and mild disruption to his operation caused by Marta's project. He had, for apparent good reason, lost faith in Víctor Zamora's ability to "fix" the situation and had decided that I was the lynchpin he needed to eradicate in order to salvage his "business" in DC

I was going back to Guatemala to get Raúl, as I was sure the Jaguar Paw was hoping. He couldn't know, however, how I would return, or in whose company I would travel. My first call was to Marta Hernandez.

"I'll be gone for a few weeks, but I've left instructions for you to have a steady flow of payments and access to emergency funds, should you need them."

"Roberto, why not let the government handle this kidnapping? I know how you must feel, but—"

"Marta, if you know how I feel and you have observed 'the government's' capacity to sensitively and effectively deal with kidnappers, then you know why I can't rely on them. These 'revolutionaries' are nothing but terrorists, and the US government policy is not to negotiate with terrorists. I appreciate your concern, but I think I can construct a solid rescue team."

"But they won't simply be trying to scare you. This thug may try to kill you both." The fear in her voice was more acute than I recalled ever hearing before.

"Yes, he probably will try. He may be underestimating my resolve and my resources. Stay well, Marta."

Next, I called Max Ramirez, whose response was not dissimilar to Marta's.

"I'm so sorry to hear about Raúl, but you're nuts to go down there, Bob."

"So why not come down with me?"

"Because two ill-equipped guys do not improve your chances. It's still suicide. You don't know the players, you are unfamiliar with the terrain, you have no idea of the Jaguar's military assets, and you are no longer a super-fit twenty-five-year-old. Other than that, it's a great idea. Jesús, Roberto, use your head. This will call for major Guatemalan brides. You know that, right? But better to trust the old corrupt way than to get Raúl and you killed." I could tell that Max was about ready to hang up.

"Max, all I want you to do is to think about who you know that might get me more information about the Jaguar's location."

The silence in the receiver was complete.

"Look, amigo, think this over for a few days. I can't help you now."

We hung up.

Next, I tried to get María Elena on the phone, but I had to leave a message.

"María, I'm coming down to find and retrieve Raúl. I know this is a scary time for you, but I'm confident that this guerilla criminal wants me and has no interest in harming Raúl. I'll contact you when I arrive. Stay calm."

I knew she'd be anything but calm about her son's welfare, but I wanted to try to prod her into thinking about key folks I was going to need to contact.

After I had Alice Brown arrange my travel, I called Guillermo Schaefer. My tight gut conveyed my anxiety about using Guillermo. I thought, however, that he would know of my arrival eventually, so I might try to see if he would uncover some useful details about the kidnapping or about who to contact "on the ground."

"I had a feeling that you would come. You know this is just what the Jaguar wants? He's merely setting a trap to be able to give you his warning 'face-to-face,' or to eliminate you as an irritant in his revenue machine."

"Sure, I know that. I don't need to be alone, however."

"Roberto, he'll never let you bring support into his area."

"Not willingly or knowingly, I agree. So, Guillermo, how are you?"

"You are crazy, Berto. Why are you doing this? If you have to, just hire some mercenaries to go in there and get the boy." Guillermo's voice had an uncharacteristic edge.

After I hung up, I kept thinking about his last question. Why had I really started the Quetzal Fund?

"Roberto. What are you, Spanish?" one of the big Caucasian boys on the playground asked me.

"No. One of my parents is from Guatemala," I responded innocently.

"That's Spanish, fool. What do they 'esspeak,' Turkey?" The big, muscular, all-American blond got into my space, two inches from my nose. I quivered visibly, I'm sure.

"You know you Spics don't blend in this neighborhood?"

"We're not 'Spics,' and I don't think you own this area. I'm just on this playground for a friendly game of basketball."

"Hey, the Spic talks real good. Must be one of them diplomat kids." The bully pushed me in the chest, and I almost fell over.

The other kids stopped shooting and began crowding around, but only two others seemed to be tight with the big bully. When the bully and his friends all started laughing, my fear turned to anger, and my anger summoned up the two years of karate training I had received. I first tried to walk away from the three, but the bully grabbed my left arm and tried to spin me around. His mistake. I spun quickly and caught him in the side of his head with an open-handed chop. He dropped immediately and looked up from his knee, more stunned than hurt or angered.

"So, you want to play rough, huh, Spic?" He held his palm up to hold back his colleagues. Then he did something I had not anticipated from a suburban tough. He pulled out a knife and lunged clumsily at my stomach. I easily sidestepped his thrust and directed a very hard chop at his wrist. The wrist snapped and the bully dropped his tool, yelling in severe pain.

His friends hesitated to come to his aid, and I stared them back down the street away from him. I'm not sure where my next words came from, but I motioned them to pick up their sprawling friend and said, "You better come get your buddy and get him to a hospital before I get angry and put you all in a bed. Tell you what—also, find another playground to terrorize."

The dozen or so other kids at the playground began clapping as the three toughs scrambled off.

My encounters with gringo bullies, black or Latino gang members didn't always end so victoriously, but playing neighborhood and high school sports helped me develop a comfortable banter with kids all over the DC metro area. I truly loved learning to mix in with all types of kids in the urban area. I certainly didn't love the rejection I often faced, but winning the challenge of "fitting in" became as important to me as winning athletic or academic competitions.

I learned to hold my own, but it was also the case that I had the advantages of being in a well-to-do diplomatic family. Few of the kids on those playgrounds or in the streets were going to have an opportunity to go to Georgetown or to end up building a multimillion-dollar business. By the time I went to college, I was fully bilingual. No one but a true linguist could tell that I wasn't a native North American when I was in the States. Similarly, when I traveled to Latin America, few could tell that I hadn't spent all of my life in a Spanish-speaking environment. Even as I climbed the ladder of economic success, blending in with Caucasian Yankees, I was fully aware of the prejudice and slights against Latinos.

The jokes at meetings, the stares when folks saw a dark-skinned laborer in an unusual setting, or the laughter about a waiter's accent in a bar seared deep into my psyche. Depending on the setting and my stage in career, I might say something. As a young professional, however, I was more often than not silent. But the pain and anger never disappeared. Rarely did I respond with physical force, since adult bullies tend to incite with more subtle forms of discrimination. But the courage to speak out came with maturity and with confidence built by my business success. So by the time I could afford to retire, The Quetzal Fund was a positive endeavor that was aligned with my beliefs.

Although I was making plans to go to the jungle to get my nephew back, deep in my gut, I knew I was going to Guatemala to save my dream in Washington. It was a dream I needed to fulfill as much for myself as for the kids in Columbia Heights.

Edward Rubin was head of the Central American desk at the US State Department in 2007, and we had become good friends since our college days at Georgetown. Our relationship had been social, but deepened only when he was posted in DC over the past couple of decades. He and I occasionally played a round of golf or went drinking after work. He had married a lovely Columbian woman and had a son. When the marriage failed, the son lived with his mother until he went off to college. Ed and I often commiserated about the difficulties of cross-cultural marriages.

"How's it going, Ed?"

"Long time, Roberto. Is it time for our cocktail catch-up already?"

"Could be. But, I'm calling about a personal matter. Got time for a drink in the next few days?"

"Well, I hit the road tomorrow. I could do it late this afternoon."

"Great. I'll come downtown. How about that steak place across from the Palm on Nineteenth Street, Sam & Harry's?"

"Perfect. I'll meet you there a bit after six," he said as he hung up.

While not the most expensive, nor the most exclusive restaurant in the downtown area, Sam & Harry's had a very tasty steak and seafood menu, a more than adequate bar, and service that made you feel like you and your guests were solving the world's most intractable problems or refining the most outrageous and enviable real estate deal on the East Coast. Its patrons felt very comfortable and ended up tipping accordingly. Ed and I were given a small, private booth tucked back in the quietest sections of the rosewood-paneled establishment.

"You look fabulous, if a little worried. Good to see you, as always, Berto."

"Good to be seen and great to see you again, Ed."

We ordered bourbons, picked at a dish of nuts, and caught up on our families. After fifteen minutes, or so, I explained the Raúl/Jaguar situation, indicated that I was heading for Guatemala, and asked for his help.

"Wow. First, my condolences. Nobody deserves this less than your family, than you." Ed paused and took a long sip. "You know our official policy about terrorists and ransom, etc."

"Yes, I'm very aware of it."

"What I can do, Berto, is contact some government and military people to make them aware of the situation and that you may be going in."

"Well, that's something. Thank you."

"I have heard of this character and know that he's not seen as a major threat by the Guatemalan government. In fact, I gather that he sweetens more than one coffer, so that he pays off some of the same entities he wishes to topple. So far, his strength isn't seen as significant. I'm just not sanguine that you'll get much support. Now, if you go in and don't come out, that may enable us to generate movement. I'm just being cold and honest."

After exchanging a few more ideas about the best approach to rescuing Raúl, Ed said, "Your best shot, my friend, may be an off-the-books commando raid using private resources."

While the meeting had not netted any direct help, Ed did reconfirm my assumption that this would have to be a private operation. Unfortunately, I didn't pay much attention to the suggestion about a "commando-type" approach.

Chapter 21

(Roberto)

"A bunch of folks don't trust you, Guillermo. More than a few people told me you might have conflicting interests in helping me get Raúl back." I let the words settle on Guillermo Schaefer as I stared at him from a most comfortable armchair in his office.

"Roberto, you didn't come all this way to tell me the obvious. Name me an influential man who doesn't have detractors."

"I just need to be up front with you, Guillermo."

"Noted. So, what's your plan?"

"I'm not sure I have one, yet. I think I need to know more about who's playing on whose team these days." I opened the top button of my business shirt, took a sip of my bottled water, and thought for several seconds before continuing.

"One thing is curious from the outset."

Guillermo seemed to sit a bit more erectly in his chair.

"How is it that this Jaguar Paw has evaded capture or death all of these years? It seems to me that our old colleagues, your friends running the military, have all the 'know-how' and more than enough firepower to locate and destroy his operation."

"Fair point, my friend. Even though the ruins around Tikal, Tulum, and others have been excavated and opened for tourism, the Petén is still quite a dense jungle. So far, no one has been willing to commit the intelligence and aviation resources needed to locate and capture this guy."

"Yes, but why not?"

"Berto, think about it. Perhaps the government benefits from him being able to run his operation. Right now, there is no really serious regional or national disruption due to guerrilla activity—certainly no more than usual. As far as his drug activities are concerned, who knows which 'official' parties are benefiting?"

"You mean payoffs or kick-backs?" I asked.

"I'm just saying it's certainly plausible. Besides, like I say, the Paw has not really destabilized any critical governmental functions. He's not harming commerce like the guerrillas that were wiped out on the San Jose coast. And he's not yet posed a serious threat to political stability nationally."

"Don't things ever change, Guillermo?"

"You asked."

"I know. It just seems so hopeless," I bemoaned.

"Berto, you realize where the demand for drugs emanates from, right? Last time I checked, the cartels' biggest markets aren't in Escuintla, Mexico City, or Medellín."

"Yes, I know. They're up north"

"And, only ten years ago, you had that terrorist McVeigh blow up a federal building in the Midwest of the good old U-S-of-A. You lost two iconic buildings and hundreds of lives in the World Trade Center, because your government wasn't sophisticated enough to understand current Islamic cultures or Middle Eastern and African colonial experience that has contributed to anti-Western sentiments; you're still in Iraq and Afghanistan with no effective exit strategy in place; Jack Abramoff just ripped off hundreds of innocent Native American investors; and how about Enron? The US, my dear friend, is not on solid ground advising on how to manage terrorism at home or abroad."

"So, if I did get close to his camp and was able to disrupt his operation, there may be those in the capital who'd be upset, as opposed to enthusiastic?"

"Seems likely."

"Well, you know I can't leave Raúl there. So what's your advice?"

"You'll have to find a way to get him out without killing the Paw or his operation."

"I can't promise that. My priority is my nephew, and I'll do whatever it takes—"

"Maybe you could give him some of what he wants from you."

"You know he wants me to close our jobs center in DC That's a nonstarter."

"Roberto, there are not a lot of options that I see."

"How about your buddies in the military helping me get Raúl out?"

"And in return?" Guillermo sighed and waited for me to respond.

"I know. God, asking someone to do what's on their job description, because that's what they're paid to do—"

"You haven't been away that long, Berto." Guillermo stood and gave me a hug.

"Let me see if I can find a couple of guys who can get you in. Getting Raúl and getting out safely will probably be on you. But I'll try to get as much help as I can. I care about Raúl too. Just don't raise your hopes too high."

"Okay, Guillermo. I'll keep that in mind and take whatever you can do."

"I'll get back to you in your hotel in a day or so."

We shook hands, and I left.

Back at my hotel room, a few blocks from the city's central square, I spent much of the afternoon organizing my thoughts and casting occasional glimpses at the TV news stories on the devastation caused by Hurricane Katrina in New Orleans. Guatemala had suffered landslides and hillside erosion as the result of a late summer storm. The loss of life, however, was nothing like that in the US The lively, bustling streets below evidenced no hint of the destruction visited on outlying areas. In fact, the bustling urban commerce surrounding my hotel offered no hint of the reality that while only 14 percent of the salaried workforce was in commercial farming, over half of the total Guatemalan population worked primarily in subsistence agricultural jobs. The per capita GDP was still, in 2005, less than $4,500. Much had changed in my beautiful hometown since I had left. The lovely beige façades and red tile-roofed historic buildings were harder to find among the ubiquitous metal-and-glass twenty-first-century ten-story boxes, and no one ever need want for North American fast food in any section of town. But income distribution, the plight of rural indigenous people, and government corruption seemed static and never-ending.

John McKoy

I left the hotel and headed for a side-street café, where I had arranged to meet Oscar del Gato, the young political scientist. He had been wary of meeting in my hotel, so I sauntered in and out of shops and up and down several blocks in no particular pattern before arriving at the pleasant outdoor table at El Tinto.

Oscar arrived wearing dark sunglasses, a well-worn short-sleeved, striped shirt, jeans, and leather sandals. He could have been a student in any Latin or European country, looking casual with a practiced serious look beneath the shades and a cigarette grasped Belmondo-like between his lips. Oscar pulled up the hard plastic chair with its back to the street but shielded from the sidewalk by a large, potted palm tree.

"What will you have, Oscar? It's on me," I assured my source.

"I'll just have a beer, please."

After I ordered two bottles, I thanked Oscar for coming and asked him his assessment of Raúl's situation.

"Senor Prettyman, I think you have to reconcile yourself to the fact that getting Raúl may not be possible, and that you will most probably get no assistance from the government," he stated bluntly.

"So much for being an honored native son," I offered, more to myself than to my guest.

"I believe, sir, that you'll find you are appreciated. Officials respect what you have done in the States and all that you have given back to communities here and up there. That is you, however, and not your nephew, who really has done nothing to merit special attention.

"While you have chosen to make your life in los Estados, many in your and subsequent generations have stayed and forced some change. The constitutional reforms of 1985 and 1993 modernized much of the old system, on paper at least. Ramiro De Leon took serious risks in mounting a popular movement to force the most recent changes. Younger leaders are proud of their victory in loosening repressive policies and slightly increasing rural power. But as you well know, the system will not change rapidly, with parts of the church and the 'establishment' digging in their heels all the time."

I stared at this youth, mature and wise beyond his years. How could I get angry at his blunt, discouraging, but honest assessment? I took a sip of beer, leaned back in my chair, and looked beyond Oscar to the street, which was now more congested than when we arrived. Rose-colored finches chirped over leftovers at the table next to us. The silence of our interaction didn't bother me, and Oscar seemed in no hurry to continue his observations.

After several minutes, he asked, "So, once you find and hopefully rescue Raúl, what does he do? Does he return to the U.S.?"

Without hesitation, I responded, "Yes. Of course."

"And his mother? His country?"

"Well, it appears to me that he is settled in Washington. I could be wrong, but he's given no indication of wanting to return permanently to Guate." I must have looked puzzled.

Oscar picked up. "It's my inexperienced opinion that once people in my generation who have options commit to staying here, they gain a certain peace and accept certain aspects of our situation. It's not that we don't see injustice, inequality, and corruption. Oh, we see it. But we accept a certain amount in order to survive and make an interesting life for ourselves. Money goes further here, and while the pace is slow, we still have modern conveniences."

"So, you think Raúl may choose to stay?" I asked.

"I really don't know. I'm just saying that it is not beyond possibility that he would do so."

"Oscar, I appreciate your counsel. Once Raúl is free, he's free to decide where he wants to live."

"Felix Gigante, after all, had many choices about his future and might have been quite successful, with what most would consider a comfortable life—"

"I fail to see how they are similar, beyond the origin of their birth." I began to look for a way to end our meeting but noticed that Oscar's eyebrows arched above his glasses.

"We need to leave," he said and placed a folded sheet of paper on the table.

I placed a few quetzales on the table and picked up the note. As we walked between tables and onto the sidewalk, I got a glimpse of two men sitting at a table inside the café trying not to appear as if they were watching us.

We stood on the sidewalk for a few more minutes, and then Oscar wished me luck; we shook hands and walked slowly in our opposite directions. When I was several blocks away, I looked over my shoulder to be sure that I wasn't being followed. I unfolded the note, which read: "A friend of mine will contact you." I smiled, tore up the paper, dropped it in a trash barrel, and continued back to my hotel.

Over the next several days, I read a lot about the presidential election consuming the political attention of the nation, walked around refurbished downtown neighborhoods that I never experienced as a boy, and met with various old colleagues who all commiserated about Raúl's situation. After I outfitted myself with backpack, hiking boots, and the most modern nutritious and tasteless camping rations, I spent long hours poring over maps of terrain around Flores. I was more concerned about finding my way out than about my trekking in. I was confident that the Jaguar would find me and lead me into his camp.

Son of the Maya

The contrast between downtown modern Guatemala City and what I imagined the Petén to be was stark. In town, I enjoyed the anesthetized bustle of a Latin capital with the commerce, transport, dining, and entertainment commonly found during sultry summer days in resource-moderate Central America. The asphalt-generated heat could always be escaped in modern air-conditioned interiors. The middle class was growing as some wealthy estates lost value at the top and more families were educated at the bottom. The streets, boulevards, and avenues offered post-colonial and modern architecture as a backdrop for attractive strolls in the late afternoons. Much of the urban environment was like a movie set that masked and hid the nation's underlying poverty.

I often recalled Oscar's point-of-fact admonition that a well-educated young man could live a comfortable life in urban Guatemala, assuming he stayed out of controversial politics. The young middle class seemed to have music, restaurants, and dancing clubs to enjoy and the accompanying electronic gadgets and hip clothing to purchase that rendered them indistinguishable from many of their North American counterparts. They pursued careers in law, medicine, and business like their parents and even invented entrepreneurial software or an agribusiness or two to place them squarely in the twenty-first century. Had I not opened a laptop, I would have not even known or cared about the horrible shootings on the Virginia Tech campus, the collapse of a bridge in Minneapolis, or the DC fascination with army projections of still more time needed to end US involvement in Iraq. These events had little impact on life in Guatemala.

Finally, about four weeks after my meeting with Oscar, a note appeared in my hotel mailbox requesting that I meet a female party named Flor at a bus stop on the main highway heading north out of the city. I was instructed to check out and to bring no more than could fit in a knapsack. I sent e-mails to the contacts I thought I could trust to inform them of my movement. With all of the outreach and contacts I had made over the last two months, however, I essentially was without an exit plan from the jungle. I was confident that Raúl was of little interest to the Jaguar Paw other than as bait to get at me, and I was fairly sure that I could negotiate his safe release, even if I remained a captive.

Life's successes sometimes breed an arrogance that is unjustified and, ultimately, unrewarded in new, foreign environments.

Even covered in khaki camouflage, young Flor was not hard to spot. Together, we must have looked like father and daughter heading off for a weekend trip to the highlands. She walked me to a navy SUV she had parked behind the bus depot. Once my knapsack was thrown in the rear and I was strapped into my seat, we took off heading north. The women had a light coffee-colored complexion, jet-black curly hair, thick, almost Angela Jolie pouting lips, and a five-foot-five body whose curves were almost hidden by her outfit. She was lovely to look at, but said very little. I gathered that she was to deposit me at a stop from which I would be retrieved by the Jaguar's men. That was a day and a half drive away, however. We pulled into a highlands village, found a motel with an adjoining café, and enjoyed a rice, beans, chicken, and tortilla dinner. We bunked in separate rooms and rose before sunrise to continue more long hours of dusty, winding roads. She was well trained, since I learned almost nothing about Flor but listened to endless radio programs featuring marimba-laced tunes.

Flor did wish me luck as she deposited me on some jungle path somewhat north and east of Flores, deep in the jungle of Petén. I took a long drag from one of my bottles of water as I watched the dust trail from the SUV disappear into the jungle. From the guide books and *National Geographic* magazines I had recently read about my own country, I could recognize the loud chatter of howler monkeys jumping about in the dense vegetation above my head. Occasionally, tropical cicadas filled the air with their own symphony. I had been left by a large cacao tree whose trunk was marred by several *X*'s carved by machetes. I was to stay in sight of this landmark and wait. Most of the sun was blocked by a green ceiling of tropical plant leaves, but it was hot and humid enough that I was sweating freely just pacing about as I explored the vegetation around the dirt road.

After about forty minutes, I sat on a roadside stump and rehearsed my arguments for getting Raúl released. It occurred to me that I would need some proof that he had reached safety prior to me giving the Jaguar any information or promises of value. That would be if I could convince him that simply holding me, or worse, killing me would not benefit his DC operation; and, in fact, might bring severe consequences to his whole operation. I had blocked out most noises, sights, and smells as I concentrated on my options, when I was startled by a rustling noise behind me. I jumped to my feet, pulled a hunting knife from a sheath strapped to my pants, and turned around quickly enough to see a large tapir retreat into the undergrowth. A shot of bile climbed my throat, but I was able to keep from throwing up. I took a deep breath and returned to my stump. Nothing of note happened the rest of the afternoon, and I finally opened one of my granola bars to eat with a couple of gulps of water.

I don't actually remember what I did during late afternoon and early evening, but I know I began to wonder if the Jaguar had lured me into the jungle to leave me as pray for some wild animal. Sounds change as the light dims, the air chills, and even fragrances differ with nightfall. Of course my imagination came to life with the new sounds and occasional citing of a fast-moving shadow. I began to consider where I might find refuge for the night and figured that elevated in some tree would be safer than on the ground, even though I would have to risk encountering the deadly coral snake. During the afternoon, I had admired a sturdy palm with reachable branches not too far off the path. So I shuffled my way toward it, feeling various trees and bushes as I strayed on and off the road until I reached my salvation. I was able to shimmy my way up the trunk to a clump of very secure branches, found no worrisome creatures in the vicinity, and was able to arrange a perch, allowing me to sleep.

I remembered how the bus wound its way over mountainous roads, through forests with different types of foliage, and then over lowland hills until my father said, "We're almost there."

John McKoy

In the distance, I first saw plumes of smoke, and then I heard church bells ringing; finally, I smelled incense burning as we approached the ancient capital, Antigua. I couldn't have been much more than eight years old when we took one of the first trips away from Guatemala City in my memory. I remember the high stonewalled houses set back from cobblestone streets and the beautiful designs made of flowers and confetti in the middle of some of the central streets in town during Semana Santa. Religious holidays had forever been accompanied by intricate and colorful murals created in the streets of the parade routes.

Our family stayed in a pension with a large interior garden that couldn't have been more than two blocks from some church's tower whose bells pealed every few minutes, or so it seemed to me. Everywhere we walked that weekend, indigenous people from every part of the country were marching, lining up to march, or finishing a march flashing their native costumes, beating animal-hide drums, and blowing different types of flutes. We visited a hundred churches and listened to scores of chants, or so it seemed. After the strangeness of this little "medieval" town wore off, I was able to enjoy the beauty and pageantry of an Easter as it is uniquely celebrated in our country. That was a very happy time, when my greatest worries were which sweet roll to dunk in my milk and coffee.

Someone called to me, and I almost lost my perch as I sat up, awake. It was dawn, and a man was standing below my tree motioning me to climb down. I carefully slipped into my backpack and slowly descended from my perch. Only when I reached the ground did I notice that the man had two accomplices shouldering rifles. All three were clad in scruffy fatigues deserving of a thorough scrubbing. To my surprise, they did not blindfold me nor bind my wrists. Ten minutes into our hike, however, I understood why. The jungle was too dense to easily find a path, much less find landmarks to remember or retrace your steps. I smashed my watch crystal when I attempted to break a fall with my left hand. I could live without a phone, but the loss of a timepiece made me feel totally isolated. By catching glimpses of the sun, I calculated that we marched for about ten hours. We camped at a site that they had clearly used before and then hiked until dusk the next day. During the exhausting two-day trek, my guides said nothing to me and spoke minimally to each other.

By the time we reached the Jaguar's mountainside camp, I had no idea whether we had traveled north, west, or east, and it would have been impossible for me to direct anyone to any point within a hundred miles of the destination. The men took me to a tent near the periphery of the campsite, opened the canvas flap, and pushed me toward a lone cot inside. I must not have moved from deep sleep for a day.

Chapter 22

(Roberto)

I slowly rolled over to the nudge of someone tapping me on the shoulder. My shirt was soaked through, my mouth was dry, and my eyelids seemed stuck together. My calves felt as if they had climbed Mt. Everest in sneakers. A man was standing next to the cot, holding a cup of water for me to drink. Instinct kicked in before reason and I grabbed the cup, gulping down its liquid without thought to the possible toxicity of its contents. The water was cool, fresh, and life-giving. I opened my eyes and rubbed away the goo. Even with a full-grown beard and shaggy mane, the man looked familiar.

"Tío, you don't recognize me?"

In the muggy humidity, the monstrous heat, totally uncomfortable and foreign enclosure, I did not instantly recognize my nephew. The man on whose behalf I had made this journey stood before me, and I reacted as if in a dream.

After another few minutes, Raúl stepped back and sat on the ground against one of the tent supports.

"It's good to see you, Uncle."

"Raúl. Oh, forgive me. I'm still sort of out of it. Are you okay? How are you?"

"A few bites here and there, and a bit tired, but otherwise fine." His smile, even through the new growth, was recognizable.

"Have they tortured you? Harassed you?"

"No, they have treated me fine. Lots of questions about stuff in DC that I didn't really know about. And, of course, I have the anxiety of not knowing what they really want or when I might be let go. After awhile, you find little things around the camp to occupy your mind."

"Well, I'm hoping to find out soon enough what they want and how we get out of here," I said.

"In good time, perhaps, Mr. Prettyman," announced a husky, well-built, fatigue-clad man of about forty who stood in the flap of the tent.

"My name is Chaco, and I'll be back in a few minutes to escort you both to dinner with the Jaguar. You'll find a wash basin behind this tent." He left as quickly and silently as he had arrived.

I asked Raúl who the man was.

"He's one of the Jaguar's top aides. Every so often, I see them discussing plans over old-fashioned maps that they lay out on these crude wooden benches."

The jungle was pretty thick at the end of the campsite housing my tent, but the air was not as hot and humid as I'd recalled it being when I had collapsed in the cot. There were men and a few women moving about the dirt paths in between tents and the jungle perimeter. No one seemed to pay any attention to Raúl or me as we washed in a basin near a cool spring behind the tent. I didn't recognize the various ferns and shrubs that formed the perimeter of the camp, but the brilliant Sparkling Blue Morpho butterflies flitting about the towering trees and siphoning off nectar from the foot-high shrubbery were unmistakable. Some kind of red-and-green parrots seemed engaged in raucous debate with the howler monkeys in those very trees.

"It's funny, Raúl, but this scene seems so natural. The campsite fits right in, since people don't seem to be hunting for sport or destroying vegetation for commerce. They're living well within the bounds of nature."

"I know, Tío, and so different from the bustle of la capital, Guatemala."

"Still, how have you avoided boredom out here?" I asked.

"I've had KP duty, foraging chores, and some occasional translation tasks. You know, satellite technology enables communication from just about anywhere today. And our Jaguar Paw likes to keep up with world events, so he'll periodically download some semi-scholarly journal written in English with lots of technical terms. It so happens that I have a much larger technical vocabulary than would be indicated by my American University grades."

We were leaning against a tree stump when Chaco returned.

"Follow me, please," he said as he led us toward the center of the camp and then up a narrow path to a structure that more resembled a cabin than a tent.

The closer we got to the bamboo-and-banana-leaf building, the more frequently spaced were the weapon-bearing guerillas. And the more intense their scrutiny of Raúl and me.

I reached down to my calf to slap at a mosquito and five carbine rifles were cocked and shouldered before I could stand back erect. I instinctively raised my hands above my head and looked at each sentry to reassure them that I had no weapon, my knife having been removed when I was first called down from my tree perch.

Our climb took no more than ten minutes under a tightly woven canopy of leaves and vines at least fifty feet above us. About twenty-five yards from the cabin, we traversed an open area encircled by crude log benches where I assumed the Jaguar held his meetings. Before leaving the open area and descending a slight grade to our destination, I looked through an opening to our right. I realized instantly why the guerrilla chief had his headquarters on this ridge. As far as one could see was a canvas of every shade of nature's green pallet. The approaching haze of dusk did nothing to mar the span and intensity of the beauty revealed through the opening.

Chaco left us at a partially closed bamboo door, and we were invited in by a soft female voice.

"*Adelante, señores.* My name is Alicia. Please, have a seat, and Jaguar will be with you in a moment."

The woman had pronounced Quiche Indian cheekbone features, stood about five feet, two inches tall, a copper complexion, and stunning green eyes. She disappeared in a side room, leaving us wondering about her perfect Midwest US English.

As we sat in very comfortable bamboo-framed and banana-leaf woven chairs, Raúl told me that Alicia was always around Gigante, sort of like a chief of staff.

Before I could take in the furnishings and accessories of the cabin, our host entered from an interior room.

"*Bienvenidos, senores. Soy* Felix Gigante. Mr. Gonzales, good to see you again, and I see you're no worse the wear for your first few weeks with us. And, Mr. Prettyman, I trust your journey was not too unpleasant." The charming man stuck out his hand in greeting. While his hand looked fragile, it was all bone, tendons, and calluses. Felix Gigante was extremely fit.

John McKoy

"My journey was nicely paced and enjoyable. Thank you." I decided to play along.

"I thought we'd eat up here your first night. Alicia, we are ready for service." Gigante spoke to the curtained doorway at one end of his cabin while escorting us onto a porch-like patio out back. From the table, we could again look out over the jungle for miles.

"This is an extraordinary perch to view the Petén," I said.

"Thank you. I picked it out myself, without a real estate agent," responded our host.

As Alicia poured some chilled white wine, I decided to get to the key question.

"Exactly how long do you think we'll be staying, Mr. Gigante?"

"Well, that totally depends upon you, Mr. Prettyman. And call me Felix or Jaguar, please."

"I'm Roberto. And what is it that I'm to do?"

"Well, for now, simply relax and get reacquainted with your nephew."

A bit later in the meal of plantains, rice, beans, and some kind of fowl, I again hinted that I'd like to know the schedule. Our host momentarily shed his congenial veneer and pointed his finger at me.

"I really don't understand you Yankees from Guatemala. Well, Yankees in general. You march in here with no real plan, as if you're so much smarter than us poor campesinos that you're sure to figure a way out. We're so primitive that tricking us will be simple. I suppose it's your colonial arrogance," he said.

152

"I meant no offense. I suppose I am anxious to begin discussing the DC situation and our US return," I offered.

"Roberto, you came of your own free will, I believe. You have no obvious immediate means of departure. So I suggest you reconnect with your native culture and your nephew. We will discuss detail in good time."

I looked over at Raúl, but his eyes said that he wanted to be a bystander in the conversation.

"And how have you found your days in the capital, Roberto?" Gigante was now sipping from what appeared to be a clay cup of very strong coffee.

"I'd say, on the surface, the city seems quite modern. The well-off seem to have all of the technology available in the States. Public transportation is no worse than in many US cities. Food is more reasonable. And, the homeless are, in fact, less evident than in Washington, DC So, all-in-all, it's quite impressive." I tried to paint an optimistic picture.

"The key phrase in your answer, Roberto, is 'on the surface.'" Gigante's mouth turned up ever so slightly at the corners. "You see, if all were as prosperous and resources as ubiquitously distributed as you suggest, there would be no need for this movement. No need to hide in the jungle. No need to orchestrate strategic attacks on the infrastructure of the regime in power. But capitalist or not, I'm sure you know that, Roberto." He took only a quick breath before he continued.

"Tell me, Roberto, do you assume that everyone, if given a chance, would prefer the US economic and political system? Do you believe the campesinos here would be better off with the 'opportunities' offered in the U.S.?"

"Well, I can't pretend to be current with all campesino life, but it does appear that the gap between rich and poor here is more extreme than many places in the Americas. Whether one is better off is relative. Being poor in the US is terrible. That's why I started the fund. But there are probably more opportunities to climb the economic ladder; I agree." I carefully studied the Jaguar's facial expressions as he responded.

"Really? I suppose being the number-one world's power breeds a sort of arrogance about the benefits of your system. Arrogance and blindness to the shortcomings of your 'democracy.' As we see in Venezuela, not every leader is so impressed with your approach. And Cuba, despite half a century of your cruel embargo, still stays committed and provides much of the developing world with its medical training." He responded as if lecturing a graduate seminar.

Raúl stretched slightly in his seat, and I sat erect and still, seeing no need to respond to Felix Gigante's monologue.

"Tell me, Roberto, do you believe in providence, fate, God, or random events in the universe?"

"It's been quite awhile since I've explored that question." I took a sip of the very bitter green tea in my cup.

"I believe we have time," he said.

"I suppose I believe in a combination of all of the above. Why?" I was more comfortable letting Gigante ramble. He seemed to be searching for aggressive political and philosophical discussion and obviously enjoyed some amount of push-back and verbal exchange.

"Tell me, Felix, do the answers to any of life's bigger philosophical questions make a difference? I mean whether or not I examine why I've accumulated wealth and am trying to help immigrant Latinos in Washington, or you are trying to mount a revolution that reconfigures the halls of power of Guatemala City on behalf of indigenous and Ladino people make either cause more just or either fighter more righteous?" I asked.

"I know you see parallels between our two campaigns. I don't. You are a capitalist fighting to create more capitalists. I am struggling to redistribute wealth and power."

I reflected for a couple of minutes, not wanting to get my "host" too energized about his situation.

"It is true that I'm a capitalist and believe in that economic system. I don't see that position as antithetical to creating opportunities for all young people to succeed. And having succeeded in the system myself gives me an informed vantage point from which to advise."

"You've succeeded, but you haven't suffered. Suffering—or at least, deprivation—builds the strength of character and the wisdom of perspective necessary to lead."

"You don't know that about me, whether or not your hypothesis is correct," I challenged.

"You're right. I don't know," he conceded. "We are different, Mr. Prettyman, in that I am fighting to end the privileges from which you and your class benefit."

"I think we both know that while the sort of equitable society you seek may be attractive in concept, in practice, humans tend to create aristocracies of the privileged and the powerful no matter the ideology. Look at China, Cuba, Venezuela, or India. 'All pigs are not equal' in those societies either."

"Orwell. Very nice, Roberto. The examples you site, however, merely show that no society is perfect."

The Jaguar rose, extended his hand, and motioned toward the front entrance.

"It has been a pleasant first chat. Good evening to you both. Alicia will put you on the path to your tent."

John McKoy

His assistant guided us back to the path leading to our tent. The security I had observed earlier had gone. After she left us, I felt we could have slipped into the jungle and not have been missed until morning.

"If we had compasses, supplies, and night goggles, we could be miles from here before anybody noticed," I said to Raúl.

"Right, and if we had energy enough, machetes to cut brush and vines, and knew where we were headed, we might have a 2 percent chance of escaping. But Tío, that's a lot of 'ifs' that the Jaguar has rightly calculated would never all break our way." Raúl sighed.

My legs and lungs welcomed my cot and were thankful that we had no immediate intention of trying to escape.

Chapter 23

(Roberto)

"I really have no idea why we're down here now," said Raúl.

We were lying on our cots listening to the quieting jungle sounds, after having returned from dinner with the Jaguar.

"Oh, I suppose he's sizing me up to see the best way to put a permanent halt to Marta and La Puerta. He'll just take some time and try to make me feel desperate." I tried to sound much more positive and assured than I felt.

"So, did you see my mother in the capital, Tío?"

"I did. And other than being worried about you, she's fine."

"God, I wish she didn't have to go through this just because of—"

"None of this is your fault. So don't beat yourself up about it. This is all because La Puerta is making the sort of impact we'd hoped it would, and it's affecting DC's drug traffic. The Jaguar needs that revenue to sustain whatever he's doing down here. I'm surprised that DC is that big a portion of the Jaguar's revenue. But don't worry about Maria Elena. She's fine, and there's nothing to be gained by Jaguar harming her, at this point. He doesn't appear to go in for gratuitous violence."

We lay for a long time in silence.

"Have you been able to figure anything out about this operation?"

"What do you mean, Tío?"

"Like who comes in and out? What are the concerns of daily communication? Are there fairly predictable routines? Have you noticed objectives or targets that get repeated references?"

"There seems to be a regular delivery of cash by two guys, who come on alternate weeks. And, occasionally, there are meetings in that space on the way to the Jaguar's tent. But I have no idea what they're discussing. In general, it's pretty boring out here."

"Well, I'd be surprised if they let you hear anything of importance to them. How about the area around the site? Are you able to identify anything that might be seen from the air, for example?"

"There are a few clearings with Mayan stone carvings, but nothing particularly unusual for the Petén."

"Well, we'll take his advice and simply chill for awhile. Keep your eyes and ears open, because eventually, we'll either send a message or find an escape."

"Tío, I hear you, but escape and survival may be worse than a long shot. Trudging through the vegetation in this aggressive heat would, by itself, be challenging. Throw in snakes, wild pigs, jaguars, or a pack of monkeys here and there, or accidentally eating some poisonous plant, and you have the recipe for certain miserable death."

"Good night, Raúl. As long as we're alive, not bedridden, and have significant players looking for us, our chances are pretty good." I tried to sound much more optimistic than I felt. I knew that my office, Max Ramirez, and Guillermo Schaefer all had political and financial reach deep into both US and Guatemalan power structures. But without knowing what was being communicated to whom, that awareness was of little real solace.

The next morning, before we could wash up and finish throwing clothes on, someone left a tray with two mugs of coffee and milk, a basket of fresh tortillas, and two bowls of black beans immediately inside our tent. Having no idea of time or schedule, Raúl and I ate slowly.

"It's really great to see you, Tío, but I'll admit that I'm now even more anxious about what Jaguar has in mind."

"Well, I'm pretty sure it has little to do with anything we can do here in the jungle." I paused to digest a couple of bites. "Raúl, how have you been able to adjust with no friends, no contact with contemporaries, no news, no computer, or books? How did you stay sane?"

"You know, we have forays for food, or wood, or medicinal plants. They even trap snakes to get venom for serum in case of bites. The Jaguar has recruited some quite resourceful troops. I think there's even a medic who trained in Havana. One guy I've talked to briefly is a software engineer, but of course he never said what his job here entails. There's more than you would imagine that goes into survival in the Petén. So, much of the time, it's been like an adventure."

A few quiet sips of coffee.

"What about politics and philosophy, Raúl? You were big on revolutionary philosophy with some of your buddies in DC"

He was pensive for many minutes.

"You know, Tío, these guys are serious revolutionaries. They live and die for the 'liberation' of the campesinos. They're also scary. One guy got caught doing something that the Jaguar thought was way out of line.

He was tied to a banana tree, coated with honey, and left as a feast for insects. I don't think he lasted two days. So, our leader can be vicious.

"I grew up here, and I guess I didn't see—or didn't want to see—the plight of the poor farmers and the urban migrants. I mean, they scrape by, while my circle of friends lives pretty comfortably. So, while I see apparent injustice, I'm neither as knowledgeable nor as dedicated as the Jaguar and his dudes. The little I have been exposed to suggests that these guys have given lots of thought to changing government and economic systems to reflect their principles. I don't think they're just a bunch of out-of-school students playing at revolution. It's like, demoniacal as Osama bin Laden is, he was no dummy and clearly thought long and hard about the implications of his type of Islamic society. Likewise, the Paw is no dummy.

"As far as the DC guys, Hector Romano and those guys are less sophisticated foot soldiers, and Victor Zamora and his thugs are puppets."

I just listened to my nephew.

"I don't know about the New York scene, but I think the only real players in this outfit are down here. These guys are way smarter, calculating, and committed than anybody I ever ran across in DC And you know what? They're way smarter than any of the government types I used to know from my mom's circle, too."

"Well, I'd be happy to stay out of his fight with the government. Smart or not, however, the government may provide our only way out of here."

At what I would guess was about 7:30 in the morning, a group of men with rifles came and escorted us to a clearing. We joined about ten men dressed in various mismatch outfits of jeans, plaid shirts, army fatigues, sandals, boots, and baseball and ranger hats.

The only common element was that all but Raúl and I had machetes. After about a two-hour hike, we reached another clearing on the fringe of some Mayan ruins. From then until about three in the afternoon, we cleared brush, chopped small trees, and bundled healthy loads of firewood. The trek back to camp seemed to take twice as long as the morning journey, and I was too exhausted to identify many landmarks. Raúl, however, did memorize unusual trees, stone configurations, even arboreal animal activity, which we later plotted on a makeshift map. Once back at camp, had I been given a choice, I would have forgone dinner and headed straight to bed. Choice, however, was not in the offing, and we ate on logs in front of several supply tents with scores of "soldiers." The hot, taxing, physical work had been spread fairly equitably, so no one was bursting with energy for even the most mundane chatter.

Chapter 24

"Hello, Marta? This is Lisa Prettyman. Roberto's daughter. How are you?"

"Lisa, I'm fine. How are you? I don't believe we've met. Are you in Washington?" Marta Hernandez responded. She added, without waiting for an answer, "Have you been in contact with your father?"

"No, I'm not in DC, but still in Berkeley. I'm calling actually to see if you have any news of Papi," said Lisa. "I've checked with Alice Brown at Quetzal's office, I've called his friend Max in New York and my aunt in Guatemala City. No one has heard from Papi or my cousin, Raúl, in weeks."

"He just left a message here that he'd be out of town for some period of time. No specifics. So we didn't worry for a few weeks, since he often travels for extended periods. But everyone is now really concerned," said Marta.

"My aunt says that he was in Guatemala City for a few weeks making arrangements to go out to the Petén to find Raúl. I didn't know until then that he'd even been kidnapped."

Marta knew, of course, that Raúl had been taken due to the success of La Puerta and the impact on Victor Zamora's gang. She never felt that made sense, since Raúl had never really participated in the activities of her center. It was clear, though, that her program had enjoyed relative peace and quiet since the police cracked down on the gang.

Columbia Heights and Adams-Morgan were again vibrant neighborhoods where folks felt safe to move about. There had been no more break-ins or harassment of club participants, and only one random shooting had come to her attention since the police roundup of Victor Zamora's gang. Raúl's disappearance and the diminished drug activity were tied together. She just didn't know how. It wasn't hard to piece together a likely chain of events. Clearly, someone sent Bob Prettyman a message about her project's disruptive influence on youth drug traffic. It had interrupted the easy flow of drug transactions among young, restless Latino men. The police, however, had sent back an emphatic rejection of the message. As of yet, the Guatemalan reception of and response to this MPD (DC Metropolitan Police Department) signal and its affect on Raúl and Bob's chances for release were unknown.

Marta didn't know how much to share with Bob's West Coast daughter. She suspected that Lisa and her father weren't particularly close, due to random comments Bob had made recently. She was his daughter, however, so Marta would err on the side of information overload and tell Lisa everything.

"Ah, thank you so much. Your information fills in big holes for me. I don't know what to do, but at least I have a better idea of what's been happening," said Lisa. "I hope you don't mind my keeping in touch. And, if I find out anything significant, I'd be glad to keep you informed," she continued.

"Please do. As far as I know, the State Department is aware of Bob's situation and is exploring various rescue options." Marta had no such information, but she wanted to keep Lisa from worrying as much as possible. She issued a heavy sigh and told Lisa to call whenever she felt the need for information or support.

Until the call, Marta had been able to focus on the work of the center and submerge her concern for Bob and Raúl. There didn't seem to be much that she could do half a continent removed from their location. Now, the potential gravity of their situation wouldn't let her concentrate on anything else.

Prettyman's office had thought about and worked on nothing but his disappearance since he left Guatemala City. From her communication with Bob's friend, Guillermo Schaefer,

Alice knew that Bob had made contact with a guerrilla leader named Jaguar Paw, who had a base hidden in the Petén. She knew Bob had arranged to make contact with this Jaguar and had set out to meet face-to-face. Her information trail stopped at that point. She had, however, gathered that Bob's ties to and influence with the Guatemalan authorities were not strong enough to command any sort of official rescue attempt. As far as she could tell, her boss and his nephew were own their own.

A second call from Lisa triggered an idea.

Alice asked Bob's daughter, "You're an MBA and anthropology student, right?"

"Economics. But, yes, basically," said Lisa.

"Well, what if we could learn more about this Jaguar? There may be something in his historical context that gives us some location clues." Alice took a quick breath. "If we knew the original Jaguar's biography and this guy's birthplace, schooling, early influences, family background, and so on, then maybe we'd be able to narrow in on motive, location, or something." Alice waited for Lisa to respond.

"You know, it's worth a shot. No one else seems to be doing any of that research. Let me do some digging and make some calls. I'll call you back in a few days. Meanwhile, if you can continue to make Guatemala inquiries, you might get some leads. Thanks, Alice."

Both women hung up with a slightly renewed sense of purpose and potential.

Why, Alice wondered, was someone of Bob's stature unworthy of serious government help in Guatemala City? Life had taught her that the web of interpersonal connections was amazingly small and tightly woven. If you were a gregarious sort and in any number of related fields, then more than likely, you could eventually get connected to someone you needed to meet. This had been true of her experience with business types in her job at the DC Chamber, and it had certainly pertained to the local government political circles that dealt with the chamber. She wondered if that axiom worked in Latin America as well. *Why wouldn't it?* she thought. But no matter how many times she pushed the tip of her ballpoint pen, no revelation, no bright new idea came to her. She fidgeted with a picture of her mother on her desk, went over her conversations with Guatemalans over the past few weeks, and played back in her mind the conversation with Lisa Prettyman. Then it hit her. There was one person who knew Bob, who might still have pull in Guatemala, who might know something about pressure points in both Guatemalan and US governments.

Mónica Sánchez: Lisa's mother and Bob's ex-wife. No one had mentioned her in any of Alice's conversations. She and Bob were not close, but Alice had never detected animosity whenever her boss had referred to his ex.

What do I have to lose? Alice thought to herself.

She found the number easily among Bob's extensive list of contacts and dialed Miami.

"Hello, Dr. Sanchez's office? This is Bob Prettyman's office calling. Yes. I'll wait."

"The doctor will have to call you back. Can you leave me the number, so that she has it in front of her, please?"

"No problem." Alice left the assistant the number. With nothing left to do on the rescue issue, she turned to some bookkeeping for various foundation accounts.

After about forty-five minutes, Alice was speaking with Mónica Sánchez. After minimal pleasantries, she gave the doctor a quick capsule of Bob's adventure to find Raúl and their disappearance.

"Impetuous fool," were the first tough words from Ms. Sanchez's mouth. "Machismo gets so many men in these situations."

Alice, a bit taken aback, didn't respond.

Mónica had awakened with a start, her nightgown soaked in perspiration. At first, she stared out her bedroom window to see if some animal had caused some REM-level disturbance. Then she looked over at her husband, Roberto. Anger, disappointment, and sadness all knotted together in her stomach. He was the disruption. Years of subtle, slight, almost imperceptible differences had finally pushed her to the breaking point. It wasn't the fact that Bob was married to his job that disturbed her. After all, she spent similar amounts of time and energy with her practice and working, sometimes together, on their real estate investments. Nor was it that Roberto didn't love her or show his affection. He was even attentive at times. The real issue was that Mónica was professionally and socially a Cuban who lived in the United States. Roberto was an American who had been born in Guatemala.

Her husband was sympathetic to her interests, but not committed. They tended to enjoy different events and gatherings, and she knew that he was often bothered by the frequent dinners and parties with her conservative wealthy Cuban exile circle. There were no fights or major arguments, just low-level friction that led to a feeling that she was being tolerated, rather than loved and respected. Her counter-resentment of his apparently exclusive focus on creating wealth was now more frequently manifesting itself in her comments about his lost soul. With

Lisa about to go off to college, it seemed so unnecessary. Why not call the relationship quits?

The sweat on her chin now mixed with tears. She knew she would leave.

"Of course, I'll do what I can. And, I know I sound unfeeling. I am a little shocked at the scene you describe, Ms. Brown. It's just that I lived through so many situations where his overconfidence got Bob into deep water."

"Ma'am, I wouldn't bother you if this were not extremely serious."

"No, of course you wouldn't. Forgive me." Mónica sighed heavily on the other end of the phone.

"The fact that neither the Guatemalan, nor the provincial governments are willing to do much is not a surprise. They are notoriously corrupt and inept in security issues. And Bob is no longer the player he was when he was contributing to various initiatives in his homeland. Nevertheless, President Colom gets considerable US aid, and I don't think the government is so stable that it would risk really angering the US State Department. Give me a few days, Ms. Brown. I'll get back to you with some ideas. I'm sorry that I was so out of it a minute ago. Good-bye." The line went dead.

Mónica Sanchez's medical practice maintained a clientele of some of Miami's most influential businessmen. She never threw out a business card nor discarded contact information, she was comfortable in any professional circle, lectured widely in the south Florida and Caribbean medical research and health business associations, and even found time to publish in national medical journals. As a result, Lisa's mother was extremely well connected in Florida, Central and South America, and the Caribbean. Had they stayed together, she and Bob would have been a formidable and very influential couple. A few discreet calls to Guatemalan friends in Miami yielded confirmation from highly placed

Guatemalan military sources that Bob's whereabouts were unknown, that no rescue effort was currently intended, and that this Jaguar was seen as a valuable asset, not a threat to the government.

"Señor Rodolfo Gomez, please."

"May I ask who's calling, please?" An assistant to one of South Florida's construction magnates screened Mónica's call.

"It's Dr. Sanchez, an old friend."

After a few seconds, the assistant returned.

"Mr. Gomez will be with you in a moment, Dr. Sanchez."

Mónica looked at the appointment schedule on her desktop and realized she had only a couple of minutes further to spare on this call.

"Mónica, how nice to hear from you. How's the practice?" Rodolfo Gomez greeted her with only slight anticipation in his voice.

After a minute of the normal greetings, well wishes for the family, and complaints about being too busy to keep up important friendships, Mónica filled Gomez in on Roberto and Raúl's situation. She then cut to the point of her call.

"I assume, Rodolfo, that you are still close with key people in Guate."

"Well, you give me too much credit, Mónica."

"Not at all, but I need a favor."

"Di me. Tell me and I'll see what I can do."

"I need to know the number, the figure it would take to have the boys in olive drab to get off their butts, find my ex, and get him out of the jungle."

"Mónica, I can inquire, but you need to be prepared for a negative response."

"And why is that? Has reform advanced so far that officials no longer care about '*el dinero*?'"

"No, you know that's not the case. From the little I already know, however, this Jaguar is not viewed as a threat, but more as an asset who contributes to the coffers and is not a serious revolutionary risk. Removing him may be seen as more harmful than just cutting a revenue stream." Rodolfo Gomez paused.

"I see. Actually, I'd like to know that you have verified that assessment, because as I understand it, this innocent student revolutionary has killed at least four soldiers in retaliation for the death of his father. So, if he's now holding a prominent US citizen, the government's inaction could threaten a far greater revenue stream to your and Roberto's homeland."

"You mean Washington? That would certainly force reconsideration. As far as I know, however, Roberto is retired and doesn't really have major chits left to play."

"That may be the case, but I'm not retired."

"I understand, Mónica." Gomez's mind was spinning. He knew that Mónica Sanchez was not just a successful physician with a passing interest in Latin American affairs. He knew that she was also a very successful, very "hardball" player, a businessperson and extremely influential contributor in south Florida politics. Gomez knew he had work to do, and it that it would not be acceptable to be sloppy or incomplete in his task.

"I'll get back to you, my friend."

"Thank you, Rodolfo. My best to Ramona and the kids. Have a good one." Mónica smiled as she hung up and buzzed her assistant for her next patient.

Later in the afternoon, Mónica had her assistant set up a call with one of her former male patients, Max Gathers, a US senator from Florida and ranking member of the Senate Committee on Foreign Relations. She also sent a quick e-mail to Roberto's resourceful assistant, Alice Brown, suggesting that she use her DC Chamber business contacts to pressure the Republican administration to at least make some well-placed diplomatic calls to line up some executive branch support for her budding scheme.

Chapter 25

While her mother began tugging at strings on the East Coast, Lisa stared out of her third-floor apartment on Hearst Street, North Berkeley. She was a ten-minute bike ride from campus and no farther from the rapid transit system, BART; everything she normally needed in daily life was within close proximity. Her focus, however, was three thousand miles away, on her mother in Miami and farther still on her father in the jungles of Central America. That neither woman wanted to unnecessarily worry the other was evident by the matter-of-fact e-mails mother and daughter exchanged about Raul and Roberto's predicament. They were both frightened, however, that any inaction could condemn both men to some terrifying death.

"He's such a selfish bastard, only caring about his damn real estate," Lisa said to her mother as she entered the living room of her new Miami condo. She was in-between her junior and senior years of high school and still adjusting to living with a single parent in a new city.

"Watch your language, young lady. He's still your father and continues to provide quite handsomely for your needs. He and I may not have made it as a couple, but he's still a wonderful man who cares deeply about you," scolded Mónica.

To her great relief, no one at her Miami high school seemed to care whether or not her parents were together. That was the good news. The bad news was that Lisa found her new classmates to be shallow and surprisingly poorly informed about the world outside of south Florida. Here she was in "the northern capital of Latin America," as some referred to the city, and few of her well-heeled classmates knew much about what was happening in Mexico, El Salvador, or Washington, DC, for that matter.

Mónica was delighted to have her daughter around but was concerned that she seemed devoid of friends and spent all of her time studying or practicing on the school swim team. And she was worried that her studious young daughter might grow more resentful of or lose touch with her father. Mónica was also insistent that Lisa engage both her Guatemalan and Cuban heritage. The latter was easier because of the number of relatives in Miami. With Bob's consent, she had arranged for Lisa to spend much of her summer vacation working in Guatemala City at the National Historical Museum while boarding with Bob's cousin, María Elena Gonzales. When Lisa returned to start her senior year, Mónica noted her new fascination with Mayan culture and, more broadly, with modern societies that were formerly world-dominant cultures.

"Mama, until this summer, it never occurred to me how ironic it is that Mexico and Guatemala produced major Aztec and Mayan governments, commerce, art, and culture before the US was 'discovered' by white men. Yet, today, much of Central America seems totally dysfunctional and trailing the US as world powers." Lisa took a sip of her Coke and looked out over the bay beyond her mother's condo. Mónica simply sat and stared at her daughter.

"There are so many post-colonial questions more interesting than what shade of lipstick is best for which occasion or which Gloria Esteban mimic one should download. My classmates are a real trip," Lisa proclaimed with a sigh.

"Really? And you think they are so different from your pals last year in DC?" asked Mónica.

"Totally."

During her senior year, Lisa continued to swim and study but increasingly spent long hours at the library and on her computer reading about Incas, Aztecs, and Mayans. She developed friendships with girls on the swim team who were also serious students from Haiti, Venezuela, and Mexico, but not Cuba or Miami. As Mónica devoted more and more time to her growing practice, Lisa grew increasingly independent, navigating neighborhoods of Miami with her friends that Mónica would certainly have considered unsafe.

During the fall of that senior year, Mónica scheduled time to take Lisa to three of her four top college choices: Yale, Texas, and Berkeley. Bob happily hosted Lisa on her visit to Georgetown. Both parents were somewhat disappointed when Lisa expressed uncharacteristic excitement after her visit to the California campus. Even more than Texas's Austin campus, Lisa felt Berkeley offered the sort of stimulating internationally populated environment within which she thought she could flourish. The swim team coach was enthusiastic, so that was further inducement. Soon after enrolling, however, Lisa realized that she neither had the skill nor the time required to compete at the intercollegiate level. Her top-notch grades and college board scores, and her bilingual background made Lisa a very good, if not exceptional candidate, without the athletic credentials.

Had she received early admittance, Lisa would have spent more time exploring Miami neighborhoods, parks, and dance spots and having outings with family and friends. She loved the range of people she was meeting outside of school and was fascinated by what made them tick. She was accepted to Texas and Berkeley, but not until April, so she remained religiously glued to her books all the way through final exams. Even so, the two years in Miami provided Lisa with an early video of the key opportunities, interests, and abilities that would later define her professional life.

"Was that your mother?" asked Lilly Chu, Lisa's roommate during her six years in California.

"No. That was Dad's office manager. She'll get in touch with mom to coordinate the DC end of whatever strategy Mom has cooked up," said Lisa.

"So, are you heading to Guatemala, or are you going to continue to fret here?" Lilly gently pressured.

"Wow, I didn't know I was so transparent. I really don't see how I can improve the situation if I'm down there. If Mom gets somewhere, maybe I can be useful," said Lisa.

"How do you feel about all of this?" Lilly continued.

"I'm sorry for my cousin, because he's the innocent bystander in this whole mess. About my father, it's more complicated. He has rarely been around for me. In some ways, he's a stranger. I mean, I really don't know what sort of person he is, other than the obvious fact that he is driven and successful. I'm not sure what he really cares about, although this Quetzal idea is cool. He's so different from Mom. She's been passionate about Latina causes all her life." Lisa turned to her friend.

"Well, the kidnappers clearly thought he was close enough to your cousin to use him as bait. He can't be all bad." Lilly affectionately squeezed Lisa's arm.

"I know that, and his work colleagues that I've met over the years think he's fair and a great boss. But real estate seems to be all about money; there's no redeeming value, like with medicine," said Lisa.

"Not to argue, but his drive and focus allowed you to go to some quite good schools and colleges. Also, last time I Googled her, your mom is pretty driven and successful herself." Lilly smiled. "And people need places to live and work. So, real estate is important. Yeah, they're both driven. But let's not have this silly argument. The point is, you need to find the best way to be helpful now. And I'll help any way I can. Although you know my family contacts are all in western Canada and Hong Kong," she continued.

"I am grateful for you just being here as a friend and sounding board. It's strange that for so much of my life, Guatemala was the land of relatives, and it really only affected me as a vacation home. The stuff I read and studied about the repression of indigenous people, the massive wealth and privilege gap, the alleged unholy alliance between the Catholic Church and the wealthy, the depressing fatalism of so many average Guatemalans, and the culture of violence that permeates authority and youth gangs were all distant news items. It's almost like the Katrina tragedy or the Columbine massacre. Tragic, scary, and foreboding in some intellectual way, but backdrop to my daily existence. Now, it's part of my reality. I don't have to be there to feel the anxiety, encounter the fear, or appreciate the ironies."

The two friends sat facing each other in silence for several minutes.

"Okay. Lilly, you know logistics, strategy, and all that stuff. What would you do?"

"Well, I'd probably be on a plane to DC, Miami, or Guatemala. I'm not sure which one. But I don't think I'd accomplish much sitting in Berkeley. That's not strategy; that's gut emotion speaking."

Lilly grew up near Palo Alto, started college at Stanford, but quickly transferred to Cal to put more distance between herself and her parents. She had majored in international studies and mathematics and was now finishing an MBA. She already had several offers to join consulting firms and global financial companies. Lilly had done well, very well. Although she could focus on analytic constructs and serial calculations with the best engineering minds in her program, Lilly was as warm toward family and friends as she was demanding of her independence.

She wanted distance from her parents, but she was unfailingly loyal to them and her younger brother. After rooming with Lisa for almost six years, she was like a sister to Lilly. She considered her as family.

"I hate to see you torture yourself like this. You're proving the counter argument to what the snooty press thinks about our generation—a bunch of spoiled brats. FOX, MSNBC, SLATE, PBS pundits say we are a self-absorbed and protected generation, but you think about the rise in Jihadists, drug-linked violence in Central America, disappearing job security all over, and I'd say we are focused on some serious issues. We are clearly as responsible as the 'beat generation' at comparable ages."

"So, I'm not concerned about being mature or responsive or whatever. I just want to do the right, most useful thing here. You know, Lilly, I have zero influence or 'walkabout' in Guatemala, and only casual acquaintances in Miami. Most of my roots are around DC. And now, most of those folks are scattered around the country. Until it's clear that I can help in one spot or another, I'm more useful here. Cal's library has some of the best resources for researching Mayan history and current Central American political dynamics."

"I hear you, but you realize that at some point, this may come down to faith and luck, and simply being in the right place to help," Lilly said.

"I know that, but I'm not quite sure what the right place is yet."

Lisa sighed and turned on the TV. Both girls watched in horror as the news bombarded them with footage of the massacre at Virginia Tech University.

Lisa looked over at her friend and whispered, "You were saying something about faith?"

Chapter 26

(Roberto)

"Tío, when you're down here in Guatemala, do you feel like or identify as 'Chapin' or 'gringo?'" Raúl asked while we rested in our tent, sheltered from the searing afternoon sun.

"That's a good question—one that I don't think I've focused on specifically. Even though I've spent my adult life in the US, I would say that I feel like a man without a country. To the degree that I feel Guatemalan, it's an association with urban middle- and upper-class folks in the capital, Antigua, or even around Lake Atitlan. Small village and highland communities were just not a major part of my early experience. On the other hand, I have never totally felt like a gringo either."

After a few more moments of reflection, I continued.

"My dad was such a patriot and Mom admired the US, so I suppose I felt American, maybe hyphenated American as a kid. How do I feel? You know, for so much of my life, I've set goals, targets to shoot for and to exceed. I wake up and my tactics and short-term goals have been laid out. Overcoming hurdles presented challenges, like in a ball game. I thrived on achieving.

"Now that I think about it, this is the first time, maybe since my mom died that I've not been able to set and meet targets on a daily basis. The

Jaguar has seen to that. I've not really allowed myself to ponder the more basic questions in a while. What do I care about? What or whom do I miss most, while I'm marooned here? I'll have to roll those questions around. My immediate response is that I miss the challenge of making the Quetzal Fund work for the kids in Columbia Heights, but I know that desire, that focus doesn't reach the level of a 'life's passion.' I guess I've become pretty good at submerging primal feelings in order to avoid struggling with issues of identity or ultimate allegiance—if there is such a thing. What about you, Raúl? What do you feel?"

"Well, I've only been away from here for five-plus years, so I definitely feel like I'm home when I'm in Guate. Although being stuck up here in the jungle makes me realize that there are many countries in our homeland. I've been up to Tikal, but I can't say I really know much about current or historic Mayan culture."

"But you know more about today's politics than I do. What do you think the Jaguar is really after?"

"My guess is that he's honestly trying to foment some sort of revolution that generates a better life for rural Guatemalans. I think he's planned out a great deal more than is evident and that he's probably taken lightly by the government and has something far greater in store for them than they imagine."

"Say more, Raúl."

"Well, the choice of his name and the likely proximity of this location to Mexico are historically and militarily significant."

"I didn't realize that you were such a scholar."

"Well, I did pay attention in school, and I still talk to Lisa about stuff on occasion."

I said nothing, but nodded for him to continue.

"In terms of history, I feel pretty sure that we are camped somewhere near El Mirador, the first, largest, and most complex Mayan metropolitan settlement back in the late pre-classical period, maybe most glorious between 300 BC and 150 AD. The kingdom dominated agricultural and urban areas in Central America during a period when Alexander was conquering Persia and the Chinese were constructing the Great Wall. This was major. And one of the significant ruler/builders was the Great Fiery Jaguar Paw, predecessor of our host's namesake. So, our boy Felix is not aiming his uprising at a few thousand acres in the Petén; I'm pretty sure he wants to conquer the whole country. It's all to benefit the poor, of course, but whatever he has planned is not insignificant."

"Is that both the historical and military significance of which you were speaking?" I asked him.

"No. I am pretty sure we are not in the immediate vicinity of El Mirador, because that's a national park and would make accidental discovery of this camp too likely. I'd say we are someplace to the southeast, somewhere in a triangle between Carmelita on the south, San Bartolo to the east, and El Mirador itself to the north. As we've seen, trails are impassable during the rainy season, no vehicle can negotiate this terrain, and it's hard to trek in here without a local guide. If you know the territory, however, it's not too far from the Mexican border and safety from the Guatemalan army. If I'm right about this, the Jaguar's location offers a safe and strategic location from which to retreat, should it be discovered."

"Maybe it's my urban ignorance, but how's he expect to foment anything stuck up here in this 100 degree heat, 90 degree humidity, insects the size of birds, and sporadic satellite communication?"

"All I know is that he has tremendous reach on campuses and among young professionals. He's a twenty-first-century Robin Hood. And you know the government is usually pretty predictable and clumsy in the way it handles anything that smacks of helping the poor. The civil war was supposed to have ended in 1996, after thirty-six years. Do you honestly think that the military oppression, the gang violence, and the constant income disparity promote a sense of well-being for the campesino or even the average urban teen?"

I had to agree with his skepticism. "Even the short time I've been coming back, it's obvious that the modernization doesn't go wide and deep once you're outside of Guatemala City. My old academic buddy Max Ramirez confirmed that over half the population lives in poverty, still."

Reflecting back on my conversations with Guillermo Schaefer and Oscar del Gato, I realized that educated and sophisticated urbanites were well aware of the tragic proportions of teenage pregnancy, single-parent households, drugs, and gang violence that falsified any claim to national security or progress out of the 'developing nation' status. They just were not going to do anything about it.

"It's interesting how we could grow up 'Chapin' in different eras, over a period that's seen major progress elsewhere in Latin America or in North America, but we are basically treading water," I said as much to myself as to Raúl.

"It's hard to argue with Felix's goal. They are not that distinct from yours in DC. I suppose being held out here has forced me to recognize the enormity, the sheer complexity of executing real social change—anywhere."

We sat quietly in a small opening among rubber trees and could see beyond the green canopy onto a lush valley floor of leafy plants and tall grasses, once the corn fields of the ancient Maya. A flock of brilliant red-and-blue parrots squawked above us across the jungle above us, demanding attention. It must have been about two in the afternoon, because most of the camp was in their tents napping.

"You know, Tío, another interesting factor about Jaguar Paw's approach is that he's basically ignored the Catholic Church."

"I don't find that too strange, because the church here has not generally been a force for change. So many indigenous countrymen are taught to bear suffering nobly and secure a ticket to a better life in heaven. The church is more a palliative than a motivator for freedom." I realized that I sounded like I was more critical of the church than I was. I didn't practice, but when I did attend religious services, it was in the Catholic Church.

"Of course, it doesn't help that priests who do try to speak on behalf of the poor are killed. What's the name of that bishop a few years ago?"

"Oh, you mean Juan Gerardi."

"Yes. That was scary."

"It would be interesting to know how Felix sees God in his revolutionary world view."

I listened to distant monkey chatter and nearby insect industry and wiped sweat from around my eyes as I reflected on the character of the man who had taken us prisoner.

"Raúl, you made a comparison between what Jaguar Paw is trying to do and what I have started. Now, granted, we know next to nothing about his grand plans, but there are extreme distinctions. And you have to give him his due.

"Here's a young man who is devoting his early adult, high earning-power years to revolution, of some sort. I am using surplus money I've made during a lifetime of high wealth accumulation. I don't live in Columbia Heights, and I'm certainly not sequestered away from friends, contacts, colleagues, entertainment, etc. What have I really given up to try to help Latino youth?

"You ask what I miss, sitting down here in this sweltering jungle? I miss not being connected to the vibrancy and excitement of a Western world twenty-first-century urban capital. I miss Internet connectivity, buzzing commerce, smart and challenging investors, dynamic neighborhoods, and thriving culture. The world I miss is one that Felix has chosen to forego. He has given it up. Given my life's trajectory and my approach, I don't have to sacrifice in order to help those kids. Not so with Jaguar."

"Comparisons aren't really fair, I suppose," said Raúl.

"Still, one has to wonder if I'm kidding myself. My dream may be no more realistic than his."

"It's strange that the Petén, in its heyday, was the center of the sort of hip urban scene you describe." Raúl's eyes shone with a new intensity.

"Yes. It's also ironic that the place in our native land most like the scene I miss is Guatemala City. On a relative basis, it's nothing like what Tikal or El Mirador were in their era. They were more like Mexico City or even Miami of today."

"But Guatemala City does have the commerce, excitement, innovative companies, music, art, and culture for the young. Well, for the affluent young of my generation," he argued.

"Then why do so many kids—educated kids—move north or south, rather than stay and expand on opportunities here?" I asked.

"We both know the answer. They assume greener pastures are elsewhere. They think there's less violence, less corruption; it's safer moving about. They feel there are so many affluent people in the US, for example, that they won't be targeted by politicians, the military or guerillas. More opportunity to become wealthy where it's seen as normal or okay. My generation is no different than yours in that respect."

"Maybe, but somehow, I think there's something missing, both materially and spiritually," I said.

"Clearly, we have a tiny middle class, and wealth distribution is not an abiding concern of my generation of educated elite," admitted Raúl.

"Nor of mine, to be fair. Rigobertu Menchu got the Nobel Peace Prize in 1992, but she had to live in Mexico to promulgate her ideas of social justice in safety. And she was certainly not a middle-class or wealthy urban Ladino," I continued. "I suppose one thing that is admirable about the Jaguar is that he has a sense of commitment along with desire for great achievement, wanting to make great contributions to something greater than himself. Chile and Argentina have much more affluence, but do they have that spirit? I feel a spirit in south Asia or South Africa; and with techies, environmentalists, black civil rights, Chicano farm workers, and immigration advocates I feel it in the US."

"A fair commentary on my generation has to include the perspective of the rebels Jaguar has recruited. As we know, all adult Chapines are not alike. Just here in camp, I've met a guy from Quetzaltenango who grew up speaking Quiche and is as well versed a historian as any upper-class legacy kid. So he was a tour guide before joining the Paw. Another guy migrated from a small Q'eqchi' village near Esquintla to the port of Iztapa, where he picked coffee, then worked as a tuna fisherman, until he tired of hard labor and low wages. Both are bright and proud fellas who've decided to try to end the wealth and power gap that they feel squashes any realistic aspirations for their buddies. Growing up, I never really knew guys like this. My crowd either didn't acknowledge their existence or thought of them as losers. They definitely have spirit. And you know what, Tío? They're actually the majority. Not the guerillas, but the young people who experience the lower end of the social ladder."

"I hear you, Raúl, but this Robin Hood action won't be the answer."

"Neither will a King John form of repression. Tío, you're just a homesick elitist." Raúl laughed.

"Maybe so, Raúl. Could be …"

Chapter 27

There were others in camp that were also skipping an afternoon nap. While most of his troops and followers slept, the Jaguar Paw sat around his table with two men dressed inconspicuously like weekend hikers. They had trekked into camp with a small group of expert guides via a northern trail that led to an airfield near Campeche on Mexico's Yucatan Peninsula. They were part of the reason for the Jaguar's extreme confidence in the success of his mission.

"Now remember, German, we don't need desertion or rebellion in the army. We just need strategic inefficiency and confusion at the critical times." Felix Gigante addressed Colonel German Cortez. He was a university friend and ideological soul mate of Gigante's who was highly placed in the Guatemala intelligence service initially under President Alfonso Portillo, but had managed to maintain status under the current administration.

"Understood. I don't imagine that will be difficult, with the incentives we've been able to distribute."

To the other visitor, the Jaguar posed a question. "Jorge, how confident are you that our targeted wealth will not be able to access their accounts on 'D-Day?'"

"I'm fairly certain now, but I will be positive after a few more tests next week," said Jorge Romano. He was the older brother of Raúl's friend at George Washington University, Hector Romano. Jorge and Felix

Gigante were childhood friends, although Romano had long since moved to Mexico, where he had built a very successful financial analysis firm. While not an ideologue, Romano had been disgusted with the politics and inequities of his homeland for most of his adult life.

"I don't have to tell you that the beauty of this scheme is that with minimal human resources, I'm convinced we can bring the government, the banks, and the major capital to their knees. Our cadre of key leaders is in place to then lead all sectors and the pueblo, of course."

Gigante's assistant, Alicia, quietly entered the tent and stood unobtrusively in an empty corner, clipboard in hand.

"Let's drink to that," said Colonel Cortez. They raised plastic water glasses filled with beer and drank.

"Okay. We've set up the usual tent on the other side of camp from our other guests, so enjoy the night. Alicia will see you over to the tent. Provisions are being made for you to get an early start tomorrow. Let's have one more really comprehensive check in a couple of weeks before D-Day, but keep messaging those reports in the meantime."

After his partners left the tent, Gigante settled in to reread the memos both had deposited with detailed status reports about their plan. Even though he had satellite computers, the Jaguar felt much more secure conducting most serious communication on paper and, to the degree possible, in person. He wanted to be fully current before he looked in on Prettyman and Gonzales again.

After reviewing his operational plans for an hour, the Jaguar turned his attention to his captives. He had underestimated Prettyman's commitment to the US and his small mission to save Latino boys in Washington. It was an admirable enough mission, but limited in scope and of questionable staying power. He had been surprised, however, that this overseas Guatemalan didn't have more compassion for indigenous people in his own country. But that was just it, wasn't it? Prettyman really saw the US as his country, so he was not motivated to sacrifice in order to help the Jaguar's goal. He would be of little help in Guatemala, because he had not provided a steady stream of support to real change in Guatemala.

Jaguar surmised that Prettyman would support reforms, but not join in any overt revolution. The most he could get from Prettyman at this point would be resumption of the critical drugs-related revenues from the DC area. Reports were that the La Puerta Abierta was more successful now than before the fire, and that the police had full-scale surveillance on his 'muchachos' in the Columbia Heights/Adams-Morgan barrio. He forced himself to focus on reopening the DC market for his operation. It was time to tighten the screws on Prettyman, time to make him much more physically uncomfortable.

On his way over to the captives' tent, Felix Gigante gave orders that the 'gringos' were not to receive solid food until he gave the order to resume their meals.

"Mr. Prettyman, I hope you and Mr. Gonzales have been well cared for," Gigante said as he entered their tent.

"Have been? Yes, absolutely. But are you implying that we're about to be set free?" Raúl asked.

"Well, that depends on your uncle and his cooperation." The Jaguar offered a slight upward curve of his lips.

"I'm just loving this tranquil vacation, thank you. I see no reason to change things or to hurry back home," responded Prettyman.

"I can understand your sarcasm and skepticism, Roberto. However, I don't understand why this government underestimates your danger. Perhaps they don't see you as valuable enough to rescue," said Gigante, as if conversing with himself.

Raúl Gonzales was about to respond when he caught glimpse of a Prettyman negative nod of the head.

"I assume they see your efforts as localized and marginalized from the major urban areas and the strategic locations in the country," Prettyman said. "So, while a few in power may be friendly, my detention by you and your pinprick rebellion are of no moment to the government."

"Clearly. How shortsighted, indeed." Again, it was as if he were commenting to himself. "Tell me, Roberto, what class of people really care about the efficient functioning of government security?" inquired the Jaguar. Before either of the prisoners could respond, Jaguar continued.

"What class cares about stability of the capital markets? Is it the rural laborers and farmers? Not really. So long as markets, prices, and currency are stable, all's well with the government, right?"

The two captives merely sat in their chairs. Waiting.

"What happens if certain levers in the governmental system malfunction and capital is no longer safe or predictable? What if markets are shaky and wealth is jeopardized? Then, gentlemen, the rich and the powerful care. But, by the time such instability is evident, it may be too late, right? Sort of like the innocent receding tide that precedes a tsunami."

Prettyman revealed no emotion or concern but asked, "This is all interesting, but where do I fit in, if I may ask? I am not a powerful cleric, a wealthy land owner, nor a well-placed diplomat. I have no real power. If I did have power, I wouldn't have been permitted to rot here for months."

"Astute points, Bob. You fit in by closing the door to La Puerta." Gigante finished with a wide grin.

"But such an insignificant revenue source. Clearly, you are substantially financed from sources other than the paltry Washington drug market." Prettyman returned the grin.

"Of course we have other sources, but DC is not insignificant in supporting our crusade."

Prettyman looked at his nephew and then back at the Jaguar.

"I can't do it. Why not tax those down here responsible for the conditions you want to change? Find ways of squeezing the rich and powerful in the capital," Prettyman suggested, partially in earnest.

"Capitalists north of the border helped create the economic conditions affecting opportunities here; they still help create and reinforce the diseconomies that cripple Guatemala. You know the results, Mr. Prettyman: 54 percent live below the poverty line, few campesinos are adequately educated, urban and rural civic leaders speak out at tremendous risk to themselves and their families. It's a suffocating situation in our homeland."

"Fine, but you are hurting Central American kids, who are equally disenfranchised in the US. And, you can't seriously believe that your DC effort in any way injures American power. Again, why not concentrate on the cause of the problem where it's most egregious and most accessible?" There was no sarcasm in Prettyman's voice now.

A bit perturbed, but ignoring Prettyman's argument, Felix Gigante stretched his five-foot-seven frame as high as he could, wiped a line of sweat from his brow, and pointed a forefinger at Prettyman.

"I got you down here, didn't I? I got you to interrupt your secure and comfortable existence in the world's most powerful city to trudge into the unforgiving jungles of the Petén. I got you to leave your air-conditioned security blanket to trek down here in the rainy season, in 100-degree daytime temperature, 85-90 percent humidity, with poisonous insects and reptiles in a jungle with no real means of escape. I'd say this little backwater rebel leader is fairly effective. What do you think, Mr. Prettyman? I don't care about those who didn't stay to fight obvious injustice. It's fine to seek better outcomes for your family by moving north, but I do care about those left behind here in Guatemala. And while Honduras, Salvador, and Nicaragua may suffer similar miseries, I am Chapin, I am Maya, and this is where I will fight. This state will improve, or I will destroy it trying.

"Roberto, you might study our history a bit more carefully. Sacrifice has always been a means to an end for Mayan leaders. The loss of a few lives in DC in order to benefit our campaign to reclaim our nation for its people is an insignificant cost."

The Jaguar stepped toward the tent flap and waited for a response. It didn't come.

"Your job, Roberto, is to fold up your DC project, at least La Puerta. Let me worry about the strategy for effectively punishing those who are robbing the Guatemalan campesino and worker of his due."

"Since you mention it, Mr. Gigante, what is your strategy for liberating the land?" Prettyman spoke in an even-tempered, nonaggressive manner.

The Jaguar took a step back toward the center of the tent's living space. He thought for a moment while his two captives waited.

"While it's no concern of yours, let me just say that for years now, we have been putting in place loyalties to build the most committed network for change seen in any Latin country in one hundred years. That network is capable and will trigger multiple coordinated strikes that will bring the power structure to its knees. The previous efforts have failed because strategies were too narrowly focused and, thus, their implementers too easily isolated. You would see a military coup here, an assassination there, industrial sabotage in one region and financial destabilization in another. Each time, often with the aid of the US, capital recovered, and government was more repressive than before. Never has the ruling class had to respond to military, social, political, and economic threats simultaneously. For your sake, Mr. Prettyman, I hope you and your nephew are back safe in DC, and your daughter in Berkeley, when the time comes. Let me know when you're ready to have us send a message."

Then the Jaguar left.

Chapter 28

While the Jaguar was annoyingly confident in the outcomes of his plan, and of his resources, and while he menacingly implied knowledge of Lisa Prettyman and her whereabouts, there was one important "family" connection he had underestimated. Dr. Mónica Sanchez was a Cuban-American with connections in the Guatemalan firmament strong enough to bring attention and pressure heretofore not experienced by the Jaguar or his movement. He was aware of her existence, but he knew it had been almost two years since Bob Prettyman and Mónica Sanchez had divorced, and much longer since they had been estranged. The Jaguar assumed that the divorce, lack of a dependent child, and geographically separate lives without evident contact meant that Dr. Sanchez and Mr. Prettyman were estranged in the most severe sense of the term. Lisa, however, knew that her mother wanted to move on from her father, but couldn't abandon him to the current circumstances.

One o'clock in the morning and Mónica Sanchez Fuentes sat, feet propped up on the railing of her twenty-ninth-floor condo, looking out over Biscayne Bay, beyond South Beach, on out into the Atlantic.

Five years back in Miami and my cosmetic dermatology practice is the largest in south Florida, the real estate I purchased with Roberto's guidance in the nineties is worth multimillions, and I love my professional life. I'm still one of the few Cuban-Americans that truly moves fluidly amongst Haitian, Latin, Caribbean, and Latingo (Cubans who have "turned" gringo) *cultures in Latin America's northern capital. But there have, of course, been costs,* Mónica thought to herself as she closed a photo album of previous years in Washington when Lisa, Roberto, and she were still together. She sipped a margarita and drifted further back to her youth in south Florida in the early 1960s.

They lived in a bungalow in the Hialeah district of Miami, along with many of the other "first wave" immigrants who fled the new Fidel Castro regime in Cuba. Mónica loved their housekeeper, Anita Dulce, because she seemed to understand and anticipate what Mónica was thinking. She could reliably lighten Mónica's mood with just the right fun activity or entrancing story. Mónica's father, Hector Garcia Sanchez, was rarely around. He seemed to either be rebuilding his cigar production business or planning a counter-revolution to recapture Cuba. Her mother, Gloria Alma Fuentes, was constantly involved with "social activities" with other well-off Cuban housewives. Mónica knew that Anita Dulce had family in Miami, but she seemed singular in her devotion to and focus on the Sanchez's only child. Anita was always there for Mónica, inventing games for them to play until the girl was old enough to want to play with school friends and cousins. Even as Mónica remembered spending more time with other kids, Anita was ingenious in getting Mónica to improve her mind, expand her intellectual reach through reading and exploring nature around marshes and waterways of the growing city. As an adult, Mónica wondered about the family and independence Anita had given up to help raise her.

"Nica, time to come in for homework," the Sanchez's Afro-Cuban nanny called to Mónica. "Okay, my little princess, get your bath so we can read some more about Jose Marti. You know, he was the first liberator of Cuba," Anita said as she lay out fresh clothes for Mónica to change into.

"But why do you say the first liberator? Who was the second?"

"Oh, child. Such questions." Anita finished drawing the bath and looked around to be sure that no one else was upstairs.

"Nica, some people feel that Fidel Castro is a liberator. Many poor and black Cubans still regard him as having made life better for them. But you'll have to decide for yourself, once you are older and can read more and talk to more different folks. Make up your own mind." Anita was whispering, even though the house was empty, save for the two of them.

"I don't understand. Mama and Papa talk like Castro's the worst person possible."

"Child, you too young to talk to them about it. Your parents are good people. They are really good people, but they are high-class, white Cuban, and they had a good life under the old ruler, Batista. When you were a baby, your family's life was better than it is here in Miami. But, hush up this talk now. You don't want to upset your parents. When you get older, do your own private studying, okay?"

Mónica could tell that Anita didn't want to talk about Castro or Batista and that she didn't want her talking to her parents about them either.

That night, Mónica watched Anita carefully when Mrs. Sanchez came home. The nanny got her talking about her day and about the preparations for the party the Sanchezes were having that weekend. When Mrs. Sanchez asked how Mónica had been that day, Anita told her about the glowing first-grade report card, which she had read; she relayed how well the daughter played with kids on the block; and she talked about her growing interest in plants and animals in books they read together. Nothing about Cuba, Castro, or Africans from Cuba. Mónica took note.

Mónica also quickly learned that it was best to keep some events and experiences that she and Anita had a secret from her parents. They became agitated, for example, if she discussed any of the playing with dolls, or burning of candles she and Anita did while singing various chants in Anita's Santeria religion. Mónica went to Catholic Church most Sundays with her parents. Mónica smiled as she reflected on the two Cubas her household had experienced. The island of her parents' memory was one of privilege and plenty, of freedom and unlimited good times. Anita often told stories of hard work in blazing fields and of a class system that repressed opportunistic blacks. She suspected that both visions were true.

Mónica stood and leaned over the balcony railing. What a journey she had had over the last forty-odd years. Although she had only moved a few blocks from her Hialeah childhood home to her multimillion-dollar condo in Brickell after returning from DC, the influence she commanded far exceeded that which her entrepreneurial father and socialite mother had dreamed of. Now Miami's top cosmetic surgeon and one of its richest commercial property owners at merely fifty-five years old, Mónica Sanchez was a true titan. Cuba meant a lot to her intellectually, but it didn't define her, as it did her parents. Her business world (wealthy Latin American clients and affluent Miami bankers and developers) was truly multicultural.

Significantly, Mónica's Miami upbringing and her early and intense exposure to Cuban culture led her to mature as a Latina with excellent gringo ties; whereas Roberto's youth as a US Army Intelligence "brat" spending vacations in Guatemala produced a gringo with deep Latino ties. On the surface, both attractive Hispanic "comers" were perfectly matched, and their distinctive backgrounds were beautifully complimentary. Those distinctive backgrounds, however, also created rifts that proved too great to mend, over time.

The phone ring interrupted Mónica's reflections.

"*Hola*, Lisa. *Como estas, mi hija?*"

"*Mama, estoy bien.* Have you had time to contact anyone about Papi? I'm really worried. It's been almost three months since anyone has heard from him or Raúl."

John McKoy

Mónica took a sip and smiled. Her daughter would do well; she was so focused.

"I'm fine, as well. Thank you," Mónica chided her daughter.

"Sorry, Mama. I'm just so concerned about Papi."

"I understand, mi hija. Yes, I have contacted some friends, and I think we'll be able to reach a few key people in Guatemala."

Mónica was a little perturbed that she had had to spend substantial time and social capital to gain commitments from Guatemalan generals and bankers about supporting some sort of rescue mission in the Petén. It was typical of Roberto, she thought, to plunge ahead with his own blind independent heroics in trying to save Raúl. Early on, she had mistaken this focus on tactics over strategy as his "adventurous nature." Bob's impulsive side had attracted her to him when she was in medical school at Georgetown University in Washington. He'd appeared bold, daring, and gregarious in some ways, and then inexplicably reserved, reflective, and private in others. She now felt that the adventurous part of her ex-husband's persona was really a dangerous impatience in nonbusiness affairs that led him to forsake careful strategic thinking for immediate actions.

She had long since given up trying to understand how this careful, strategic businessman could be so tactically impulsive in his personal life. She smiled when remembering their escape from a guerrilla blockade on a mountain road in Guatemala.

Whether his behavior annoyed her or not, Roberto and Raúl were in real danger, and she would do whatever she could to help rescue them.

Her conversations with Rodolfo Gomez in Miami and Guillermo Schaefer in Guatemala City had been very helpful in terms of validating her ideas about the key power levers in business and in the military to help back any rescue effort. While the government didn't know of the

Jaguar's specific location, they could provide coordinates that narrowed the area for his camp within a hundred-mile radius.

"Mom, I also have some unexpected good news," Lisa continued.

"Oh? I could use some right now." Mónica finished her drink and turned full attention to the conversation.

"You know that I have been in regular contact with Papi's assistant at The Quetzal Fund, Alice Brown? She's been great with background on what's happening on the ground in DC, with the police, the grantees, key resources, etc. Anyway, she put me in contact with Papi's biggest grantee and project, La Puerta Abierta. It's the one whose effective work with Latino youth got this drug dealer in Guatemala ticked off."

"Mónica, this is all very interesting, but—"

"Hold on, Mama. So, the head of La Puerta, Marta Hernandez, is super worried about Papi. She feels like he's facilitated her saving scores of kids' lives and all that. Anyway, her main youth worker, a guy named Manny Cortez, is an ex-marine. And he wants to … no, he insists on helping us."

"Lovely. How does some DC city kid, who happens to be a tough guy, help with your father lost in impenetrable jungle in el Petén? In the rainy season, no less." Mónica's voice offered none of the excitement of her daughter's.

"It turns out that Manny Cortez spent most of his early youth in a Mexican port town." Lisa took a breath.

"Lovely. I still don't see how this eager beaver helps us."

"His hometown is Chetumal, a port town above Belize, on the Caribbean side of the Yucatán Peninsula, and a bit northeast of Tikal. As a boy, he spent time exploring the area we think the Jaguar now inhabits."

John McKoy

Mónica stood up, padded into her living room, spun the globe on a modern glass end-table, and located the Yucatan.

"I see; the Quintana Roo region abuts Guatemala in the Petén. Oh, my goodness. And he's a marine, you say?"

"Marine or Ranger; I'm not sure what Marta said. One of those. But a trained and experienced Harrison Ford-type character."

"Wonderful, Lisa. Maybe you could find out more specifically what his background is while I continue to put the pieces together for the other resources we are going to need. I need to get some sleep. I love you, mi hija."

"Love you too. Good night, Mama."

Lisa had trouble sleeping, so at 5:30 in the morning Pacific Time, she placed a call to La Puerta and reached the receptionist as the office opened in DC.

"Let me put you through to Mr. Cortez, Ms. Prettyman."

"Manda. Aquí, soy Manuel."

"Señor Cortez, aquí hablo Lisa Prettyman. Yo—"

"Yes, I know. How are you? Any news of your father?"

"No. Actually, that's why I'm calling."

Lisa heard Manuel sip some sort of drink. Then silence.

"Marta Hernandez told me that you grew up in Yucatan and might be able to help us." Lisa waited again for some reply.

"Lisa, I am sure what Marta told you is true. And yes, I would very much like to help. Unfortunately, I am not in a position financially to be of much assistance on the ground."

"Please, Manuel, my mother and I will foot the bill for whatever effort we have to mount and will reimburse La Puerta for your time."

"In that case, I think you'll find that my training and subsequent service in southeast Asia, as well as my younger days in and around the Petén, equip me to be of assistance. I would suggest, however, that we meet rather than try planning over the phone, or by e-mail."

"Great. Let me talk this over with my mother, but in the meantime, could you send me a resume and some references, so I can be better informed when I speak to her?"

"Absolutely."

Later that morning, Lisa received a dossier and contact numbers for several Army Ranger references. Manuel also sent a couple of Mexican references of family friends and church people from his teenage years. Without giving any specific detail, the military references provided enough feedback to give Lisa comfort that Manuel had, indeed, adequate experience in search and rescue missions in Afghanistan to be a capable asset in Guatemala. Three days later, both she and Manuel were on planes heading to Miami to put a plan together with Mónica's friend, Rodolfo Gómez.

As she drove along Biscayne Boulevard and the Dolphin Expressway to the Miami-Dade Airport to pick up her daughter and Manuel Cortez, Mónica flashed on some of the history that brought her to this point.

In the late 1970s and early 1980s, prior to Lisa's birth, Mónica enjoyed her medical studies, as well as the people in Washington that she and Roberto met and with whom they spent time. There were plenty of people in both the medical and the real estate fields who were young, ambitious, and interesting. As Roberto's projects grew in size and value, she noted that her geographic interest in Latin America was much stronger than his. At first, she noticed small, and apparently insignificant, things, like her not being able to go more than a couple of weeks without Cuban or Mexican food, her preference for speaking Spanish when they were alone at home, or her stronger desire to travel to Florida or Latin America on vacations.

Roberto never objected to her wishes, but neither did he have a strong enough preference to initiate these choices. Gradually, she noted that more and more of Roberto's friends were gringo. She paid only slight attention, because the property, development, and financial fields around DC were so predominantly populated by white Americans that his selections seemed natural. Mónica, however, was clear early on that she wanted to have a Latin practice to the degree possible. So, her school and casual contacts were often with the wealthy from Central and South America. Both wanted money and financial success, but Roberto's concern for and focus on Latinos developed late in their relationship.

She smiled and reflected warmly on her former husband. They had simply grown apart, and the valuable family time when they weren't working was no longer stimulating; in fact, it was only their attention to Lisa that kept them together. He was now much more immersed in a Latino culture, but his reorientation was focused on Latino boys, and he was truly concerned about helping the less fortunate. Mónica's attention to the poor in Miami was normally limited to the few hours a month that she worked in a burn clinic in the lower-income section of Little Havana.

Pulling into the short-term parking at the airport, Mónica wondered how the different career and social paths of Roberto and herself would influence the life choices of their daughter.

While she had had him send a picture, Mónica didn't recognize the tall and handsome bearded, coffee-colored young man at the United luggage belt as Manuel Cortez. He, however, had no problem identifying the attractive, stylishly dressed middle-aged woman scanning the newly arrived DC passengers.

"Señora Sanchez?" he asked hesitantly.

"*Si. Mónica, por favor. Me llamo Mónica.*"

"Mucho gusto. Soy Manny."

"Sorry to keep you waiting. Your flight must have gotten here right on schedule," she offered.

"We were a bit early, actually."

"Is this your first trip to Miami?"

"Well, I've been to the airport many times, but I think this will be the first time in quite a few years that I have actually been in downtown Miami."

"Well, welcome. We will certainly try to make this a pleasant memory, even though the occasion is quite somber."

"I've been looking forward to meeting both you and Lisa, and I am anxious to help locate and rescue Mr. Prettyman. He's literally saved many lives up in DC."

"Well, it's a pleasure to meet you. Your background is not too shabby either. Perhaps we can walk over to the Delta luggage belt and meet Lisa, and then I'll get the car."

"I'm ready."

By the time they located the right Delta Airlines conveyor belt, Lisa had retrieved her luggage and was standing by a newsstand nearby.

"Hello, Chula. How are you?" Mónica said, embracing her daughter.

"Lisa, this is Manuel Cortez."

"Hi. Manuel. Nice to meet you in person."

"The pleasure is certainly mine."

Cortez recognized the similarly shaped nose and mouth with mother and daughter, but Lisa was even more stunning than her mother, he thought. Her skin was a darker tan, and her light green eyes were larger and more striking than her mother's violet irises. He had to make an effort not to stare.

"Why don't I get the car, and—"

"Oh, Mama, we can walk with you."

"Absolutely, Ms. Sanchez … Mónica. It seems that we both have light bags."

"Then, if you don't mind, let's stop by the office for a bit. We can get Rodolfo Gomez on the line and sketch out a plan."

"Perfect," said Manuel.

Lisa nodded her agreement.

Chapter 29

(Roberto)

The cave was within a quarter mile of the Jaguar's camp, and the first hundred feet or so inside the entrance were damp, dark, and frequented by large brown bats. I knew, however, that Felix Gigante had space deep inside for his romantic encounters. I had followed Felix and a revolutionary courier named Graciela Donoso after they left camp unescorted by guards. It was early evening, so I assumed they weren't straying far. They were easy to follow, and the raucous croaking of wood frogs provided perfect cover for any missteps I might have made. Once they were inside the cave, I hid on a shrub and tree-covered lip over the entrance and loosened the knot on a bag containing a very poisonous blue-and-green tree snake. I chewed some tasteless extract from a rubber tree to keep awake and focused on the task ahead.

When, after about two hours, I heard the lovers approaching from the depths of the cave, I readied the bag. Graciela exited first, allowing me a clear path to drop the snake on Felix as he passed below my perch.

At first, he must have thought he'd been brushed on the neck by a bat or large insect. He flicked the snake off of his neck, but not until after it had sunk its fangs into him and injected some of its lethal venom. The Jaguar was able to walk a thousand yards or so back toward camp before his legs buckled. He must have quickly realized that he had been bitten and motioned for Graciela to inspect his neck; then he instructed her to get the group's medic and anti-venom.

I approached Gigante and could hear his laborious breathing and his painful moaning. I knew he would die before help arrived. I stopped fifteen feet from him and was quickly overcome with sickening guilt. I was in the process of taking a life. Although my father had been a soldier, and I had had my share of tough fights, I had never killed. I knew that I had to get back to camp via another path, but I couldn't tear myself away from the stricken figure in front of me.

Finally, he stopped moving. I took a step backward and prepared to take another path back to camp, when I heard a rustling sound behind some palms to my left. As I stepped onto my escape path, I came face to face with a crouching cat of almost leopard-like proportions. It stared at me for agonizing seconds; then, claws extended, the Jaguar attacked.

In a split second, I rose from my cot, gasping for air and perspiring quarts of sweat. I scanned the tent. Raúl was on his cot, still sound asleep, and his light snoring provided the only break to the serenade of reptiles and insects harmlessly patrolling our camp grounds. I was weak and lay back down. We hadn't been given solid food for at least seven days. My physical strength was further eroded, however, by the panic induced by my nightmare. I knew that Raúl and I had to be fully committed to whatever escape plan we devised and that we would have to initiate that plan within the next few days. Our strength reserves were dwindling with every day of the Jaguar's rationing. My dream now revealed another concern. I knew that I could defend myself, maybe even kill in self-defense, but I now realized the depths of my reservations about taking another life. Our plan would have to build on diversion and not violence. Any indecision when facing a lethal human combatant could be fatal for us.

As I lay on my cot in the early dawn heat, I tried to picture my father. He was a warrior whom I knew so little about. He had been a family rule-setter and disciplinarian. And he had encouraged me to adopt traits that enforced a dogmatic adherence to Catholic principles. "Obey the rules, study hard, learn from older accomplished people, respect others, and trust in Christ, Son. You'll do well," he would advise.

He missed many of my school activities, like sports or theater. But he did show interest in my progress and in the events he missed due to travel or office work. I suppose he was a good dad, but like many of the fathers in DC in the military or foreign service, he just wasn't as present as my mom. Even on summer vacations in Guatemala, Dad rarely stayed the whole time Mom and I were there. It was clear, however, that when the three of us were together, Dad was very happy. Trips to Guatemala also made him relax and be more present for both Mom and me.

"Are you awake, Uncle?" Raúl asked, rising slowly from his cot.

"Yes. I've been awake for quite awhile. How did you sleep?"

"Fine, but of course, I don't have much energy. I wonder how many grains of corn will be meted out for breakfast?"

"I don't know, but I think we need to hatch an escape plan today."

"Tío, I've been thinking that Gigante has to have some access to cellular or electronic communication. He's coordinating events around the country and is planning to orchestrate system-wide catastrophes, if you listen to his boasts. Further, he wants you to have Marta call off the youth training project in DC; yet, he knows we don't have phones or computers."

"I follow you so far," I said.

"So, if he has some modern means of communication, he must be assuming you or I would use it to communicate with Marta. If that's the case, we should be able to use that communication to send her a message about our location, and maybe even about the Jaguar's plan." Raúl took a breath.

"I would agree, in concept. The guy's very smart, however, so I don't yet see any foolproof way of sending a signal."

"Well, it seems to me, based on elementary communications policy stuff I've had, that we break this task into three steps. The first is to decide on the message we want to send. The second is to identify the best recipient. And finally, we need to figure the code or disguise for the message that can only be interpreted by our recipient." Raúl seemed to find energy from the challenge, because it certainly wasn't from the meager amount of protein or carbs we had been fed.

"The message should convey our location, to the degree that we can estimate, and perhaps the size of the Jaguar's force."

"Again, to the degree that we can count them. On any given day, that number could vary from twenty to fifty or seventy-five," chimed in Raúl.

"Okay, so what do we know about location that can help narrow in on our part of the jungle?"

"Well, we've seen smoke to the northeast. That suggests farming or cultivation within, say, fifty miles," Raúl estimated.

"Based on that *Lonely Planet* guide book I studied before I got out here, on the distance from Carmelita where I figure I was deposited before being picked up for the final leg of my trip, based on the lack of any signs of human existence in any of our daytime forays with our hosts, and based on the lack of low-flying aircraft from any direction, we're somewhere between Carmelita and Tikal."

"Given that Gigante grew up in Flores, I'd guess we're far enough north from there so that he doesn't risk being recognized by the random explorer from his hometown. And given the tourist traffic around Mirador, we're southeast of that area. I was brought to the peninsula by boat, but I could have docked anywhere from Veracruz, Mexico, to Belize City. I doubt that information helps us," said Raúl.

"If I can picture that guide book map again, I'll bet we're in the neighborhood of latitude 89.5. It would also make sense that we were hiking distance from Belize and/or Mexico, for quick escapes from Guatemalan authorities." I was straining to recall the colored map that, luckily, I had studied frequently while waiting to be summoned in the city.

"So, putting it all together, I'd say we're in a triangular part of the Petén whose corners are defined by Carmelita on the west, Tikal to the south, and Rio Azul to the northeast."

"Tío, I agree, but that's a huge area."

"Yes, but if they have aerial surveillance and the camp is unaware that their movements might be spotted, we have a chance." I was more exhorting than I was spouting fact.

"All right, my guess is that there are no more than twenty-five people in Gigante's camp these days. But it seems like he can bring in another fifty with short notice," Raúl said with hesitance.

"I would agree with you. I suppose if that's our 'what,' then Marta Hernandez is the target 'who.'"

"Tío, I think Lisa is actually a better focal point."

"Why?"

"Well, Gigante probably knows less about her. She has more research resources, has a more diverse network of possible helpers, particularly if you consider her mother in Miami, and I think we know more about her upbringing, giving us more data with which to craft a disguised message."

"It is also reasonable that I would want to let her know that I'm alive as part of any deal to shut down La Puerta." I was impressed with Raúl's cleverness and quickly agreed to begin working on the coded message.

"Tío, when I was recuperating at your condo earlier, didn't you say that you and Lisa were supposed to take some camping trip later this year?"

"Yes, so—"

"Well, you could let her know you're all right and are still looking forward to the trip. Only you bury our location in that message. Then, insist that the Jaguar brings you back a response, so you know Lisa got the message, before you send anything to Marta."

"That's quite smart, Raúl. That will give her a head start on finding us." I sat up on my cot and began to visualize a sketch of the Bay Area. As my mind's eye traveled the coast from Half Moon Bay down toward Carmel, I formed an idea.

"We think we're in a triangle formed by Carmelita, Rio Azul, and Tikal, right, Raúl?"

"More or less, that's right."

"So, if I have my geography correct, Carmelita could be San Francisco, Rio Azul would be Berkeley, and Tikal would be Oakland Airport for a Bay Area triangular equivalent. What if I said I wanted to do our trip later this year, but instead of heading up to the wine country, we covered a triangular area starting in Carmel, or better yet San Francisco, then up to someplace like Berkeley, and finally down to the Oakland Airport?"

"She would think you were nuts."

"Exactly, and therefore, she would know there was a code in the suggestion. If I added that instead of a AAA recommended route 101 and 580, we'll take *Lonely Planet's* 89.5 and have a blast stopping at every vineyard along the way?"

"She'd know you never use AAA maps and that there's no route 89.5 North, so she might go to Guatemala Lonely Planet and, hopefully, she'd see Carmelita and get the clue about the triangular relationships.

And, while he would guess you were sending a message, Jaguar hasn't spent enough time on the West Coast of US, that we know of, to get the references. It could work, Tío."

"Now we need to figure out how to signal timing, which is ASAP."

My spirits began to sink, since I realized that although I flew down to Guatemala in early May, between two and three months ago, I had no idea of the exact date. Given the extreme daily temperatures, the afternoon rains, and the mosquitoes, I assumed we were still in the height of the rainy season—June through early September.

"Tío, I have been trying to keep count of my days in captivity. I might be off by a week or so, given the boat trip and days blindfolded in a car, but I'm pretty confident that it's early to middle of August now."

"That fits my estimate, given the climate and my arrival date."

"Bingo!" Raúl practically shouted.

"What's wrong?"

"Well, isn't Lisa's birthday in late August?"

"Yes, the twentieth."

"Why not say you hope to be back in the US and out to California to start your trip by her birthday? That gives a sense of urgency, even if we're off by a few days."

"I like it, Raúl. Now we just have to get the Jaguar to send the message and hope we can stall sending his instructions to Marta."

After a skimpy breakfast of corn meal and coffee, we made a morning group trek to gather corn from a small field a kilometer or so below our hillside perch. I was so exhausted from the walk in the baking sun that I had to rest after picking only a few ears. I noticed the guards smiling as I labored to get through this simplest of chores. Once, I looked up and saw two king vultures gliding above our field. The sun made their black-and-white tipped, seven-foot wings look the width of a jet airplane. I fantasized that I must be emitting some deathly odors, since those birds usually feed only on the spoils of jaguar kills. I could also hear spider monkeys in the nearby jungles squawking about some serious matters. My death?

I made it back to camp slowly and collapsed on my cot for an afternoon nap, unsure if I'd ever awaken.

Late that afternoon, after the sun had almost disappeared, Raúl and I were visited by Gigante, accompanied by his aide, Angel Chiapas. The young aide carried two canteens of chilled spring water. It was the most delicious drink I could recall swallowing in recent memory.

"I trust you've had a productive day in the fields," Gigante said as we drank and he sat alone at our table, guard outside the tent.

Raúl and I were mute while insects and monkeys provided the only sounds in the background.

The Jaguar leaned back in the wooden chair as far as he could safely tilt, while the aide stood motionless in the corner.

"You know, you and I are very much alike, Mr. Prettyman—Roberto."

I didn't respond. I was tired and had no idea what he was thinking.

"You see, you built an empire in the land of the great capitalists, and you seek to turn around some of its major injustices with respect to our people." His eyes remained fixed on mine. His confidence filled the room.

"*We* are not alike, at all," I heard my voice say. "To be honest, I built an empire, as you call it, for selfish reasons—to see if I could do it and to acquire substantial wealth. It is only afterward that I began to think of how to help others. I'll grant you that you are building your empire to benefit others from the inception of your effort. I don't know you well enough to assess whether you have some other motivation for yours." The little voice called "self" warned me against referencing Jaguar's revenge killings.

The Jaguar allowed a smile to form at the corners of his mouth.

I continued. "But, in another way, we are fundamentally different. I have not taken lives, destroyed families, or destroyed other humanitarian efforts to further my cause."

The smile disappeared.

"Fair enough, Roberto, but your effort is focused on one or two neighborhoods in a single city. I am trying to liberate a country. The costs will naturally be higher here. Clearly, you see that."

"Felix, you made the comparison, not I."

While the exchanges became more frequent, they were without animus from either party.

"Tell me, Jaguar, why not simply destroy transportation and communications infrastructure? Create the typical revolutionary chaos and havoc. You may be amassing some drug profits in the US, but commerce and the daily lives of well-to-do Guatemalans seem unaffected by your actions. You and your colleagues seem to be sacrificing lifestyle to no apparent tangible end."

He rose from the table and paced about the room. Then he stopped and stared at both of us. Again, I heard my voice speak.

"Even if you do successfully drive out the government and engineer some Castro-like takeover, do you really imagine that the US will idly sit by and risk another leftist regime on its southern border?"

He waited a few minutes and then pulled a couple of articles from his canvas vest and dropped them on the table. The lighting from our one bulb was weak, but both Raúl and I edged over to the table and scanned the articles. The Jaguar sat back down.

Spread before us were computer copies of articles from one of Guatemala's main press, the *Prensa Libre*. As the Jaguar smoked a cigar, it took us easily half an hour to absorb the gist of articles covering about sixty days worth of news. In each of the major urban areas of the country, one of the following events had occurred:

- Citywide electrical failure
- Traffic light failure
- Commercial bank mysterious withdrawals
- Army garrison bombings

There was no connection noted in the press, but based on Jaguar's previous hints, he was orchestrating these events. Jaguar had strategically placed either electronic or personnel resources capable of creating countrywide chaos over a relatively short period of time. However, I was not convinced that he had yet amassed the control he needed to crumble the government.

He picked up the articles, placed them in his vest again, and turned to us.

"Roberto, I must concede that you are strikingly accurate in your assessment of our likenesses. The loss of life, while lamentable, even condemnable from a certain moral perspective, is nevertheless necessary to achieve great social ends. It is usually imperative to make real social change."

"But weren't you raised Catholic? How about the teachings of Christ versus killing?" I persisted.

"And what about the Crusades or any of the other pogroms and massacres conducted throughout history in the name of religion,

Roberto?" Agitated, the Jaguar continued to preach. "Let's not insult our intelligence. We both know that the church has been complicit in subjugating the poor, or at least weak in protecting them. In Guatemala, those brave prelates who dared follow the true word of Christ have been silenced."

He ground his cigar into the dirt floor, moved to the tent flap, and bid us a pleasant evening. Chiapas lingered for a moment, staring at Raúl. In a loud stage whisper, he said to my nephew, "You don't remember me from my Guatemala City days. We once helped each other out. I'm going to give you one more favor. Leave as soon as possible and head northwest."

Then he was also gone.

Stunned, Raúl and I looked at each other for several minutes.

"What was that about? Who is Angel Chiapas?" I asked.

"As I recall now, he's a former gang tough I met in high school. Totally filled out and bearded now, but it's him. We saved each other from beatings by our respective crews. I would believe his warning," said Raúl.

I reflected a moment longer on the encounter but then turned back to our cots.

"Well, the Jaguar will let his message sit for a day or so and then ask you to send that communication to Marta. That's my bet," offered Raúl.

"I get the commitment, the fervor, and even the whole master plan. If he's got this all figured out and has enough resources in place to cause the disruption he's claiming, what's holding him back? Why does he need the drug funds? He seems to have national catastrophe well in hand," I said to no one in particular.

"I am only guessing, but the disruption he intends to bring will require sustained action, and that will require large strategic bribes. He needs more cash to ensure his plan works over a long enough period. That's why he wants La Puerta shut down."

"Not bad, Raúl. I think you may have hit it on the nose. So we'll still have leverage to get a message to Lisa. I'm just wondering if we shouldn't add more about the chaos he's already causing."

"I don't think so, because the more that's in there, the more content for the Jaguar to decipher and the more likely he'll get some of it and crush the message altogether or rewrite it so that he destroys our code," said my nephew.

"You know, when your mom and I were teenagers and I would visit from Washington, we saw how chaotic guerrilla activity and military crack-downs can make daily life. It's not as stifling as it must have been up here under the control of the early Mayas, but it could get pretty brutal and scary. The constant random acts of violence leave you anxious about venturing out in some areas, and at its worst, you'd hesitate to make simple daily trips or transactions at all. It's paranoia unlike any that North Americans, gringos, have ever experienced, even after 9/11. Maybe it's akin to what southern blacks experience after Reconstruction and during the dark days of segregation and the rein of the Ku Klux Klan. I remember kidnappings, murder, assaults, blackouts, and roadblocks without warning, provocation, or remedy. Your anxiety and tension were never far from the surface, and if sustained long enough, countries can implode from bickering, distrust, malfunction, and general disorder."

"Tío, I have experienced some of that, and my mom has certainly told me those same stories, but I think the Jaguar is far from being able to cause that sort of disruption."

"I don't think either of us wants to find out for sure. So, we not only have to get out of here, but also have to find a way to stop our would-be Mayan King."

We heard the tray with our dinner being left outside the tent. Rice porridge and beans and a good night's sleep were the only fuel I had to power my thinking about a more detailed plan of escape.

The next morning, our hosts had us in a cornfield early but then back before noon and told everyone to rest because of expected torrential rains. After I jotted down notes from which to construct our message to Lisa, I lay on my cot in a semiconscious state.

"Raúl, what do you see yourself doing when we get out of here? Going back to the US?"

I could hear my nephew breathing and almost hear his mind working, but he said nothing for several minutes.

"I've obviously had a great deal of time to think about that question, Tío. I can't say, however, that I have a firm answer. I'm pretty sure that I want to go back to DC for the time being. And, while I thought about international relations when I was an undergraduate, I now think real estate may be a better fit."

"Why's that?" I leaned up on an elbow to look directly into his young, bearded face.

"There's so much guesswork and chicanery in politics, local or international. You have to really understand cultures, national and individual histories, as well as current events, to make good decisions in international relations, it appears to me. It's too flexible, and there are no real rules—too many moving pieces. In business, particularly real estate, there are factors you can assess, there are reasonable probabilities and ranges of certitude with decisions. I like that sense of security."

"Well, what about recessions and dips in the markets? Every decade, in every metropolis, developers, agents, and bankers lose their shirts in residential and commercial markets."

John McKoy

"Sure, Tío. Nothing is certain 100 percent. I just now feel that people and institutions in markets are easier to predict than people and institutions in politics."

"Fair enough. I suppose I felt similarly when I was your age. My father tried to encourage me to enter international relations. He didn't think the military would provide me with enough reward. 'You're good at reading people, and you like languages—do international business or relations and foreign policy when you grow up,' he'd tell me."

"So, why didn't you, Tío?"

"I took courses in foreign policy at Georgetown, but by that time, I knew I wanted to make money. I guess my best contacts were in the DC area, and I always did very well in real estate finance. Then, when I had my own firm, work in the DC area became all-consuming. I suppose I never had the driving urge to build an international practice."

Without being accusatory, Raúl continued. "And you don't have a desire to stay and find a legitimate way to bring about the changes Gigante seeks?"

"I have to admit that I think his assessment of the wealth gap and the intransigence of power is accurate. I'm just not clear what a successful, peaceful revolution would look like, or how one would bring it about."

"While I am also skeptical, history might be instructive. You've read about Gandhi's nonviolent tactics leading to India's independence from Britain? Two decades ago, Czechoslovakia had its 'Velvet Revolution' leading to the election of Vaclav Havel. Closer to home, Chile had a socialist peacefully elected for a hot second in 1973. Then again, the US is not too tolerant of leftist governments in this hemisphere. Nevertheless, one could argue that all three countries are currently more democratic than they were prior to those events."

Raúl stared at me for several moments.

"How about just taking on the reform of one sector, like education? Let others deal with corruption," I offered.

"Isn't it all so interconnected? I'd want some evidence that others were, in fact, reforming other sectors."

"I don't know, Raúl, but it seems clear to me that change of the magnitude you're envisioning requires risk. Doesn't it stand to reason that waiting for others generates stagnation?" I waited momentarily for his response. "Are you considering working in concert with the Jaguar?" I finally asked.

"No. That would be too extreme for me. I guess I'll have to keep thinking about this, Tío. As you can tell, I feel there are downsides to real estate, or any business, for me. I like the security, but I can't see spending my life without trying to address some of society's glaring injustices. Yeah, I'll keep thinking about my choices. I'm assuming, of course, that we get out of here."

"Well, let's hope you get that time back home, and not too much longer down here."

The rain came in a steady downpour and began to stream under our tent flap, so I got up to see if anything needed to be moved off of our dirt floor. Satisfied that nothing important was in the path of the brown stream meandering across our floor, I sat at the table. Looking about our canvas world, I noted for the first time a carved wooden cross high up on one of the tent's support posts.

"Raúl, do you go to church in DC?"

"No, not really. I sometimes go to mass, and I'll go for Christmas and Easter services. Why do you ask?"

"I was just thinking again about how ubiquitous the Catholic Church is here, as it is in most of Latin America. Yet, it doesn't seem to have infused the elite population with any obvious spirituality or Christian values. And some of the practices of the military, as well as of some guerrillas, are as barbarous as the blood sacrifices of the ancient Maya."

"So, show me where the church has truly captured most of the population. I've come to believe that humans all have a spiritual need, but that formal religion often misses the mark in terms of filling it."

"Interesting. I think that describes my belief as well. I've never been terribly comfortable with all of the killing that's done in the name of one god or another. Looking around, I notice that Fundamentalist Pentecostals have grown in number since I left. It's not clear, however, that the quality of the poor's' nonspiritual life has improved," I said.

"I know it sounds a bit Marxist and similar to the Jaguar, but it really does seem like the church here devotes so much pulpit time to having the poor accept their lot in this life by preparing them for the promised rewards of the afterlife. It's almost as if there is a conspiracy of power—government, wealth, the church—to keep peasants laboring away for subsistence. It's also partly why youth gangs are becoming so much more prevalent."

"You sound like you're ready to join the Jaguar."

"Hardly. You would have to be blind, however, not to recognize the deep inequities in our society. Even my privileged friends and I recognized the inequities early on. The odds against change always seemed so high that it was easier and safer just to go along and continue to lead the privileged life."

"Raúl, I'd even say that I respect some of the Jaguar's aims. The lack of income distribution and the totalitarian grip the government has over most of the people has not really improved since my childhood. It's no wonder that more kids are risking very dangerous immigration to the US, even though, in many cases, they don't have the skills to succeed up there. Alternatively, there's plenty of opportunity in trafficking of narcotics, it appears."

"Right; and in some few cases, there are people like you and Marta that are trying to provide them with skills needed for the legitimate economy."

"Thanks, Raúl. But, we all know El Quetzal can only offer a drop of support, when what's needed is buckets full."

"You know, I can't but wonder how true to his Mayan heritage Felix Gigante intends to be once he reinvigorates his DC revenue stream."

"What do you mean, Raúl?"

"Well, as I remember, Mayan kings could be totally unforgiving with the lives of their enemies and quite cruel in their punishment."

"That's why we have to have a plan that allows Lisa to generate action before we're forced to pull the plug on Marta. I don't intend to find out if this Jaguar is as bloodthirsty as his predecessors."

"Right, Tío. But we know that the generals and land owners aren't going to improve the plight of 'the people' to close the wealth gap just because some kids march on the national palace, or a few public services are inconvenienced, or even a few of their number are kidnapped. They've resisted change for decades."

"One thing at a time. Let's get out of here; let's survive first," I urged.

Chapter 30

(Roberto)

The rains came in the morning the next day, so the Jaguar had most of his crew hanging around the campsite, waiting for the weather to clear. When he came by our tent to ask that we send the message to El Quetzal to close down the La Puerta project, we were ready.

"I have a request to make of you first," I said.

"Tell me, Roberto. I promise to restore a reasonable diet once you have sent and gotten confirmation that the project will be closed," Felix said, anticipating my request.

"That's good news indeed, but that's not my request. I need to let my daughter know that I'm okay. I don't even know how long I've been down here and I'm sure she's worried to death. Let me send her a message that I'm okay, and then I'll initiate the El Quetzal process. Besides, if it's August already, I'm supposed to join her for a trip out in California. She'll be wondering why I haven't contacted her. No point in having another Prettyman family member making calls and inquiries down here."

The last point seemed to register with Gigante.

"Okay, but make it short, and we'll give her a couple of days to respond. I can have it e-mailed."

I wrote out the message that Raúl and I had crafted and gave it to Gigante.

"Please, send it in English if you don't want her thinking it's strange. Her generation of Latinos doesn't normally communicate in Español," I suggested.

The Jaguar looked over the message, stared at us for a moment, and left.

"What do you think, Raúl?"

"I think he's going to send it. If he had found it out of bounds, he'd have rejected it. He didn't seem to think it such a strange request. And he's super confident about the security of this site."

Tired from hunger and the little anxiety-producing exchange with the Jaguar, I lay back down on my cot and dozed off. The heat and humidity were so draining that I experienced little benefit from cool water or coconut milk. Vitamins and minerals evaporated in sweat, and sleep rarely left me refreshed, only feeling less drugged.

"Mama, I don't want to go to the playground. The white kids make fun of my accent, and the Negroes call me names."

"Berto, you're ten years old. Do you know what black or brown boys your age have to go through in Belize or Esquintla or even here in Virginia?" My mother was about to repeat her lecture on how lucky we were to be in the US, in the nation's capital. "Do you want me to come out with you?"

"No, Mama. I'll handle it."

"Unfortunately, son, you have to earn their respect. And if they try to bully you, stand up to them."

John McKoy

"Okay, Mama."

"And Berto, you know whose son you are, don't you?" She began another well-worn refrain.

"Yes, Mama; I'm a child of God, and no one on earth is better."

Silly as it seemed, just repeating her mantra buoyed my spirits. That and looking into the steely eyes of that five-foot-two fireplug that I knew would move heaven and earth to protect me, if things really got scary.

The slights and insults that bothered me never seemed to faze her. She ignored the words, lectured the offending clod, or pitied him/her as some poor, ignorant lesser being. Given another set of genes, she might have suffered mightily, if she had allowed the small-minded prejudice of pure Spanish blood Guatemaltecos, or snooty white Washingtonians to diminish her self-worth. She didn't ever allow the barbs to disturb her equilibrium and sense of value. Never. Whether due to her parents, some teachers, or the church, she embraced her Negro, Spanish, and Indian heritage with pride and exuded a confidence and faith in the future I've not experienced in many people—anywhere.

The early days of the leftist guerrillas in the late fifties created anxiety over the safety of middle-class Guatemalan folks that seeped down to young kids, who were surrounded by barbed wire-topped residential walls and carefully shuttled to supervised play dates. My youthful years in Alexandria and DC were not sheltered from TV drama and dinner table discussion (by my parents and their guests) about vicious racists in Alabama, Mississippi, and Georgia, of segregated facilities in DC and the early, testy days of desegregation after the 1954 Brown Supreme Court decision; anxiety at our dinner table about the growing danger of Khrushchev and the communists in Europe and Cuba, of bombs that could blow us to smithereens; of the Kennedy assassination; and of the growing peril of the Vietnam war. As a "foreign" kid, I experienced mild prejudice on my own in Washington, and I was not too young to absorb some of the impacts of all of the local, national, and international turmoil. Through it all, Mama enveloped me with her love and confidence.

"Those gringos may think you're white, but you have blood of black, brown, red, and white people in your veins, Berto. You have to learn to be comfortable with all kinds of people. It's the Christian way to live; it will make your life richer and more fulfilling, and later in life, you'll be well served by that ability," Mama would lecture.

Without my knowing at the time, she made arrangements for parents of friends to accompany us to ensure we were safe on various public field trips, like to the DC Zoo or the Smithsonian museums. Over time, I learned to deal with the nastiness I did encounter on my own, without involving my mother. If I did slip and mention being picked on as a "Spic" or "nigger lover," she would smile and ask for the child's name. When I dodged her request, she'd remind me of what village kids in Guatemala or black kids in my neighborhood, much less far down south, had to deal with.

When my father was around, he'd say I needed to build my body and learn to defend myself. He taught me a bit of karate and showed me exercises to build my chest and arms.

He also arrived at breakfast on occasion with reading lists of "classics" he thought I should be reading and understanding.

"Bob, you can't make a living in the world you're going to face unless you know how to experience what others—friends or adversaries—are experiencing. You learn that by keeping your eyes and ears open and by reading widely."

Even when I was only eight or nine, he'd ask me about some event that was in the local news about local civil rights leaders like Walter Fauntroy or Julius Hobson. He challenged me to understand the events and to imagine why different figures acted the way they did.

"Tío, Tío, wake up. You're about to roll off of your cot." Raúl was shaking my shoulders.

"Wow, I must have been dreaming. Thank you. Did I say anything intelligible, Raúl?"

"Not really, but I guess you were seeing your mother and father. You kept mentioning their names. What were you thinking about, Tío?"

"I suppose I was reflecting on how they shaped important parts of me when I was way too young to understand what they were doing."

"You know, I have vivid memories of my great-aunt from your Guatemala visits and from my mother's stories. She must have been quite a strong lady."

"That she was, Raúl."

"But I really don't remember your father."

"Well, he died almost twenty years before you were born, and I don't know how much the Guatemalan side of the family really knew about him. He was in the US armed forces, part of the time in intelligence. He was very principled, very tough, and cared a great deal about his small family. I don't really have relatives on Papi's side."

"Was he religious like your mother?"

"Not religious, no. He was also Catholic, but he rarely went to church. He was, however, very principled and had a strong moral code. He and Mama agreed on basic issues of right and wrong."

"And what about Aunt Mónica? She seems to be principled, but not really Catholic."

"You mean my ex-wife?" I hesitated, and Raúl nodded.

"Well, she's like my father in that regard. In Cuba and early on in Miami, she was exposed to Santería, as well as Catholicism."

"Oh, that's that Afro-spiritualistic religion that sacrifices the blood of animals—"

"Yes, whereas Catholicism symbolically drinks the blood of Christ," I added.

"Anyway, I think she's like me in that she appreciates the moral footing of the church but is less captivated by the rituals." I took a moment to sit up on my cot. "She's very principled and very hard-driving. Her medical practice allows her to satisfy her strong intellectual curiosity and do some good, as well as makes her a very wealthy woman and gives her access to people of power all over two continents. Yes, she's an extraordinary person," I said.

"And you still love her, Tío?"

"Probably." I responded instinctively. We had grown apart, and I'd realized a few years back that I found it more difficult to anticipate her moods or satisfy her emotional needs. Did I still love her and miss her company? Yes.

Even though the rain was still steadily driving the light-green ground cover into the shape of a slick carpet, I needed to stand outside briefly and breathe the jungle air. The humidity sapped the little strength I had stored up, so I returned inside and lay down again on my cot. I was hoping that a square meal would restore my strength, but the closest approximation of a well-balanced, nutritious meal I came upon was in my dreams.

"Suppose the Jaguar is right, Tío?" Raúl was sitting, wide awake, on the edge of his cot.

"Right about what, Raúl?"

"Well, I have to admit that since I've been captive in this makeshift village, I've given a great deal of thought to how much of my own country I don't know. Even though I was sympathetic to guerrillas and political movements that would create a more equitable society, I never really knew campesinos or poor Ladinos in the capital. My associations with the left here and in college at George Washington University were safe and purely intellectual. Chatting with these guys here, who've risked everything to join this movement, I have a better sense of the real prison the military and government cements around millions of poor Guatemalans."

"Are you sure this isn't the hunger and weakness speaking?" I asked him with a tiny grin.

"No, Tío. I am weak, scared, and feeling a bit helpless, sure. But listening to the young rebels reflecting on their life choices and comparing them to mine and my buddies' down here makes stark the gap between the poor and the middle class, between the city-dwellers and the campesinos. For example, these guys or any of the kids you see in DC from Langley Park, Maryland all have '*desaparecidos*' in their families, relatives that they'll clearly never see alive again. The only times I've known friends whose relatives have been kidnapped, they were returned for ransom."

"Let's hope that streak continues in our case." I sighed.

"Tío, it really is all about greed and power, and the average Guatemalan is merely a pawn in this class game."

"That said, you keep sounding like you're ready to join our host?"

"No, but I now recognize his gripes as legitimate. As I've said, it's complicated, and I don't have answers, Tío. If I didn't think I had other options in life, if I had grown up in some highlands village, or La Limonada in Guatemala City, you bet joining the Jaguar would be appealing."

I rolled over on the cot, stared at the tent ceiling that pulsated under the storm, and thought about Raúl's perspective. His assessment looked at life from the front lens of a telescope where all images are large and out in front of you. While I agreed with the nefarious grip the "system" had on the poor, I somehow looked at the situation from the other end of the telescope, through which all images seem small and illusive. I was stuck focusing on the Jaguar's methods, the harm he perpetrated via the drug trade, and less on his noble, larger goal.

As I drifted in and out of consciousness, I began to recognize and accept that the magnitude of the changes the Jaguar sought would probably never be realized peacefully. The "system" that ensured a life of privilege for Guatemalans like me had been in power too long and insinuated its tentacles so deep into every facet of the culture as expressed in daily life, of the "Chapin" way of life, that its guardians could not conceive of giving up anything willingly. As in the past, no change would come nor power be redistributed voluntarily in the land of the Maya.

I finally had to ask myself if I wanted the Jaguar to succeed. I knew and saw clearly that what I wanted was impossible. Like the Jaguar, I wanted justice for the poor, equitable opportunities for all Guatemalans, and even a redistribution of wealth. With these goals, I was totally comfortable.

What was unrealistic, to even a semiconscious and drained intellect, was how to achieve these ends without reducing status or lifestyle comfort to my family, friends, and colleagues. While I believed that my circle was innocent of grievous day-to-day acts against campesinos and the poor, they were beneficiaries of an odious system. I didn't want to acknowledge that wealth gaps can only really be closed with a shift from the upper classes. Taxing the poor to increase their wealth is ludicrous on the surface. Clearly, should a revolution come, there would be no innocent bystanders.

So, while I couldn't see aiding the Jaguar, I couldn't pinpoint, to myself, the reason. Perhaps I simply didn't care about change enough to be willing to have my circle of family, friends, and colleagues suffer. I knew that my discomfort and unsatisfactory conclusions weren't really influenced by my exhaustion; our captivity had forced me to face a

John McKoy

dilemma as old as recorded history. I begrudgingly granted the Jaguar his due for his courage and moral conviction.

For the time being, however, I convinced myself that the Jaguar should be opposed, because he had fomented negative and destructive activity in the lives of hundreds of kids and families in DC's Columbia Heights and Adams-Morgan neighborhoods. I couldn't see building the Guatemalan revolution on the backs of innocents in DC. My subconscious wouldn't let go unchallenged, however, the proposition that real social change can take place without violence or without collateral damage to innocents.

"Mama, who is that angry man who is blaming peoples' unrest on Communism?"

My mother joined me in front of the black-and-white TV.

"Oh, that's that nasty J. Edgar Hoover. He's head of the FBI. Do you know what that is, Berto?"

"It's the Federal Bureau of Investigation. They're like supercops. But I don't understand why he's blaming Negroes. It's those white bigots who are causing the problem. He thinks Rosa Parks, or Medgar Evers, or Dr. King actually made up stories about how nasty, violent, and hurtful segregation is," I said.

"I know. I agree with you, mi hijo. But, because Castro has now taken over Cuba and defeated rebels we supported at the Bay of Pigs; Khrushchev and the Russians are invading Europe; and the Chinese are moving south into Vietnam; it's easy for some people to use 'communism' as a shorthand to identify enemies and scare folks. Even back home, President Montenegro is saying all of the Guatemalan rebels are communists."

Five years later, in 1968, after Poppa had been killed in the Vietnam War, my mother and I watched more horror on live TV, as Dr. King was assassinated and Bobby Kennedy was gunned down. The Democratic Convention in Chicago was like a soap opera written to portray a political system totally imploding into chaos and violence. Nor could we escape mounting national anxiety by focusing on home. US Ambassador to Guatemala John Gordon Mein was shot to death there, causing heightened panic within the upper classes and the ex-pat community. While still grieving Poppa's death, Mama was stoic about the turmoil we witnessed daily on TV.

"You know, Berto, that the Bible doesn't condone violence, that Jesús was a man of peace and nonviolence. Let's pray that those nonviolent civil disobedience tactics and national strike against produce work for Cesar Chavez and the California farm workers, that they aren't taking the beatings and abuse for nothing."

"Yes, but—" I tried to respond.

"Yes, but there are times when people must defend and fight for what they think is right. That's why your father went to Vietnam."

"So, King, Gandhi, Chavez, and all the pacifists are wrong?"

"No. That's the complicated and important thing, mi hijo. If you truly believe Christ's gospel, and you are willing to stand up for what you believe is right, even to suffer at the hands of violent and evil people, you can also achieve great things. It's not that there is one right way. And whichever approach you take, people, innocent people, will die. So, one has to be sure the challenge is truly evil and that the situation that's hurting thousands of people is insufferable, then you fight or protest the best way you can. You understand?"

"Not sure that I do."

"You will figure it out in time, Berto."

"Raúl, I think we're going to have to either make a stand or try to escape in the next few days. We may not be able to wait for Lisa's response. Let's hope she figures out where we are, contacts Guillermo Schaefer or somebody down here who can mobilize help, and that they find us out in the jungle."

"We're not even clear where we are, Tío."

"We know enough from what we told Lisa. Besides, I don't think these guys are going to allow us to get any stronger, so we might as well take our chances while we can still walk."

I remembered looking over at my nephew, as I fell back asleep.

Chapter 31

Miami was hot, humid, and sultry as mother and daughter returned to Brickell Avenue after a morning jog along Biscayne Bay. They cooled off in the air-conditioned elevator ride up to Mónica's condo.

"Mama, it's gorgeous here, but how do you take the humidity?" Lisa wiped the sweat from her arms, legs, and face.

"What humidity, mi hija? The sun's barely up yet."

"Okay. I think I'm spoiled by the Bay Area. I need to take a quick shower," Lisa said.

"What hotel is Manny at? I'll call and have him come over for breakfast. We can plan the morning before I have to go to the hospital."

"It's the Hampton Inn over on Southwest Twelfth."

"Oh, that's just west of South Miami Avenue. Very close."

Mónica placed the call, reached Manny, and arranged for him to come over for breakfast in forty-five minutes. She then called a nearby Intermezzo Café and Deli and ordered bagels and lox to go with the black beans and *plátanos* she was heating.

John McKoy

"We'll have a healthy international meal, although these bagels are not like New York's." Mónica realized that she was speaking to herself, as the showerhead was cascading tepid water down on Lisa behind a closed door.

Manny had been up for hours before he got Mónica's call. He put on running shorts and a T-shirt and jogged north up Biscayne Boulevard, through some of the "downtown," into the Wynwood District, over the Sheridan Avenue bridge, over to Collins Avenue, down to South Beach, back over MacArthur Causeway to the mainland and down to his hotel. He took his time, because so much of what he saw was new to him. Actually, he was a bit overwhelmed by the gleaming glass-and-steel towers that punctuated downtown, the ultra-modern Metro Mover, an overhead railway that seemed to connect key points in the downtown, the manicured lush boulevards decorating every vista, the accessibility of the bay's crystal-blue waters and the proximity of fresh-smelling ocean, the distinct feel of South Beach and of the painted splendor of its art deco buildings. To Manny, there were signs of wealth and leisure everywhere. And, even early in the morning, there were folks heading to the beach passing others in summer business dress heading to the office towers.

As he spotted his hotel several blocks ahead, Manny slowed down, found a park bench, and completed a routine of cool-down stretches. Looking around him, the young Mexican American was struck by the diversity and the similarity of people he had seen during his run. There had been business executives, shopkeepers, tourists, elderly domino players, young roller bladers, groundskeepers, and yachtsmen—people of every station in life. And all of them had been Latinos. He realized that he'd heard no English, seen no blondes, nor heard any standard US hip-hop or pop music. When he flipped on the TV last night, and when he caught a bit of radio in the morning, it had all been in Spanish. The feeling was different from any he'd experienced as an adult. He was not in an urban minority community as in DC or in a poor rural Latino environment, like the one he'd grown up in; this was a majority twenty-first-century, sophisticated, affluent Latino environment. He looked around him like a kid in a candy store who had just realized that the toy figures and dolls were real avatars with powerful potential. Exciting and frightening.

"What am I doing here? How could I possibly think I'll be able to lead a mission in this world?" Manny questioned out loud.

"This metropolis swallows up even the most urbane and sophisticated people. Others get trampled by the heavy crime scene. God, I'm just a country boy with a few years of Army Ranger experience."

By the time he had returned to his room, Manny had calmed down and began to regain some of his modest DC swagger.

"I'm not going to be looking for some criminal protected by smooth Florida crime bosses. My job is to find Mr. Prettyman and his nephew in a jungle where I grew up. Then I get on a plane and head back to Columbia Heights. Enjoy this ride, Manny."

By the time he exited the hotel to walk over to Mónica Sanchez's condo, his full confidence and smile had returned.

"Wow, you look all rested and fresh, Manny. Did you just get up?" Lisa asked as he entered the sunlit living room.

"No. I had a nice run up to Wynwood, over to South Beach, and back."

"Impressive," said Mónica. "Tonight, we'll show you the neon sparkle of Ocean Drive, a little of Fairchild Tropical Gardens—no time to go down to the Everglades, but you should see a taste of our wildlife—hit a couple of Coral Gables neighborhoods, and finish off with dinner in Little Havana, so you can see how real Miami Cubans live. Sound good?"

"Awesome, as they say up north."

"Down here too." Mónica smiled as she set plates and cutlery on the table.

The phone rang, and she okayed the delivery of their breakfast.

After they had placed items on their plates and poured juice and coffee, the team assembled around a glass table on the balcony overlooking Biscayne Bay.

"Okay. I have made initial contacts with friends in Guatemala, and I'm hoping to call in some favors from wealthy players here. So financing a small rescue effort and signing up 'soldiers of fortune' will not be a problem. Finding Bob and Raúl and successfully extricating them, on the other hand, will take some doing," Mónica said, looking directly at Manny.

"It's been awhile since I ran rescue operations in Afghanistan and even longer since I hiked around in the Petén, but I have an idea of how this can work," said Manny, taking a slow sip of coffee.

"Before we call anyone else, it might be a good idea to all be on the same page with respect to the basic plan. So we could start with what we know and what we assume about their situation," said Lisa, placing her laptop on the table.

"Well, we know that Raúl was taken by this Jaguar guy," offered Manny.

"Whose real name, according to Guillermo Schaefer in Guatemala, is Felix Gigante," Mónica interjected.

"And he's organizing some uprising that is partially financed by a North American drug operation, located partly in DC," added Manny.

"To date, he's made no ransom demand," said Lisa. "The situation is complicated by the fact that the Guatemalan government and army have turned a blind eye to Jaguar's movement, because he's not disrupting trade or the economy for the powerful, yet has quieted other guerrilla activity in the north and central part of the country. And he's undoubtedly greasing the palms of various government and military officials."

"That may be changing, given the string of disruptive events that people have recognized in the past few weeks. If all of the attacks on the financial market, electrical grid, and protest activity are not random, but are actually being coordinated by the Jaguar, then the government will rapidly lose patience with him," chimed in Mónica.

"Yes, but given what I've gathered about military sophistication, it could take some time for the army to find and shut him down. They're sort of used to outright bullying people for information to locate guerrillas hidden in population centers, or permitting unofficial rogue campaigns to terrorize villagers into giving up hiding places. If he's as smart as I guess he is, the Jaguar's campsite will have minimal numbers of permanent guerrillas, like a couple of dozen. And it won't be found easily by traditional army tactics."

"I'm betting you're correct, Manny," said Mónica.

She stood up and took her dishes into the condo.

"I don't really know much about Guatemalan topography, rural culture, land economics, or even regional politics, so I can't be much more help with this part. I've got to get over to the hospital, and I will check in with you two later this afternoon. If you get something concrete, then we'll get on the phones tonight or tomorrow."

After Mónica left, Manny and Lisa spent a couple of frustrating hours gathering as much data as they could to narrow in on the location of the Jaguar.

"Let's take a lunch break. I know a nice outdoor place over near Wynwood Walls, so you could see some cool murals and walk a little for a change of scenery," Lisa suggested.

"Let's do it," agreed Manny.

Later, seated at butcher block tables at Wynwood Kitchen and Bar, Manny sipped a beer.

"You didn't mention that this place had galleries, shops, and amazing murals. The colors on the walls alone could keep me occupied for hours. This is special."

"Well, I'm glad you like it. I didn't know what your taste was."

"You mean because I work in Columbia Heights and come from rural Mexico?"

"No, because you seem so comfortable planning a risky expedition into the jungle to rescue two people from a band of guerrillas of unknown size and strength. I mean you might be more comfortable at a gun show."

"Well, I'm glad that you took a chance and brought me here. I'm quite at home among these murals. It's not Diego Rivera, but—"

"Well, *no me digas*," said Lisa, a bit taken aback.

"Yeah, actually, my brother was a mural artist and settled in Mexico City. What about you; where does your interest come from?"

"Well, it's hard to be a cultural anthropologist, live in the Bay Area, have middle-class Latino parents and not be somewhat interested in art. Remember, I spent a lot of formative years in DC with all of those great free museum resources."

The early afternoon passed quickly without a word mentioned about their critical task.

"I feel like we're at a dead end in terms of narrowing in on a location, but I suppose we should get back to Mom's and struggle some more," said Lisa, rising from the table.

Back at Mónica's condo, Lisa sat down immediately at her laptop to check e-mail.

"This is strange. I don't recognize this address, but it's addressed to me. Probably junk."

"I don't know; you might try to open it. I have a funny feeling—" Manny couldn't finish.

"Oh, my goodness. It's from Papi. He says he's okay. But I can't make heads or tails out of the rest of this."

"Let me have a look." Manny sat next to Lisa on the short corduroy-covered sofa. "This is some sort of code. He's trying to tell us something. Most likely, it's information about their location."

After another minute of staring at the screen, Manny continued, "This has got to be based on something only you can decipher."

"Well, for starters, he is referring to a vacation we were to take in August in California. The reference to Carmel, San Francisco, Berkeley, and Oakland Airport for the trip is absurd."

"That's why it's clearly a code. He's trying to signal that he's in an area somehow similar to the one he cited." Manny was almost hyperventilating with excitement.

"And this. Following a *Lonely Planet* map taking route 89.5? There is no such road."

"Perfect. It's another clue," said Manny.

"This part, asking me to respond, makes sense," Lisa whispered as she pulled her legs under her in lotus position and leaned farther into the screen.

"Yes, but I'm sure we need to decipher this first. Once Jaguar knows that you think your father's okay, he's onto the next step, whatever that is. We have to assume that your father feels the situation is about to change. The timing of him being permitted to send the e-mail suggests something is about to change. We have to solve this riddle first, even if it means forcing them to send another message."

"Can the address be traced?" she asked.

"I doubt it, Lisa. I'd be totally shocked if Jaguar didn't have some techie in his base camp who could help prevent detection."

"So maybe I should go online here, find a large-scale map of the Petén, and print that out."

"Let's also print out a map of the San Francisco area. There's either something in the words, the tourist attractions, the geography, the topography, or the positioning of those cities he mentioned that will give us a clue," added Manny.

"Well, Papi knows I know nothing about topography and my geography is weak. So, it's either the names themselves, tourist attractions in those spots, or the positioning that is the key."

"Or some combination."

The two cleared an area on the floor and spread out two color maps spit out from Mónica's large printer.

"Luckily, there aren't too many urban sites in Tikal," Manny said, studying the Guatemala map.

"Look. I bet Carmel somehow refers to Carmelita. They are the only two locations with similar names." Lisa was warming to the challenge.

"Why Oakland Airport? There is a landing strip in Tikal, so maybe that's the reference. That's southeast of Carmelita. But on your San Francisco map, the other cities are north of Carmel." Manny ran his hands through his thick, jet-black hair and exhaled.

"Manny, none of these other names bear relationship to anything in the Tikal area. Maybe the airport is to throw others off. Oh, this is frustrating," said Lisa matter-of-factly.

"Okay. What about this 89.5 reference?" he asked.

"That sounds more like a radio station. Do you think … there's a Pacifica radio station that sometimes plays jazz, in DC. I think it's 89.3." Lisa sighed in frustration.

"I suggest we quit for a bit, give some thought to dinner, and start again when your mom gets home."

"That could be midnight, and she wants to take us to dinner, but all right. Let's have a drink and watch the sunset. That should give us a mental break." Lisa moved to her mother's liquor bar.

Manny couldn't help watching Lisa closely as she leaned over behind her mother's bar to pick through a few large bottles. She was a mature woman, older than he'd assessed at the airport. She was, however, only in her early twenties and had yet to venture out into the world beyond a university. "Focus on your job, Manny," he said to himself while closing his mouth.

The table held a small floral-pattern plate displaying slices of pepper jack cheese and rice crackers. Lisa and Manny were leaning back in wire chairs, their feet pressing the top of the balcony railing, each clutching a frosty drink.

"You would think that two pretty savvy people could figure out a code that's only a couple of sentences long. But, then again, if your father made it too obvious, the Jaguar would figure it out and probably never let the message stand," said Manny, sipping a can of Tecate beer.

Lisa licked the rim of her mojito glass but didn't respond.

"It's strange that when I suggested to Marta that I come to help find Senor Roberto, I thought the tough part would be raising the money and finding a team that's rescue-qualified and knows the area." Another long sip.

"Now, it's clear to me that that part may have been taken care of by your mother, with her amazing contacts. I'm just wondering whether I've underestimated how difficult the trekking, site identification, and extrication might be. You know that jungle can be very dense, and the insects can be ferocious during the rainy season."

"Manny, I want to go with you and the search team." Lisa roused from her trance.

"Lisa, I know you're concerned, and I know I may seem like some random youth worker, but let me assure you that this will be very, very dangerous. That's just finding them. Then it will be scarier fighting our way into camp, securing them both, and getting out alive. That's all assuming we solve this riddle as to where the camp actually is in time. I've done this a few times, and this won't be the place for an untrained graduate student. No offense."

"Well, I have been to Tikal—"

"As a tourist, right?" He stared at her, seeing a younger Lisa than he'd been talking to.

"Yes, but—"

"Again, no offense, but that's like comparing an afternoon at a Disney theme park to trekking through the Serengeti without a guide or a jeep. Way different experience." Manny crushed his empty beer can.

"Well, at least I can go to Guatemala City. I do know some of these folks Mom has talked to, and I could also be of comfort to my aunt while you're playing Boy Scout in the jungle."

"You know, the Petén will feel like it's on the equator at this time of year. Not your average North American Boy Scout outing."

"What did you say about—" Lisa sat up straight.

"I said it's not going to be like a—" Manny started to repeat.

"No. I mean, you mentioned the equator?" Lisa now stood in front of her chair.

"Yes. So, what's that got to do—" Manny looked confused.

"That might be it. Let's get that map out again. Better yet, I'll bet Mom has a *Lonely Planet Guide* for Central America, or even Guatemala. Didn't the message say something about *Lonely Planet's* route 89.5 W?" Lisa was taking control and was looking in a living room bookshelf.

"I still don't see what you're getting at," Manny said, trailing behind her.

"Just help me locate the book, please."

"I remember clearly how Papi and Mama always consulted a *Lonely Planet* book before any major trip when I was little," said Lisa as she knelt in front of the wall-length bookshelf.

"Here's a 2004 edition," said Manny.

"Terrific. Now, let's see if there's a map here in the front with geographic measures."

John McKoy

It took several minutes, but Lisa finally found the map she was looking for.

"Here it is. Look. Carmelita is right about on longitude 90 degrees west. So, the area they're in, by Papi's estimation, is toward 89.5 degrees west, or toward Belize," she said.

"How's the equator fit in?" Manny asked.

"It doesn't. Your mentioning the equator made me think of longitudes and latitudes. Since 89.5 is not a road designation, and not likely a radio station, I guessed that it was a map coordinate."

"Awesome. And those other Bay Area cities in his fake itinerary are in relationship to Carmel as similar towns would be to Carmelita, moving east toward Belize."

"Bingo." Lisa held out her palm to be slapped by her co-investigator.

"Okay, if we are right, I can draw a triangle between the biggest landmarks east of Carmelita." Manny's mouth drooped as he estimated the number of sites and the size of the likely area.

Another Tecate and mojito into the evening, the pair almost simultaneously let out a holler.

"Rio Azul to the north and Tikal to the southeast have to be the other corners of the triangle," they yelled and clinked glasses.

"While that's a big area to cover on foot, the camp has been there long enough and the Jaguar has to have had supplies and information trekked in, so I bet there will be signs of human activity around. And I know from exploring as a kid and from a few plane trips with my uncle that there is farming intermittently scattered in the plains. Campesinos may have noticed smoke, or even animals being spooked. Something out of the ordinary. We'll find them. The question is time. How much do we have?"

Lisa and Manny were relaxed and hungry when Mónica finally returned at 8:30 that night.

After a whirlwind tour of a bit of Coconut Grove's finest houses, a drive into the neon tapestry and the party-time activity of South Beach, a gander at some of the cruise ships anchored in the harbor, a brisk walk along the glass palace canyon and through the shops of Bayside Marketplace, Mónica parked off Calle 8 in Little Havana.

"Let's walk a few blocks so you can see the best domino players in the world and get a flavor for the way Miami was when I was a kid," said Mónica.

"It looks like you have to tint your hair blue and carry a copy of the latest *Bohemia* magazine, if you're over sixty here," remarked Lisa with a smile.

"That's right, mi hija. I don't have too many more years of brown highlights left," laughed her mother.

"It also seems like you're not a man if you don't smoke stogies," said Manny.

"You have to remember that many of these guys relaxing in the park and on their stoops are cigar rollers at some factory during the day. For some, cigars are as Cuban as beans and rice. Okay, this is it," Mónica said.

"El Cristo's? It looks a bit funky." Manny held the door for the ladies.

"First things first," said Mónica as they were seated at a simple wooden table facing the street-front window that permitted them to feel like a part of the lively scenery without the pedestrian and vehicular noise.

"What will you have to drink?" their server asked.

"I'll stick with beer," Manny quickly responded.

"Might I suggest you try Hatuey? We only recently have been able to get it from Cuba."

Before Manny could respond, Mónica turned to Lisa and said, "Have you tried the Bacardi mojito they make here? It's delicious."

"I guess that's what I'm having, then," smiled Lisa.

"We'll have a Hatuey, a Bacardi mojito, and a *Canchánchara*, gracias," said Mónica to the waiter.

"I know you guys are dying to get to the plan you've figured out, but let me just suggest a few things on the menu; then we can talk leisurely," Mónica insisted.

"Is that a Dorsey band over the speakers?" Manny asked about a new jazz orchestral number that filled the restaurant.

"I didn't realize you liked jazz," said Lisa.

"Actually, since we just met, there's a ton we don't know about each other." Manny caught Lisa's eyes.

"Sweet, you two. Anyway, that's Desi Arnaz, the Cuban bandleader of the fifties who was married to—"

"Lucille Ball." Lisa finished her mother's sentence.

"Very good, sweetie. That was way before your time, almost before mine."

"Yes, but I watch old movies and an occasional rerun on YouTube," said Lisa.

"Ah, the drinks." After they all toasted the evening and had a sip, Mónica resumed. "Actually, this rum drink of mine was a favorite of Desi's. Now, everything here is tasty; however, I'd recommend the paella, *pomodoro* fettuccini, chicken apple salad or *marisco* salad, *arroz* imperial, and gran *churrasco* as particularly fine."

After placing their orders, Mónica stared at each of them for several seconds.

"Now, what's the plan?"

Mónica and Manny took turns describing their deciphering of the e-mail and of their estimation of Roberto and Raúl's location.

"That's great work. And I'm willing to bet that Lisa will soon get another e-mail allegedly checking on her concurrence with the vacation plan laid out by Roberto. Your response will start the clock ticking on whatever this Mayan king, this Jaguar has planned," said Mónica.

Manny looked as if he were about to speak but then took a minute to look around the restaurant, as if carefully formulating his words. The décor couldn't have been of much assistance, for although tastefully arranged, the watercolors, framed awards, flat-screened TV, and mounted wine bottles on the wall told no particular story.

"So, what's next?" he finally ventured.

"I'm glad you asked. I, too, have been busy today. My colleague, Rodolfo Gómez, got busy when I suggested that the senate might look dimly on a noncooperative Guatemalan government. Anyway, your contact in the city will be Guillermo Schaefer. He's a friend of your father's and mine and will be the point person for the resources you will need, Manny. Specifically, you will have half a dozen top-notch ex-Guatemalan army rangers, one ex-US marine flying in from Mexico, a couple of heavy duty four-wheel-drive vehicles, weapons and supplies, and a small plane at the Tikal airport." Mónica took a breath.

"Wow. That's fantastic. How much did this cost?" asked her daughter.

"You don't need to know—either of you," Mónica responded.

"Mama, is this all above board?" asked Lisa, suddenly sounding like a middle-class, isolated grad student.

"Mi hija. Your father's life is at risk. In fact, we don't know if he and Raúl are still alive. And while all of that crime and violence you've seen on TV—*Miami Vice, CSI Miami*—depicts made-for-TV incidences and intrigue, much of modern-day Miami was, in fact, built on the drug trade. And that trade started back in the forties and fifties with Batista. Then, Fidel practically emptied mental hospitals and jails as he let large families emigrate in the 1980s. Those good folks didn't suddenly become Rhodes Scholars on landing in Miami. But, violence and vice around drugs has been an equal opportunity industry here—Jamaicans, Haitians, and Cubans have all carved out a part of the less glamorous parts of our history. While the skyscrapers, yachts, and mansions offer the patina of legitimacy for the rich and famous, many of those fortunes were built on the shoulders of former heroine kingpins. So, in pulling this raiding party together, I've not solely tapped people who are 'above board.'" Mónica tried to smile at her young daughter.

The silence and dazed gazes at their tables might have drawn attention from other diners had it not been for the jazz overhead, and the drunkenness of the hour.

"Mama, I am going too." Lisa voided her previous pledge to a frowning Manny.

"I thought you might say that. Neither you nor I are of much use down there on a venture like this, but you might want to go console your aunt, María Elena."

"I mean, I'm going to the Petén."

"I know it's your father, Lisa. And, while you are a very accomplished and mature young lady, this is going to be above your pay grade, sweetie. It will be quite rugged getting there and more than likely extremely dangerous when they make their assault. Plus, one doesn't usually leap from the books of Berkeley to the jungle without serious training, even in Netflix-streamed videos. Wouldn't you agree, Manny?"

The former army ranger merely nodded in agreement.

Lisa looked at both, drained her drink, and relented.

"Okay, I'll stay in the capital. But, as soon as you get Papi out and come back to the city, I—"

"Once we're safe, I'll e-mail you, and you should take a plane to Belize. That's going to be the best rendezvous place. If we get out without much bloodshed, the guerrillas will likely follow, expecting us to head back to the capital." Manny cut her off.

"Okay. I'll spend some time with my aunt." Lisa didn't like feeling like a little kid in someone else's grown-up scenario, but she begrudgingly recognized that the others were right.

"Well, people, we'd best get back. You have an early commercial flight tomorrow."

Chapter 32

The sign outside the immigration portal at Guatemala's international airport read *"Bienvenida Señora del Prettyman."*

"Well, they got the last name right, anyway," whispered Lisa as they lifted knapsacks onto their backs and marched over to the young man in a black suit, white shirt, and narrow black tie.

"Hola, somos la Señorita Prettyman y el Señor Cortez," said Lisa.

Without a smile, and after flipping down a pair of obscure black sunglasses, the driver said, *"Soy Juan Molina. Mucho gusto."* He then asked if they had baggage other than the knapsacks.

"This is it," said Manny.

Molina was clearly trying to assess who was in charge, whether they were more than a business couple, and probably how old they were. He led the two Americans to the parking lot, walking ramrod straight to minimize the height differential between Lisa, Manny, and himself. In order, they were five feet, six inches; six feet, one inch; and five feet, four inches tall. After an uneventful but scenic forty-minute drive, Molina parked and escorted Lisa and Manny up to Guillermo Schaefer's suite. He left them in Schaefer's foyer, bid them good luck, and left.

"Can I get you anything to drink while Mr. Schaefer finishes up this call?" asked his pleasant receptionist/assistant.

"I would love to be able to plug my laptop in to recharge its battery," responded Lisa.

"And I would appreciate a glass of water, if it's not a bother," said Manny.

"Not a problem for either request," said the receptionist.

After about fifteen minutes, Guillermo came down the hall and greeted the two.

"I'm so sorry to keep you waiting. Mr. Cortez, so nice to meet you. And, Lisa, my dear, wow, you're now a grown-up, gorgeous woman," he said, kissing her on both cheeks. "Let's go inside, shall we? We have an hour or so to chat before the team we've assembled for you, Manny, will arrive."

Once seated, Lisa opened her laptop on a teakwood coffee table and said, "As anticipated, I've just received a request to acknowledge his e-mail from my father."

"Perfect. Let's go over everything with the team and then decide how and when to respond," said Guillermo.

They had just finished going over a plan when a group of four muscular, bearded young men arrived. They all sported trimmed black beards and hid behind opaque black-lens sunglasses. Once the door was shut and introductions had been made, the four superhero mannequins showed some teeth and became somewhat approachable, if not actually pleasant. Manny the youth worker morphed into the professional military officer who took over the meeting. He summed up the plan for driving to Tikal, testing all of their equipment, retrieving the plane, the reconnaissance flight, the more detailed mapping, the trek into the jungle, and the rescue operation. Lisa sat, mouth agape, because Manny repeated their scheme with enriched detail perfectly, as if it had been researched for several months. Felipe Santos, an ex-marine retired to Mexico, provided a topographical map that they marked up with most likely path into the area that Manny and Lisa had circled on the map.

The other three ex-Guatemalan army rangers added bits and pieces of information about what to look for from the air, since each one of them, Jesús Cantada, Pedro Cuevas, and Miguel Visadora had spent time patrolling in or near the area.

After an hour, the group agreed to meet in front of Schaefer's office at 6:30 the next morning. The four more local raiders were anxious to hook up with friends to "relax" before the mission. So, after it was agreed that Lisa would send her father a brief response expressing her excitement about his coming trip to California and her relief that he was safe on some business trip, the party split up. Guillermo offered to drop Manny at a nearby hotel and Lisa at her aunt's.

After dropping his belongings in a functional room at the Palacio Royal Hotel, Manny took a walk around the Zone 1 neighborhood. More than viewing any particular landmark, he wanted to become adjusted to the urban beat and feel of a twenty-first-century Central American city. Since his time in the service and his immersion in Columbia Heights, DC, Manny had not had many extended visits to Mexico or Central America. He was enjoying the images, sounds, and smells of moderately affluent urban Guatemala, even though he knew they would be abandoned the next day for terrain that would more approximate the dense jungle near his hometown—territory he had assumed would remind him of his past.

As the sun began to set, Manny hailed a taxi and headed down Avenida Reforma and then east into Zone 10 toward an unassuming restaurant with a famously authentic Guatemalan cuisine. The ride provided Manny with glimpses of the traditional Spanish stucco, as well as the modern glass-dominated architecture of the city. He was struck by the mix of high- and low-rise buildings, seemingly placed on street blocks with little concern for streetscape design or uniformity, with an almost random choice of building material or color. It seemed ultra modern in spots and early twentieth century in others. Though alive and witness to lots of activity, the streets just didn't seem to pulse like the scene he'd left in Miami. The clusters of street vendors, the array of beautiful *huipiles* that differentiated indigenous groups, perpetual background of marimba music emanating from every other store, and the pronounced lilt of the melodic Spanish heard on Guatemalan streets whet Manny's curiosity about the unseen complexities of this society.

After ordering a dish featuring rice, beans, stewed chicken, and tortillas, Manny leaned back in his chair, sipping *aguardiente*, a local sugar cane liquor. Across the dining room, he spotted a familiar face, and without thinking, he rose to say hello. A few feet from the table, he realized that the man of the couple in the corner was not some rediscovered friend, but Jesús Cantada, one of the rangers with whom he was about to enter the Petén. It was too late to turn back, so Manny grinned and said, "What a small world."

Jesús graciously offered Manny a seat as he introduced his dinner guest, Graciela Donoso.

"Nice to meet you, Mr. Cortez. Jesús was being quite circumspect about this adventure you are about to undertake. I'd love to hear your version."

Manny avoided the temptation to frown at Jesús and instead declined the invitation to join them, citing some "thinking" he had to do prior to their trip.

"A pleasure to meet you, Ms. Donoso," Manny said, as he bowed, turned, and returned to his table. He had no idea who the young lady was, but he hoped that Jesús had the sense not to talk any further about the mission.

The rest of the meal was uneventful for Manny, as he spent his time thinking about a laundry list of items to anticipate upon arrival at the rendezvous site in Tikal.

Lisa was able to be much more forthright about her knowledge of the mission, as she settled in for a visit with Raúl's mother and her aunt, María Elena Gonzales. They stayed up early into the morning talking about old times, Lisa's distant relatives, transitions in Guatemala, and Lisa's life in California.

As planned, early the next morning, Miguel, Pedro, Jesús, and Manny met outside Guillermo's office and were driven by Juan Molina to the airport for the trip to Tikal. Once at the jungle airfield, they checked out the small plane that had been rented for Pedro, a one-time aspiring fighter pilot, to fly. They picked up their jeep and headed for a nearby motel to complete their planning.

"A plane, guns, bug spray, sunblock, snake anti-venom, compasses, flares, provisions. It looks like we've got everything but a clear idea of where our target is," said Jesús.

"Well, given the coordinates that are estimated, I'm guessing we'll spot some clues from the air," countered Felipe Santos between puffs on his Marlboro.

"Think about it, friend. If it was so easy to spot this guy's camp, he'd have been wiped out a year ago," responded Jesús, this time, smiling.

"No offense to your former employer, but I wouldn't put 'search and destroy' capabilities at the top of the army's resume," said Felipe.

"True. And word is that this character is not really hurting the big deep pockets, nor causing any strategic harm or destabilization, so let him be. This way, the campesinos feel like somebody is paying attention to their grievances, but the government really doesn't have to change anything," chimed in Miguel Visadora.

"I'm not Guatemalan, but I'll bet if there are too many more blackouts, bank heists, and computer viruses affecting financial markets, the government will, all of a sudden, recognize that the Jaguar is more dangerous than some jungle cat," Manny added.

Laughing, Pedro Cuevas offered a practical contribution.

"If we find this camp, rescue these two dudes, and put a dent in the Jaguar's operation, I'll be happy. Not because I agree with *el presidente's* politics, or because the fat cats have ever done me any favors, nor because I'm against the left and the poor." He paused, took a sip of his cold Corona, waited until all eight eyes were on him, and grinned.

"I'll be happy, amigos, because I'll get paid," he concluded.

The group roared, finished their drinks, and dispersed to separate corners of the suite for a last night's undisturbed sleep before their mission was due to go live.

Pedro took the group up early the next morning into a hazy blue sky dotted with occasional thin clouds. He used most of his first tank of fuel in systematically crisscrossing a triangular area outlined on Manny's map. They noted jungle clearings, random patches of open cornfields, scattered farm buildings, and sporadic stone formations covered with jungle vegetation that they judged to be Mayan ruins. He even spotted random trails exiting the thick jungle. Felipe Santos marked promising areas to explore on the ground on a topographical map.

For the next two days, the team canvassed small settlements and entered likely sites by jeep and on foot. They had an occasional campesino acknowledge that he had seen guerillas in the surrounding jungle, but they gathered no really useful clues. On the evening of the fourth day, while sitting around sipping beers at a dilapidated motel near Tikal airport, the team tried to eliminate areas from the search target area.

"Well, it seems clear we have to move into the interior, away from any settlements. These citings that people provide us are of zero value. We will have to do more serious trekking and leave the vehicle behind," said Miguel.

"Now that we have a hands-on feel for normal activity in this part of Petén, we should be more sensitive to the abnormal. We can better identify real from false clues." Felipe sounded more confident than his colleagues thought was merited by the situation. Manny said nothing for more than an hour. Then he broached a subject with Jesús that had clearly been on his mind for some time.

"That was a fine friend you were with at that restaurant the other night. What does she do?"

"She's an old high school sweetheart. Just a friend now. She's a biologist at Landívar University."

Chapter 33

After breakfast the next morning, the rescue team headed out in pairs. Manny and Jesús headed for an Indian village whose smoke they had spotted from the plane. Filipe and Miguel were to trek toward Mayan ruins reported to be a recent archeological dig, while Pedro was to continue surveying from the air in successively tighter circles. They were to meet at a hilltop identified on a topographical map they all carried. Each pair started off cheerfully with excited apprehension that they would uncover "the missing clues" that would lead them to the Jaguar's camp.

After two hours through heavy underbrush and steamy jungle, Jesús heard faint signs of inhabited space.

"Did you get that? That clanging sound like a blacksmith's pounding on an anvil?" Jesús stopped and turned to Manny.

"Now I do, yes. It's hard for me to tell how far off it is," said Manny.

"My guess is less than half a mile, but we'll see. Are you locked and loaded?" Jesús asked.

"I am, but I'm not looking for a fight at this village," Manny said with a hint of disbelief.

"I've scouted in these hills all my life. You got be ready," responded Jesús matter-of-factly.

They had only walked another five minutes when the trail widened and displayed more obvious footprints and other signs of frequent use. As they approached the first wood-and-straw structures, Jesús said, "My Q'eqchi', though not good, is better than yours. So, let me do most of the talking, okay?"

Manny quickly nodded agreement. The first few encounters were with friendly women finishing preparations for the noon meal. They were very pleasant, but clearly either didn't understand Jesús, were brilliant actresses hiding their knowledge, or really had no idea of who or where the Jaguar was. In any event, at least a half hour was spent chatting with villagers, yet gathering no useful intelligence. Jesús was growing frustrated, while Manny seemed to take these results in stride. Both men hoped that a conversation with a carpenter who was building some sort of farming plow, thus the clanging metal sounds, would be more fruitful. He, however, was more reticent, perhaps distrustful, and revealed nothing. They then approached an open area where women were selling vegetables and where it appeared, by the distinctively different patterns on their blouses, that some of the customers were from another village.

When Jesús got no better results from the first couple of vendors, he lost his temper and kicked over a couple of stands. Manny grabbed his colleague by the arm and pulled him from the market area.

"What's wrong with you, dude? These folks may or may not be concealing something, but they're not the enemy here. Chill." Manny was calming and friendly, but deadly serious. Jesús saw a depth of steel determination in Manny's eyes that he only associated with the toughest soldiers he'd worked with in combat. He leaned against a tree and took a couple of deep breaths.

"Okay. You're right. But you're not from here. You can be detached and cool. These are, in some ways, my people. For centuries, farmers like these have played the victim and allowed violent thugs to subdue them. The guerrillas and street gangs thrive off of the weakness of folks like this." Jesús's anger rose again.

"And let's not forget the army and some of its upstanding psychopathic hotheads. So are you saying the corruption, military violence, youth gangs, and revolutionaries are the fault of and enabled by these undereducated, unarmed, hard-working peasants?" Manny's voice remained calm.

"No. You know it's more complicated than that. I just wish these campesinos would be tougher."

"Yes, but blaming them and pushing them around even more doesn't seem to work. Not from my viewpoint." Manny stared hard at Jesús.

"I was a ranger in the damn Guatemalan army, remember? I know how nasty, vicious, and evil some soldiers can be. And I grew up on the south coast in a tough neighborhood, without the benefit of a silver spoon. There's no excusing some military behavior, but you have to demand respect." Jesús returned the stare.

"You mean like the Jaguar teaches."

Jesús was caught short.

"Well, in a way, he is better. He's trying to create change. And he doesn't take crap," admitted Jesús.

They turned to cross the market space, which was once again buzzing with activity and oblivious to the intruders, and headed for another path to leave the village. As they stepped onto the path, they were approached by a farm boy of about seventeen or eighteen and an older man. Before Jesús could say anything, Manny addressed the older man in Spanish and asked if he was familiar with the surrounding area. The younger man responded in halting Spanish, saying that he would interpret, since his uncle didn't speak the language.

Manny thanked him and asked them both several general questions in an open, friendly, and inquiring tone. Once the residents seemed at ease, not put off by the rescuers' weapons, Manny explained that they were looking for some friends thought to be captives of the Jaguar. The older man freely offered that one or two strangers came to market regularly, once a month, to buy food for a much larger group. Often, a man and a woman came, at least one speaking a bit of Q'eqchi', and always entered on this path. He didn't know, however, where they lived, nor the number of people in their group. Manny and Jesús thanked them and resumed their trek.

After about fifteen minutes, Manny pulled out his map and compass to plot their route to the meeting place.

"I think I know the direction from here. And point well-taken, Manny," said Jesús, smiling. The men bumped fists and headed into thicker jungle.

By the same time in the early afternoon, Miguel and Felipe had reached and scouted the Mayan ruins. Pushing aside brush near a mound of dirt pointed out by a villager they had talked to about two hours earlier, Miguel stopped and stared at a jumble of crumbling steps, moss-stained granite platforms, and six-foot-high stelas with illegible rounded figures etched on each of their four sides. Felipe followed him into the space, wiping sweat from his brow and feeling thankful that they could rest for a few moments.

"Wow. I'm not sure I've ever seen a dig from a Mayan period this old," said an admiring Miguel Visadora.

"This old? I can't tell the difference between this and Tikal, or like *Palenque* or *Chichen Itzá* in Mexico. It's called old, in various stages of disrepair, and from a civilization that's long since died," said the former US Marine.

"Now, you're showing your ignorance of important history that, for all you know, could be part of your gringo heritage," offered Visadora.

"Dude, my folks are from Puerto Rico and the Bronx. No glyphs or stelas playing a role in our lives. I didn't learn about this stuff until I moved to Mexico."

"Well, since we're here, might as well pick up a little information. This place, for example, I bet is part of *Tintal*, an area built between 500 and 350 BC. Yeah, there's a university sign on that wall, identifying this site." Miguel smiled proudly.

"Okay. I'm impressed, but what's this got to do with our search?" asked Felipe.

"Hold on, mi amigo," said Miguel. "Parts of Mexico and Guatemala were the center of the western universe in those days. Do you realize what was happening in Europe or Asia then?"

"No, but I bet you're going to tell me." Felipe took a long drag on his water bottle and leaned again a prehistoric rock.

"Alexander the Great was swallowing up huge chunks of the Middle East and Asia, the Greeks were building the Parthenon, and the Chinese were just starting to build the Great Wall. While Europeans and Africans had no clue that the Americas were here, we were dominating, you hear me?"

"Congratulations to you and your Central American brothers, and maybe even to my ancestors. Why, then, are you so down on and skeptical about the Jaguar's revolution? How come you aren't fighting with the guerillas?"

"That's easy, Felipe. I don't think his pissant group of Boy Scouts or the peasants he's recruiting have the moral strength to topple this obviously corrupt regime. They aren't up to it."

"So, why not help them, Miguel?"

"I guess I'm not sure I have what it takes either. In the meantime, I got to feed my family. I don't think I'm happy with where I am on this, but for now, I guess I'm a mercenary."

Neither man said anything for several minutes as parrots, monkeys, and insects assumed the soundtrack.

"To answer your question about the connection to our search, I was hoping that we'd find local workers or foreign archeologists at an active dig who could give some clues to the Jaguar's whereabouts," said Miguel.

"With all due respect to previous greatness and lingering sanctity, this place seems abandoned and unhelpful."

"On that, Felipe, I must now agree," grinned Miguel.

After consulting their maps and compasses, the two head out in a northeasterly direction toward the rendezvous site. About a half hour's march from the site, they stumbled over some tin cans, corn husks, and broken marble carvings.

"This is a fresh campsite. I wonder if it's from the workers we had hoped to meet?" asked Felipe.

"My money is on thieves. These broken carvings are worthless, and trained diggers would know that before they even tried to move them," Miguel speculated.

"Makes sense. The site has growth on it, so whoever it was has been gone for weeks or months. Let's push on, but we probably need to be quieter, in case there are folks in the area," Felipe concluded.

By early evening, all four rescuers had reached the hilltop rendezvous site, debriefed, conferred with Pedro Cuevas, and realized that they still had no definitive sense of where to head next.

"Miguel and Jesús, it's really your call, because you know this green maze better than the rest of us," said Manny.

Both Guatemalans looked at each other and nodded.

"Based on Pedro's smoke sitting and my gut, we should head north toward El Mirador," said Miguel.

"I'd agree. Unless we trip on some contrary evidence, that would be my plan," Jesús concurred.

"I have a suspicion that we need to get lucky soon, or we will find dead bodies, if we ever do find this hideout." Felipe sighed.

A few minutes before dawn the next day, the hikers began trekking in a northwest direction through light underbrush, under a heavy forty-foot canopy of palm leaves. By daylight, it was so humid that Felipe's shirt was soaked and his Central American colleagues' brows and underarms were beginning to sweat. By noon, they had to slow down to rest. But as they were searching for a relatively cool spot, Miguel signaled the others to lie down and remain still. Two minutes, then five, and then ten minutes passed without a perceptible change in the environment. Felipe was about to stand up and begin walking when they all heard a twig crack about twenty-five yards ahead. Then a second twig, and finally, a man in city clothes (jeans and a cotton shirt, with sneaker-like boots) came toward them. He was by himself and offered no resistance and only shock when the four surrounded him and took his old-fashioned carbine rifle.

Jesús immediately suspected that this man was out of place, was not an archeologist, nor a ruin-site fortune hunter, but was, in fact, a courier for the guerillas. While Felipe and Manny scouted out the trail from which the captive had come, Jesús and Miguel subjected him to blindfolded interrogation that involved a mixture of water and honey occasionally poured down his nose. Within an hour, the captive had given them enough information for them to know how to get to the Jaguar's camp.

"So, do we leave him, take him with us, or kill him?" asked Miguel in Spanish.

The growth of the captive's pupils revealed that he thoroughly understood the national language.

"I will take you to the camp, but please, do not force me to lead you inside. They will kill me," he pleaded.

The four conferenced and agreed to use the captive as a guide, but to leave him loosely tied near the entrance to the site, so that he'd be found and saved after they finished their chore. So, after another three hours' hike, the mercenaries found and surrounded the campsite. They waited until sunset to attack, giving them ample time to confirm logistical details given them by their captive.

On an agreed-upon whistle signal, Manny and Felipe attacked from the west and north, while Jesús and Miguel waited two minutes to close in from the south and east. Manny and Felipe quickly shot and injured seven guerrillas, while two fled into the jungle. The injured were disarmed and tied within ten minutes of the initial shots. Jesús chased, knifed, and killed one of the guerrillas on his side of the camp after a brief gun battle forced six men back into the center of the camp, where they surrendered. Miguel captured five with but a few shots fired. Once all eighteen hostages were corralled, Felipe and Manny searched the camp. Roberto, Raúl, and the Jaguar were gone. They had clearly been in separate tents recently, but no other live bodies, beyond those captured, remained. Additionally, all tents and hiding places had been swept of computers, files, and anything else that might have been useful to authorities.

"Looks like we not only missed the elusive Jaguar, but he must have had enough warning to move any useful information. Question is: Are Roberto and Raúl with him, or did they escape on their own?" speculated Miguel.

"Give me fifteen minutes with a couple of these fierce guerillas, and I'll get our information, or they'll never produce anymore children." Jesús stood and walked toward the captives.

"Hold on, cowboy. I've already gotten what we need from one of the dudes I wounded. Let's get a message to Pedro so he can direct the army to air-drop some rangers nearby and pick up these prisoners in the morning. We can bed down here, rotate watch, and head out after Roberto and Raúl before midday. They escaped a day after the Jaguar left for another camp. I doubt they'll be too far ahead of us. Apparently, they left a couple of days ago but were in very weak shape. Here's a crude map of the direction they headed before these guys gave up the search. They assumed the jungle would finish Roberto and Raúl before they reached safety," Manny reported.

None of his colleagues had appetite for more adventure that night, so they made arrangements by phone with Pedro to have their "guide" picked up in a second airlift to protect him from possible reprisals from other guerillas.

At about midnight, Manny approached the campfire to relieve Miguel of watch duty.

"Everything okay, amigo?" Manny asked Miguel as he took a seat on a log twenty-five feet away from the fire.

"Quiet as a morgue. Too quiet. Several times, I've had the feeling that we were being watched, and not by an animal," said Miguel with tension palpable in his reddened eyes.

"I'll move about the perimeter occasionally. These guerillas don't look like they are going anywhere except in their dreams. Get some sleep," Manny said with more confidence in his voice than he felt in his gut. The night, however, passed quietly without incident.

Chapter 34

(Roberto)

Despite our best intentions, camp-site activity and rain delayed our departure for almost a week. I spent restless nights, and the mornings provided little relief. The air was always thick when I stepped outside into a steamy, hot and muggy campsite. Mosquito activity would subside during the night, so we could move about freely without repellant or hats. The early morning sun, moisture, and humidity outside our tent soon sapped the little energy our bodies had restored during the night. I heard monkeys, birds, and insects that I felt I'd heard all of my life, instead of for only a few weeks. They didn't seem disturbed by the rainforest's oppressive climate. I looked through our tree-framed emerald window out over the jungle canopy below our bluff and caught a glimpse of smoke. Undoubtedly, some farmer was burning his field, as his forefathers had done for ages.

Finally, whether it was my low energy, the sign of civilization off in the distance, or simply some sixth sense akin to horoscopic predictions, I decided that tonight was the time for Raúl and me to escape. I had gotten a response from Lisa to my e-mail several nights ago indicating she was anxious to see me in California, but with no indication that she had cracked our coded message. The Jaguar had been preoccupied with other activities and had ignored us for several days. But, Raúl and I knew that he would soon be demanding I send a message to the

Quetzal Fund to shut down La Puerta funding immediately. Gigante may not have been as crude, crass, and violent as the drug lords who made life horrific for many Central American families. He may not have been as untutored, unethical, or as low on Maslow's Hierarchy of Needs, but he was nonetheless a determined despot intent on ordering the world to suit his priorities. Waiting for rescue no longer seemed like an intelligent option.

As if he was reading my thoughts, Raúl stepped into the morning and whispered, "I think we should head out this afternoon, while the camp is napping. We probably won't be missed until dark; and by then, we will have a good start."

"My thoughts exactly. Let's pack some things. Hopefully, the morning tasks won't be heavy and energy-sapping."

"I think I've learned enough about the surrounding plant life to know how to survive for a couple of days," said Raúl.

"Yes. And there's always bush meat clamoring through the jungle canopy." I laughed.

We quickly packed essentials in two nylon hammocks we had secured from a pile of miscellaneous items behind the kitchen. We bundled our things, tied them so that they could be slung over our shoulders, and hid them under our cots.

The Mayan gods were smiling on us, because we were ordered to help with kitchen duty for the morning. Raúl was able to steal some coconuts, canned sausages, and water bottles from the storage area. I pilfered several ears of corn and a tin of leftover cooked rice. While helping stew tomatoes and fry beans for lunch, I overheard one of the guerillas mention that the Jaguar was headed for another of his camps nearer to Tikal and not expected back until the next afternoon. We had long observed that guard and camp attentiveness slackened when he was away.

John McKoy

The Jaguar had long since relaxed the schedule for a guard checking on our tent and even the clearing in front of our space, so once the assigned guerilla vacated our area during an afternoon shower at about 3:30, we knew we probably had our chance. Raúl and I were deep in the jungle and well away from the camp before my fatigue and weakness slowed my pace. We were fairly confident in our direction toward the farmers' smoke and eventually toward Rio Azul and Belize, but we were slowed by thick vegetation once we left paths we had memorized during our weeks of captivity. Yet, jungle sounds that might have freaked either of us months earlier were welcome background music, registering no alarm as we trudged northward.

We stopped near sunset for a rest in a cool Eucalyptus grove.

"Tío, my hands are getting scratched, my shirt is soaked, and my knees hurt, but I'm happier than I've ever been to be in the jungle and free."

For a moment, I was so exhausted that all I could do was lean against the smooth tan tree trunk, sip water, and smile. The leaves on the ground behind me moved, and I froze as a long python slithered near my tree, showing no interest in Raúl or me.

"If we don't hear indication of being followed before dark, we're probably safe until the morning." I uttered my thoughts out loud.

"Safe from humans, maybe, but the night shift of animals means we'll soon need to figure out our shelter for the night," said Raúl.

"Let's give ourselves another fifteen minutes' rest and then see how far we can get in the next half hour," I said. I was slowly dredging up camping lessons from my days in the Boy Scouts in Maryland's Catoctin Mountains. The lessons about making fires, boiling water, and securing our food from animals were easily retrieved. But rural Maryland didn't have Jaguars, giant spiders, powerful and stealthy constrictors, or crocodiles. And the feral pigs we might have encountered as kids were like pets compared to the boar down here. My thoughts about nighttime protection generated adrenaline that fueled my next half hour's trekking through ferns, vines, and annoying underbrush. By the time we reached another small clearing with trees that might support the rope hammocks we had packed from the Jaguar's compound, my feet, legs, knees and hands were all pleading for rest. We made a fire; sucked in beans, rice, and plantains; built a perimeter of sticks and thorns to ward off predators; tied up our hammocks; and passed out.

Hours later, I opened my eyes to catch the yellow glow of two nickel-sized globes staring at me from about ten yards away at one of the break points in our perimeter. I leapt out of the hammock and grabbed a sharpened walking staff I had lay on the tree next to my head. By the time I brought the stick up to shoulder height to point at our visitor, it was gone.

"Tío, what's the matter?" asked Raúl while tumbling out of his hammock.

"We had a visitor of the cat variety, but I couldn't tell if it was ocelot or jaguar. I doubt that it will return, in any event. You go on back to sleep. I think I'll stay alert for a bit. I don't think I'll be able to sleep much right now."

"Tío, I don't mind standing watch."

"Thanks, Raúl, but I'm wide awake now anyway. We'll likely have a long trek in the morning, so build your strength."

My nephew quickly dropped back to sleep. I was exhausted and couldn't keep my eyes open, but neither could I really sleep. Now, every natural night sound seemed magnified—a bat's flapping wings sounded like a thousand migrating crows; a puma's distant cry was like a tiger's roar from a nearby riverbank; and the snap of a twig under some tiny deer's hoof seemed like the approaching charge of a family of enraged boar. I was in no condition to stand watch, but I felt that it was most important to have Raúl be fresh in the morning.

After an early start following a quick breakfast at daybreak, we were able to make headway toward Rio Azul, but after the sun had been overhead for a few hours, my strength seemed totally sapped.

"Raúl, I need to catch a nap. Why don't you go on and let me catch up later?"

"Why, Tío? That's a terrible idea. If you don't get surprised by some animal, the inevitable search party might get you, or you could get lost, and ... no, we have to stick together. We'll both rest."

I was so grateful that Raúl was thinking more clearly than I, as I closed my eyes while leaning against a rock covered with moss. I inhaled the sweet smell of honeysuckle-like flowers from a nearby branch. My relaxation, however, was almost ruined by the rancid smell similar to a popular gym's locker room after an afternoon and evening of heavy use. The jolting smell was that of my own body. I must have been too exhausted during the night, but resting still, with no breeze permitted my odor to envelope every thread of my filthy clothes. Luckily, exhaustion again won out, and I was able to drift off.

After about an hour, Raúl woke me and forced me to drink some coconut water that was thankfully cooler than the jungle below our canopy of palm and banana trees. In my DC life, my running and gym schedule keep me quite fit. The last few weeks in the rainforest, particularly the recent days of a punishingly minimalist diet, had left me feeling like a hospital patient in the first hours after major surgery. Without Raúl's encouragement, I'm sure I would have perished. He locked his strong left arm under my right, lifted me up, helped me reposition my shirt-pack, and led us in what we assumed was a northwest direction.

Occasionally, we'd scare a patrolling Petén turkey, stop to gaze at the flight of a brilliantly colored toucan, or marvel at the arboreal gymnastics of a family of spider monkeys. During the daylight, even though we were not sure of our direction, we felt comfortable and unafraid of our natural surroundings. We were fairly confident that no carnivore was likely to attack two fair-sized humans in broad daylight, unless provoked. Our biggest fear was that we'd simply dehydrate, fall and break a limb, or expire due to exhaustion. Hour after hour, we trudged through brush, forest, and an occasional clearing, but no farm, no town, no well-worn path, and no sign of other humans appeared.

I had begun to trail Raúl by twenty-five yards or so, when I spotted a gorgeous red snake with yellow and black rings making its way down the bark of a large Spanish cedar beside our makeshift path. I stopped to admire its markings and then realized that I was within a few arms' length of the very poisonous coral snake. I instinctively backed away, tripped on a tree root, fell in the brush, and began descending down an embankment. I couldn't grab anything that held my weight, and I began to pick up speed until my foot caught in some vine or root and suspended my slide. My surroundings were vegetation-covered rock, like the wall of some sort of open cave. The top, a small hole through which I had fallen, looked distant and bright. The sunshine that shone through the opening was refracted by layers of jungle canopy, and then by the ground cover, which had obscured the opening.

"Help! Raúl, help!"

My call drew no answer other than the song of some macaw high up in a mahogany tree near the opening. No response from Raúl. I was able to safely disentangle my foot, fashion a stirrup from vines growing on the hole's wall, and support my body for what seemed like half an hour. Every few moments, I called for help. As the sunlight began to rapidly fade, I began to panic. There was no way I could continue suspended on the side of this hole for too much longer. I had no idea how deep it was, nor what surface covered the bottom of this new prison.

A large centipede, which had no trouble clinging to the wall, began making its way down the vines and rock toward me. Whether it had enough venom to kill me or not was not my worry. I was convinced, however, that any more added discomfort would likely weaken my grip, sending me to the bottom. The centipede must have lost its normal protective stealth and remained uncovered for too long. Before it could

John McKoy

get close enough to investigate my arm, the insect became diner for a hand-sized rodent that looked more like a mole than a mouse. Whatever its classification, the rodent quickly separated the head of its prey and carried off the remaining wriggling catch into the rock-and-clay wall above me.

What felt like an eternity to me was a mere five minutes, according to my nephew. Raúl had apparently been answering my calls, saw the hole, and had already fashioned a crude rope of some vines and was lowering it to me when I first caught sight of him. He'd knotted a loop on the end of the cord, into which I could place one foot. With all of the feeble strength and with the energy I had not yet sweated away, I clung to the rope while he pulled me to the surface.

"Are you able to walk, Tío?"

"I suppose so," I said between breaths.

"Okay, let's put that sinkhole incident behind us, because we have very little daylight left." Thankfully, Raúl wasn't panicked; he was purely matter-of-fact.

Within an hour that second afternoon, we discovered boulders, carved stones, and open areas that seemed to be the scattered remains of some Mayan ruin. I rested, and Raúl scouted the area. We both determined that this was some outlier relic of no particular significance, since there was no evidence of architectural digging or signage. We decided to risk making camp, starting a fire and resting for the evening in a corner of what appeared to be part of an ancient ball court of some sort. Howler and spider monkeys kept us company from a distance as the sun set. We were reassured that our direction was at least approximately correct based on the position of the setting sun.

"Tío, did you notice how low we are on canned and dried supplies?" Raúl asked me after we had finished some ears of corn, papaya, and canned beans.

"I did. I'm afraid things must have fallen from my backpack when I dropped into that sinkhole. We may have to hunt down a monkey, pig, or maybe a snake for protein soon."

"I'm not that desperate yet. Are you, really?" Raúl was clearly hoping I'd say no.

I didn't get a chance to answer, because I thought I heard voices in the jungle back in the direction from which we had come.

"Did you hear that?" I asked him, while leaning on an elbow.

"I did, but I couldn't make out any words."

We were both silent for a few minutes as we assessed the drastic change in or circumstances. Both of us came to the conclusion that they must be pursuers from the Jaguar's camp.

"Well, we've got two options. Hide here or nearby, hoping they'll pass us by. Or try to outrun them," said Raúl.

"I can't out-walk anybody, much less outrun them. So I think we need to make it look like we broke camp and left, but hide in some crag in the walls or maybe some nearby tree."

I didn't wait for Raúl to respond and kicked dirt on our fire, tied my bundle, and headed for a corner of the court that had a clump of eucalyptus and ceiba trees on its perimeter.

"Why don't I walk off in the other direction, making obvious footprints, and circle back to you in the jungle?"

I stopped in my tracks and followed Raúl.

"Why don't we both do that? Otherwise, they'll split up and follow both trails until they spot us," I said.

John McKoy

"Tío, do you have the energy?"

We heard voices again but couldn't judge how much closer they were. I ignored Raúl's question, as we quickly created a trail into the far corner of the ball court and started doubling back through the brush, tree roots, and vines hanging from cedar, palm, mahogany, and ceiba trees in our thick surrounding.

We had found a suitable ceiba tree and pulled ourselves up to its lowest branches as a group of four men entered the ruins. They immediately split up to search the grounds, and my anxiety shot up to the treetops above us. I was sure they would find us. It seemed like an hour that I held my breath and listened to my heart pounding at triple its normal rate. I couldn't control my thoughts and began to smile at the irony of our situation. If this area was a Mayan ball court at one time, it may well have been where the powerful threw prisoners from high walls to their deaths in order to rev up their audiences. Were we to die here, after all we had endured?

Somehow, neither our low perch, our body odor, nor my pounding heart gave us away. The group reconvened in the center of the game space to confer on next steps. It was too dark to make out faces, but something about their size and manner suggested to me that these men were not from Jaguar's camp. They slowly walked toward an opposite corner of the space, and Raúl and I stared at each other, signaling that it was safe to descend.

While climbing out of the tree, I slipped and fell a short distance.

"Señores Prettyman and Gonzales, is that you?" one of the men asked, turning around to face our location.

We froze and looked for another place to hide. The men started toward us. All I could do was sit on the ground. I almost wept from exhaustion. I was spent.

"It's me, Manny Cortez! We're glad we got to you, finally."

Chapter 35

(Roberto)

"It looks like good timing. You look like you can barely stand up. But you did pretty well, considering the heat and the thickness of this terrain." Manny helped me to a sitting position, while his colleagues quickly reconstructed the fire.

Almost in unison, Raúl and I said, "You're not half as glad as we are."

Manny introduced us to Felipe, Jesús, and Miguel. Their colleague, Pedro Cuevas, had been contacted via cell phone and was going to fly a small plane to meet us at a nearby field in the morning.

The rescue party cooked a fabulous meal of corn, green papaya, and beef strips. Real beef.

"I know this area pretty well, and I'm amazed you made it to Xultun," said Miguel.

"Wow, we're nowhere near Rio Azul," Raúl said between bites.

"Is that where you were headed? That's quite a hike," said Manny.

"Originally, we had targeted some random farmer's field where we had recently seen smoke," I said.

"That must have been very random, because it's too late in the rainy season for farmers to be using slash-and-burn cultivation. Generally, they burn a month or two earlier."

"Well, clearly, he stopped. We must have passed right by without noticing a thing," I said.

After some light chatter and a lifesaving campfire meal, the whole group sipped on warm beers that tasted as if they'd been frosted for days. Our imaginations were vivid.

"So, you have a Mexican, Chapines, and a gringo working together. Clearly, an impressive combination," I joked with the group. My energy was beginning to return.

"And a Cuban. Your ex-wife gets big credit for pulling this together," Manny said.

"My ex-wife? *Monica* has been involved?" I sat up, alert.

"Yeah. Without her resources, this operation would never have come together. Certainly not in as fast a time as it did," said Manny.

Felipe added, "The little we saw of your daughter, we can tell that she's also a force. Right now, she's with your mother, Raúl, but she'll meet us in Belize."

We had counted on Lisa, but I had never imagined *Monica* would be asked or willing to play a role. I couldn't hide the quick, thin smile my reflection brought to my tired, grizzly jaw. I looked into the tired faces around the fire and returned to the present.

"So, what happened at the camp? Was there a big firefight? What about the big boss, the Jaguar?" I was revived enough to absorb all details.

Manny began to narrate. "There's not much to tell. By the time we located their hideout yesterday morning, there were only eighteen to twenty, no more than a dozen guerillas there."

"None of the women?" Raúl asked.

"No. We surprised these armed guys, because the trail into camp was well hidden, but the ascent up to it from about a quarter of a mile outward was fairly well worn, and we were able to encircle the area without much difficulty."

"There was only ten minutes of fighting. One of them was killed, fifteen surrendered, and maybe a couple escaped," added Miguel.

"We sent coordinates to Pedro, the last member of our team, who had arranged for a few army backups to come in and pick up the captives. I should add that he was able to make that arrangement thanks to your ex-wife's support." Jesús finished off their story.

Manny said, "Apparently, they had only halfheartedly set out to track you. They soon gave up, assuming the jungle would kill you before you had a prayer of reaching safety."

"They were almost correct," I added.

"So, no women in camp, and, I assume, no Jaguar." Raúl made more of a statement than asked a question.

"Definitely, neither were present," Felipe affirmed.

"So, their operation is still intact." I sighed.

"Well, it may be awhile before the Jaguar can operate at his previous levels. We captured a bunch of communications equipment and notebooks that they overlooked in their attempt to remove all sensitive items. Hopefully, they will help with intelligence on the various attacks we suspect he's recently planned. Based on feedback from Guillermo

Schaefer, there's now at least part of the military hierarchy interested in closing down the Jaguar's operation," Felipe continued.

"When we're rested and can more fully debrief, we might be able to add to the picture of his plans. The Jaguar revealed, actually bragged about the disruption he was capable of causing to banking, communications, and other systems. Whether overconfident or not, he's more thoughtful than one's prototypical 'drug lord.'" I had to pause to catch my breath.

"Yeah, I feel that he thinks more like a revolutionary. He sees himself as a twenty-first-century Che," Raúl piped up.

"Regardless, he's no longer operating under maximum cover, and he will have a hard time finding out how much of his government and army network has been compromised. He can't be sure of who's still on his side, and your ex-wife and daughter have arranged for a reliable army unit to post a half million-dollar reward for assistance directly leading to the Jaguar's capture." Felipe clearly felt that the various pieces of this strategy were worthy of applause.

"I might as well throw this good news in the mix," said Jesús. "Manny, the woman you saw me with the other night is an agent for us. Graciela Donoso is close to Felix Gigante."

"Wait a minute. Tío, isn't that the woman who periodically visited the Jaguar up at the camp?" Raúl turned to me.

"I believe it is, yes."

Then I looked at our rescuers. "She may be your agent, but she's probably the one who tipped off the Jaguar about your raid. She's more than likely the reason he took off, or at least didn't return from his trip the day before we left."

Jesús stared down at his beer.

"Okay, Okay. There will be plenty of time to analyze and track the whereabouts of the Jaguar. It's probably safe to say that the goal of this mission has been achieved. Don Roberto and Don Raúl are safe, and the Jaguar's operation in DC is shut down—certainly for the foreseeable future. For that, amigos, I raise my bottle to all of you." Manny stood before the fire casting a much larger shadow than I'd ever seen him cast in the neighborhood.

Clearly, Marta had been so much more perceptive than I had been about the young man's capabilities.

After Pedro Cuevas picked us up the next morning, the flight to Belize was brief, if bumpy and uncomfortable. Lisa met us with a medic she had hired to tend to Raúl and me. They wanted to keep me in some rundown hospital in Belize City for observation and rehydration. I convinced them that I was well enough to make it to Miami. We agreed that various loose ends needed to be tied with different parties and that Mónica was critical to every knot. Lisa booked Manny, herself, and me on a flight to Miami and called Mónica to set up a debriefing headquarters. Raúl flew back to Guatemala to spend a few days recuperating and visiting with his mother. Manny called Marta, and I called Alice Brown to update her. Before we boarded our various flights, we exchanged permanent contact information with our rescue warriors. At the very least, I was going to augment whatever fee they would receive from Mónica.

Chapter 36

(Roberto)

She was waiting at the baggage claim and immediately gave Lisa and then Manny a hug. I didn't wait for any awkward pause and gave Mónica the biggest, warmest hug I could remember ever giving her.

"You know that words can never express my gratitude for what you did. We wouldn't have survived another week there. And I doubt that we would have made it out of the jungle alive if Manny, Felipe, and crew hadn't found us when they did."

Mónica stared back at me with a broad smile and said I would have plenty of time to repay both Lisa and her. My emotional intelligence was running on low, and I was exhausted and very dehydrated. I remember reaching out to touch my ex's shoulder, covered in the long sleeve of her hospital jacket. I don't think my hand ever reached her shoulder, because my knees buckled and I dropped in a heap on the airport floor.

My next recollection was that of waking up in a bed in a hospital room at Mt. Sinai Hospital, Mónica's home base. I stayed awake long enough to recognize the Mt. Sinai logo on a chair, note the IV stuck in my arm, and see that my room had a sunny view of Biscayne Bay. Then, I passed out until nighttime.

"Well, you look a bit stronger," said Mónica from the side of the bed when I next awoke.

"Lisa and Manny are resting at the condo, and we'll pick you up when you're discharged in the morning," she continued.

"Morning? Why can't I get out now?" I asked, while attempting to swing my legs over the side of the bed.

"As your legs have probably informed you, you don't yet have the strength."

"Mónica, I can't allow myself to burden you any more than I already have."

"Hush, Bob. I haven't seen Lisa in an age, and I haven't really visited with you in, well too long. You know that I haven't stopped loving you. I … we just can't live together. So, I'll see you in the morning."

She was gone. I looked for a phone for a minute and then decided to forget about The Quetzal Fund, La Puerta, and DC for the moment.

"I still love you," she had basically said.

I knew there were things about Mónica that I missed being around. There were parts of myself that I couldn't share with anyone else. There used to be times that I had wished I could roll over in bed and touch her soft skin, but did I still love her?

I wasn't sure. I certainly hadn't thought about her in those terms in many years, even before she moved back down to Florida. Clearly, no other woman had replaced the partner I'd once had. I was, however, a different person than I was a few years ago. And my whole orientation to life had shifted since retiring from the business and starting The Quetzal. I turned over and looked at the stars above the bay. The view was mitigated by the inevitable chemical odors that float through every hospital. Sleep came easily again.

I was released the next morning, with a few meds and written instructions. Mónica had a driver dispatched to ferry me over to her condo, where I was greeted by Lisa and Manny.

"Both of you look like I wish I felt," I said, giving them both a big hug.

"Mom has treated us fabulously, and she's set up a guest suite for you," said Lisa.

"We've picked up some soup and light sandwiches to have on the balcony, when you're settled in," said Manny.

"Just give me ten minutes. I am hungry," I said, feeling rejuvenated.

After a couple of bites of a ham on rye, I leaned back in one of Mónica's comfortable wooden deck chairs and let the warm Floridian sun do its work. Lisa and Manny did the same for a respectable number of minutes.

"Okay. I know you two have been sketching out something. The saga doesn't just end. But before we delve into post-mortem and plans vis-a-vis the Jaguar, I've got a question that Raúl and I tossed around several times," I said.

"Yes, Papi." Lisa smiled at both of us but didn't roll her eyes.

"Manny, you grew up in Yucatan, Mexico, but have now lived much of your adult life in the US. Lisa, you have always been basically an American. A US North American. I'm a naturalized US citizen whose early memories of Guatemala were from summer visits to relatives, like Raúl's grandparents. My point is that we're all tied to Central America through blood. After this experience, do you feel any differently about Guatemala or Mexico?"

"Señor Prettyman … Roberto, the rescue part of this trip holds more similarity with my experience as a ranger in Asia than anything else. The terrain is different, but the preparation, difficult climate, uncertainty about the search, and anxiety about engaging an enemy brought back strong sensations from those days in the service. What was new for me was the couple of days in Guatemala City listening to the marimba, seeing colorful fruits and vegetables in the markets being sold by rubber tire-sandaled farmers working with their wives who were making fresh tortillas in the background.

"Between the businessman we first met, the rangers on my mission, the young twenty-somethings hanging out in 'hip' restaurants, and the campesinos from different indigenous groups we saw as we drove to the site, I got a glimpse of how diverse this society is. I don't know that the range of residential architecture between ritzy neighborhoods and working-class ones is any starker than in the US, but the gap between favelas, like La Limonada and mansions up by my hotel, is crazy. I must admit that it's far more varied, complicated, and confusing than what I experienced with migrant youth in Columbia Heights."

"But, Manny, the real question is, how does it make you feel?" Lisa cut in.

"I don't know that I feel any differently. I appreciate that part of the world more, but I never really 'dissed' C. A. And I suppose I've always been comfortable with who I am, where I'm from, and, for that matter, what I'm doing with my life. So, no; I don't feel any differently."

Lisa jumped back in. "Maybe because I have fewer life experiences at this point, I think this has had a huge impact on me. I haven't been to war, and I'm not working in a community, yet. And I'll admit that my Miami, DC, and Berkeley world is a far cry from what I've experienced in a few days with Aunt María Elena. I don't think I feel any more Guatemalan than I do Cuban, but I know I want to meet more people, learn more about Guatemala, and spend more time there. It's like it's a part of home that I want to learn so much more about. What about you, Papi?"

"I suppose I've had a range of reflections. First, I'm thankful to be alive and to have the life I have in DC. I am so thankful to have my daughter, nephew, former wife *and* new friend, and Columbia Heights buddy in my life. I think basic identity questions were settled a long time ago, for me. I'm an American with Guatemalan roots. I grew to appreciate the complexity you speak of, Manny, when I was much younger. The most interesting change stimulated by this experience, however, might be some additional verification that the Quetzal is the right mission at this stage in life. Before this odyssey, I was clear that what I'm doing with Quetzal and what you and Marta are doing at La Puerta are spot on.

"This experience, however, has made me confront the inequities that persist in Guatemala. It's hard to deny Jaguar's claim that characters change, but the class distinctions remain fixed and odious in Guatemala. It's hard to deny that gradual, measured reforms have not worked. If you have substantial means there, you may be inconvenienced a bit, but the probability of being injured by drug gangs, military or par-military troops is much less than if you're an average Guatemalan. The chances of losing someone close if you are a campesino are huge. Further, even without exposure to violence, the chances of achieving fruitful life outcomes (as we would view them) if you are born to the poor majority are slim to none.

"When the Jaguar compares the benefits of Guatemalan structural change against the cost of a few lives lost in the US, his choice is obvious. Missionaries, random priests, even volunteers have tried nonviolent reform, with resounding failure. The army has permitted 'democratically' elected governments to rule periodically, only to take control again if they threaten the status quo. And, big surprise, the rich thrive, and the poor survive."

"So, Papi, are you thinking of joining the Jaguar?"

"Heavens, no. I am thinking that I need to expand the Quetzal's mission to more directly benefit other immigrant families. Maybe work in the Guatemalan community in Hyattsville, Maryland, or fund Raúl to do work in Guatemala, if he decides to stay. The Jaguar experience leaves me feeling that our work is inadequate, but absolutely necessary. Necessary, but not sufficient," I said.

"What about his revolution? Where do you come down on that?" Manny asked.

"Good question. Nothing has had sustained positive effect, yet. And I wouldn't take bets that the army changes reported to us will result in the capture or derailment of the Jaguar. I think, if he builds back his network and continues to damage financial, electronic, and governmental systems, he'll garner attention. Change and redirection are, as we know, much more complicated. I suppose if he can make things so dysfunctional for the rich, such that they think he can bring about 'Armageddon,' then he might generate the leverage required to demand real change. Then again, the US probably still wouldn't tolerate that disruption to its hemispheric sphere of interests."

"I think it's safe to say that this guy won't simply go away. If not captured, he'll continue to push, somehow. At least he's not inspired by the jihadist approach I saw in Asia." Manny sighed.

"As in the conversations with Raúl, there are no simple answers, once you acknowledge that the wealth gap in Guatemala creates unacceptable consequences for most Guatemalans. Well, thank you for indulging me in that discussion. Okay, what have you guys come up with?" I sat back, prepared to listen.

"Hold on, Papi. How can we just leave it like that? That country, those people, our people are in a mess. And, from what you and Aunt María-Elena say, it's likely to creep along with no real change for the vast majority of people. At least the Jaguar is trying to create change," said Lisa.

"You realize, Lisa, that the people most affected by any redistribution of wealth will be your kin, your childhood friends and their whole set? There's not some unclaimed pot of gold in the sky waiting to be collected and handed out to low-income *Guatemaltecos*, free of charge to anyone."

"Papi, I'm young but not stupid." Lisa pulled her legs up under her chin and tried to look offended and indignant.

"Sorry, pumpkin. I suppose, intellectually, you know better than most how the economics of Central America work."

"One thing seems clear to me from this experience," Manny offered, trying to relieve the perceived tension.

"And that is?" Lisa turned to him.

"The Jaguar is not responsible for, nor basically interested in, the vicious grip that drug gangs have on much of Guatemala. If successful, his revolution would wipe them out, along with the gap in wealth and privilege he sees as the core cancer down there. It's hard to fault him." Manny looked perplexed.

"So, we're all arriving at the same place about the Jaguar but are at loose ends on what to do next."

No one said anything for several minutes. We were all content to look out at the bay, breathe deep of ocean breezes, and let our minds drift. I don't think the blessing of developed nation comfort and security was lost on any of us. Nor was the ache to help escaping us.

"So, let's debrief," I said finally.

Lisa listed out the few loans that had been made and the IOUs Monica had incurred to finance our rescue.

"If you monetize everything, it's over three quarters of a million dollars," she concluded.

"I think it's reasonable that I cover this. Raúl's in no position to chip in."

"Secondly, we have to consider whatever appropriate follow-up is with respect to the Jaguar," added Manny. "While his cause may be just, we were hired to kill or capture him if we encountered him in the rescue, and we had at least benign collaboration from the army. So I've prepared a report on what we found at his camp and on its location."

"I think that's fair. And it's not likely to help the authorities, unless they get a lot more serious than I think they are or are likely to get about the Jaguar. I'd suggest you send the report to Mónica and Guillermo Schaefer to decide who else needs a copy. Guillermo will know if and who in the government needs to know."

"I am sure that María Elena is not interested in these details. She's just happy to have Raúl back and safe," Lisa added.

"Manny, have you had a chance to think about La Puerta and what you and Marta will do next?" I didn't really expect an answer, but I needed to ask.

"A little bit. Somehow, I think we should add more discussion about the history and current status of Salvador, Honduras, and Guatemala for the boys in the program. It's important that they understand and wrestle with what's happening in their countries. Now, it's all about escaping the drug trade, but there is so much more to learn about and discuss."

"I'm not sure where that will lead, but it sounds like an idea worth working on."

The front door opened, and Mónica swept in, perfectly attired in a peacock-green business suit.

"Mama, you're home early," Lisa said.

"Well, I couldn't miss all of this intense reporting. After all, I really don't know much about what happened to Roberto and Raúl before the team got to Tikal, or how the rescue proceeded, or any of the exciting details," said Mónica, stepping out of her shoes and grabbing a mojito offered by our daughter.

"I can tell you that before the guys arrived, Raúl and I learned a great deal about jungle fauna, which plants to eat and which to avoid, how to sleep on uncomfortable cots in extreme heat and humidity, and how to stretch dull conversations into daylong discussion. Oh, and we also learned how to live on little to no sustenance for an extended period."

"It must have been terrifying out there," Lisa said with a seriousness that ignored my lighthearted reportage.

"How is Raúl? Is he traumatized?" Mónica asked after a long sip.

"Actually, he turned out to be a stalwart of physical and mental toughness. I bet he'll be fine."

Manny added, "Yes, that's my observation too."

"Well, let me put some dinner together," said Mónica, rising from her chair.

"Mama, you sit. I've got dinner, and they can brief you on our report and suggested next steps," said Lisa while collecting hors d'œuvre plates.

The three of us spent another hour bringing Mónica up to speed on more of the rescue details, Lisa's assumptions about paybacks, our thoughts for notifying her colleagues, and plans for enhancing the work in DC.

"Bob, you don't have to pay me back for my input—"

"I appreciate all you did, and I know you didn't have to lift a finger, but I can't let you pay," I said firmly.

"Well, I'm glad everyone is safe and that the Jaguar's operation is at least temporarily stalled."

"I doubt he'll come back to DC, at least not with a similar operation. One outcome of all of this is that the DC police really cracked down on the 'trade' in our neighborhood. And, with any luck, by the time

Jaguar or anybody else can build a similar business, we'll have most of the vulnerable youngsters heavily involved with productive programs," I proffered.

"I'll drink to that." The warmth of her smile reminded me of the Mónica I'd met and married decades earlier.

Lisa prepared an exquisite Chinese meal that we all enjoyed with a cold, crisp pinot grigio from Chile.

"Wow, where did you learn to cook like that, mi hija?" Mónica asked.

"Well, Lilly Chu and I have done more than study for the last few years."

Later that night, as I was falling asleep in her guest room, Mónica quietly slipped through the door. She stood, silhouetted against a rippling white curtain that was the only barrier between the room and the quiet night sea breezes. As she quietly approached the bed, the unique fragrance, that of blossoming plumería, grew stronger.

"Are you just going to stand there?" I asked.

She lay on the top sheet with a thin cotton nightgown that revealed every important curve of her model's figure. We kissed lightly.

"You always have slept with the windows open," she said as she tugged at my undershirt.

My weary limbs were revived and my muscles responded as we made love as if we had fallen in love for the first time.

"Did you ever find that Latin hero to love that you were seeking?" I teased.

"I did at one point, but he didn't want to be a full part of my world," she said, smiling. "Tell me, Berto, now that you've been rescued, what about Guatemala? I mean, conditions are better than in Cuba, but only for a few, as you saw." Mónica leaned on an elbow, naked and serious.

"For so many Guatemalans, health care and education is much worse than for Cubans. And most Cubans don't experience the violence and the threat of violence Guatemalans live with. So I'm not sure we're better off than your Cuban cousins. Nonetheless, I can't believe the only models for change are Fidel on the one hand, or Cesar Chavez on the other. Maybe some combination. I really don't know, and I surely don't have any idea about what my role might be. Right now, I'm happy to be alive and thankful to a beautiful person for her kindness."

Monica had her questions queued up. "So, what about women? Is that Marta your current flame?"

I laughed and sat up, head against the headboard.

"No. She's a bit young, and my former wife set such a high bar that I really haven't even tried to find a serious partner since she left."

"Well, if it's any consolation, she would say the same about you."

We embraced and our eyes spoke. "Maybe now, we can at least be friends."

Mónica rose to go back to her room and turned at the door.

"Sleep tight. There's lots of life left to be lived, Berto."

"Indeed, and it's bound to be complicated, my sweet," I said, blowing her a kiss.

Chapter 37

Two years after being freed, Bob Prettyman sat in his office at the Quetzal Fund having a late-afternoon cocktail with his friend Max Ramirez. The friends were reminiscing about some of the world changes that had occurred after Bob had returned to Washington. The World Bank issued a report in 2008 critical of the slow social progress in Guatemala on social and health service and other public institutional reforms outlined in a United Nations-brokered 1996 Peace Accord. While it was critical, the bank found that slow progress was being made. That same year, the Ford Foundation awarded a two million dollar grant to La Puerta to help accelerate employment. Notoriety from the Guatemala kidnapping and significant assistance from Max in New York had propelled the grant along. And the world changed in many ways when Barack Obama was elected the first African American US president in November of 2008.

"Max, I almost feel guilty for the good fortune that has followed the projects and my family since my run-in with the Jaguar Paw. I mean, having survived the kidnapping; having been able to save La Puerta and to have Marta build it into an awesome, life-changing community jewel; being alive to see my homeland creep toward stability and crawl toward equity. That ain't bad. In fact, pinch me, Max."

Prettyman took another sip of scotch as his subconscious raced, warp speed, over the past two years.

John McKoy

Lisa returned to Berkeley to finish her doctoral work and secured a post-doc in Quetzaltenango comparing the experiences of different indigenous groups with information-age technologies. She and Manny have visited each other several times, and he's taking a three-month sabbatical from La Puerta to help her get settled in Guatemala.

Raúl quit his housing job and returned to Guatemala to set up a project similar to La Puerta in Guatemala City. Bob gave him a huge startup investment. Although the US has sent in a large number of military advisors to help stabilize a tenuous guerilla situation outside of the major cities, Raúl's operation has remained off-limits to all fighting parties. Even drug gangs have left him alone. Typically, he has not shared details with his uncle, but Guillermo Schaefer reports that Raúl has been brilliantly strategic in building alliances across warring parties.

Roberto and Mónica have maintained e-mail and occasional phone contact, mostly about Lisa's activities. They consult, now and then, about politics and real estate investments. More than one conversation has focused on getting the new Obama administration committed to more engagement in both Cuba and Guatemala. They are cordial and friendly, but by no means intimate.

All indications from the poplar press, journals and websites, and friends and family suggest that the Jaguar has remained active, but with diminished capacity. The military seems not to be paying much attention to him, although sporadic disruptions continue to plague normal comings and goings in urban areas. And he seems to have developed an accommodation with major drug gangs that permits him to operate unchallenged in their territory.

Prettyman has added community activists and social policy experts to his board of advisors to help the fund think through program expansion beyond its employment focus, but that was only after he increased investment in La Puerta to enable Marta Hernandez to augment her administrative and training staff. He also paid for a series of courses

Manny wanted to take to build his business skills. His relationship with Marta remained professional and friendly—what one would expect with the director of his flagship project.

He spent a fair number of hours maintaining business, political, and professional relationships. Quetzal became Roberto's life. An occasional movie, ballgame, museum visit, lecture at Brookings or Carnegie, date, reception or party with old friends augmented his routine. By and large, if an activity didn't help the Quetzal Fund, fit his exercise routine, or feed the occasional need to connect with family or friends, Bob didn't do it.

To the casual observer, life for Roberto Prettyman was good.

"Bob, I'll be honest with you."

"Is this something new?" Roberto laughed.

Max grinned. "Funny. No, I expected you to succeed with the fund, but I never thought you'd be this effective so quickly. Here's to you, mi amigo. *Salud!*"

"By the way, Bob, I need to get this scotch. It's tasty."

"Thanks. I got a bottle as a gift. It's Shieldaig."

Both men swiveled toward the busy street scene of the revitalized Columbia Heights three floors below and tapped their feet to a Carlos Santana tune coming from ceiling speakers Roberto had recently installed.

"Got time for dinner this trip, Max?" Roberto set down his glass.

Before Max could answer, Roberto's assistant, Alice Brown, burst into the suite and headed for the wall-mounted television. She turned the set on, switched to Al Jazeera, and blurted out, "You have to see this."

The screen showed the Guatemalan National Palace ablaze and first responders trying to attend to the fire among a chaotic scene of pedestrians, motorists, and police. The commentators were describing similar fires in Antigua, Quetzaltenango, and the south coast. Roberto and Max stared.

"I have to finish up at my desk, but I knew you'd want to follow this," said Alice.

"Thanks, Alice. I think we'll stay with this for awhile," said Roberto, not turning from the screen.

"By the way, I almost forgot. Here's a card and package from Guatemala. It came via FedEx. I'll leave it on your desk. I'll check back in before I leave," Alice said, but no one responded.

"Let's bring in our correspondent, Lydia Fuentes, from Huehuetenango, out near Chiapas, Mexico," said the lead television anchor.

"Humberto, this crisis seems nationwide. Even out here, the banking system has collapsed due to some computer virus; all airline flights are cancelled due to another virus; there are rumors about the water system being contaminated. Worse, there are troops and advisors roaming the streets with no apparent clarity of mission. It's total chaos. Back to you in the capital, Humberto."

"Max, let me try Guillermo on my cell phone," said Prettyman while dialing. Roberto's phone rang twice and then disconnected. He next dialed Raúl. The same result.

"Somehow, cellular communications is also affected," he said.

Max looked at his friend. "Try CNN to see if they have any more coverage," he suggested.

"Go ahead. I'm going to open this package that Alice brought in," said Roberto.

Prettyman ripped open the envelope accompanying the box, read the note, and handed it to Max. Ramirez held the red-and-orange-flame colored card, which had the Guatemalan national bird, the Quetzal, printed in the top left-hand corner. Typed in the middle was the inscription:

Since at least a century before Christ, the Greeks and Romans believed that the Phoenix had risen in Egypt from the ashes of his own father every 500 years. Thus began the legend of the indestructibility of the Phoenix. There is such a power in the land of the Maya. However, it's not the lovely national bird. It's more ferocious and indestructible, isn't it, *mi compadre*?

"Berto, aren't you going to open the box?" Max asked.

"I don't have to; I can guess what's in it." Berto Prettyman paused and then started gathering up his cell phone, laptop, and other effects for the night.

Standing up, Berto motioned to his friend, "Max, we've got a lot of work to do."

Half an hour later, Alice came into Roberto's office to see if Max and Roberto needed any final items before she left for the evening. As she pushed the door open, she noted that the television was now tuned to CNN. The two occupants, however, had gone, and the back door was ajar. She approached Roberto's desk noting two empty scotch glasses and a half empty bottle of Shieldaig Single Malt. Next to them, on top of the envelope, was a bright-colored note card, which she assumed came with the box. The message about the Phoenix was clearly pertaining to Roberto's work and the situation in Guatemala. How it pertained was a mystery to the assistant.

The cardboard container, however, remained unopened. Strange, she thought. Alice picked it up and folded back the flaps. She looked inside the box and immediately lost her balance. Alice stumbled back a couple of steps, dropped the package on the desk, and covered her mouth to prevent from screaming.

Inside the box was a carved wooden animal head that was beautifully embroidered with thousands of multicolored beads. The beads were tightly strung on thread and then craftily wrapped around the head, so that the piece looked like a painted figure from several feet away. The piece, while stylized, was clearly that of the head of a large cat with open jaws showing oversized teeth.

Alice had seen the news. She knew details about the Quetzal's projects and Roberto's captivity in Guatemala and about the characters involved. She connected dots instantly. Now she knew the meaning of the note. The figure on the desk was the head of a jaguar.

CPSIA information can be obtained
at www.ICGtesting.com
Printed in the USA
LVHW112342190219
608131LV00002B/203/P